NI-4

4-
bb

A CLEAR CONSCIENCE

Frances Fyfield

A

CLEAR

CONSCIENCE

PANTHEON BOOKS NEW YORK

All rights reserved under International and Pan-American Copyright
Conventions. Published in the United States by Pantheon Books, a division of
Random House, Inc., New York. Originally published in Great Britain
by Bantam Press, London, in 1994.

Library of Congress Cataloging-in-Publication Data

Fyfield, Frances.
A clear conscience / Frances Fyfield.
p.   cm.
ISBN: 0-679-42666-3
1. West, Helen (Fictitious character)—Fiction. 2. Women lawyers—
England—London—Fiction. 3. London (England)—Fiction. 4. Crimes
of passion—Fiction. I. Title.
PR6056.Y47C54   1995
823'.914—dc20   94-43092

Manufactured in the United States of America

First American Edition

2 4 6 8 9 7 5 3 1

To the ever gorgeous
Clair Friedman,
with love.

ACKNOWLEDGEMENTS

Thanks are owed to the staff of the Domestic Violence Units at Plumstead and Hackney police stations, for their generous help with information and insight. Thanks also to Mike Shadrack for the introduction.

PROLOGUE

L ife was dull, monochrome. Live dangerously. It was her own
perception of herself which made her take the risks. Such as
not looking left or right when she crossed the road, staring
straight ahead and moving slowly. She did not walk deliberately
into the path of the bus, simply did not seem to notice the squeal
of horn and fart of brakes. The same sloppy attitude, fed by
exhaustion, made her take short cuts, although all she really
wanted on the way home was to postpone getting there. It was
hot inside her second-hand coat. The pub which she would have
passed on the main road would have crowds against the windows,
a few pretty girls drooping like half-dead flowers around the pool
tables, waiting on busy youths with pectorals like carvings and
small muscular bums; the girls so bored, they were looking for
something to scorn. Someone ugly. One of them would notice
her, point, sneer, and although she seemed to have mislaid the
habit of thinking, she knew she did not want to be the subject of
comment. In any event, concentration was limited to ten seconds
a time.

So she went through the back of the leisure centre instead, into
the park. There was a running track round the edge: she liked the
feeling of the cinders beneath her feet, the shoddy barrenness of

it all, and the sense of importance she got unlatching the gate at the opposite end and walking through as if she was the only person who knew it was there. The park avoided the street. Once, she would have chosen the route rationally. That point in time was a long while ago.

The leisure centre was run like a gospel church and looked like a warehouse from the outside. Local children, disbarred from the place for less than total devotion to either the architecture or the mystical purposes of the building, seemed to haunt it, inspired by a kind of envy for the mysteries within. The leisure centre was not really for the untouchables. She knew the reputation of this particular part of the neighbourhood – she lived here, could read the local paper as well as anyone else – it simply did not make any difference because it did not apply to her and she did not care. This was the way she was going to go.

Muggers on a warm, spring night were unlikely to be fussy animals, she had to concede that. They cared as little as dogs round dustbins. They would knock her down for the contents of her small and bulging shopping bag, but if all they wanted was two bottles of bleach, assorted cheap groceries, a packet of washing powder and her front-door key, good luck to them. And if the motive was rape, they would obviously turn back as soon as they saw her, look around for a better target. They would have to be blind to persist; youth could be wicked, but, surely, never so desperate. Not even a male on heat would do more than sniff at this small woman, twenty-five going on sixty, plodding down the alley which cut alongside Smith Street, led her round the edge of the kiddies' playground, wired in like a prison compound, whether to keep them in or keep them out she did not know, flanked by the tennis courts, also wired in, and skirted by the path which led to the gate, and then up a terraced road to her door.

She could have looked at the tower blocks looming to the left and felt gratitude for not having to live there, never again having to trudge all the way to the top of such spartan splendour. They were like the stars in the darkness – oddly glamorous unless you knew better, which, after a fashion, she did. Bevan was the most ominous, sticking up into the sky; but she was not in the mood for counting large mercies, let alone the small. The hurt, with grief and bruises, was all she knew as she trudged, feeling the slack skin of her arms rub against the worn cotton of her blouse. Her skirt rode up between her legs, bunching in the front under the coat, emphasizing the slight prominence of her stomach, however slowly she walked in her training shoes. She had the beginning of a double chin, pasty cheeks, hair pulled into an elastic band and eyes already laced with fine lines. She walked with a slight stoop. Rape? Don't make me laugh, she told herself, to hide the first *frisson* of fear. They'd pay me to go away. You want good looks, find someone like my brother. He got them all. The niggle of fear persisted, despite her coughing to clear it. It grew like a bubble of air in her chest, felt like indigestion, at first merely uncomfortable, then becoming sharp, sticking in the throat like heartburn.

It was the sudden sound of the wind in the trees which began the alien sensation. Whispering branches, full of budding leaves set too high for vandals, added sibilant volume to the sound of bare limbs. Maybe there was nothing new in the sound, simply a novel ability in herself to notice the symptoms of the seasons. She registered summer because it was hot, winter because it was cold, that was all, but now the sound of the trees made a noise like a whispered command. Don't, don't. The fear grew larger, enraged her.

'Don't do what?' she shouted back, stopping to draw breath. The trees seemed to obey, falling silent for a minute, then began again, moaning. Trees were alien here, belonged in another place. They shed dirty leaves in autumn: they made a mess. She had never rejoiced in their triumph of survival. Now she did not look up or down, only straight ahead and did not allow herself any distraction: she would be fine if she kept going at the same pace with her eyes ahead and, all the same, she found herself walking faster.

There was always a point where she had to decide which way to take round the perimeter fence, left or right, to complete the circle, reach the other end and emerge through the gate. One way was longer than the other and she had chosen it by mistake, flustered by the trees. Walking faster with her ungainly stride, she tripped over the lace on her shoe, an accident, because of trying to hurry and the laces being too long, that brought her heart into her mouth, the shock of nearly falling, lurching instead like her brother did when he was drunk, bouncing off the wire fence, the almost falling always worse than the fall itself. She steadied herself, adjusted the bag which bit into a calloused palm suddenly

9

slippery with sweat. Her skin, as dry as the washing she ironed most mornings, felt the texture of rough parchment. She could imagine a knife going through her plump, papery cheek: it would not bleed, not now. What was the matter with her? Come on, come on! No-one could possibly want her for anything, no-one knew her enough to think she deserved malice; there was nothing to fear, but the fear still grew from somewhere. The short route ahead seemed endless, lengthening in proportion to her silly attempts at speed, with the bag heavier all the time and the bathroom bleach slurping about in its bottle. And then when she reached the gate out of the park, it was shut. Not simply shut, six feet high and locked. Keep them out, keep them in.

Turning round with a deliberate, deep breath, she saw him then, slinking away behind a tree. Just someone, some youth who would climb the fence with ease. Probably a black boy: they could climb like monkeys, robbed anything which moved, so she'd been told and so she believed, although she would not know. She only knew that without making any conscious decision, she was beginning to run in the other direction, round the link fence back towards the trees. As soon as she started she knew this was a mistake: there were no lights this side, and it had been the lights which had drawn her to the longer route in the first place. Here there were only dusty bushes by the side of the track, the cinder laid thickly, which made her slip. He was after her now; she did not have to turn to know he was there, jogging along behind her, his feet crunching, his wide, white eyes watching her graceless progress, waiting in the knowledge that she would never manage a real turn of speed. The shoelace snapped; she tripped again, righted herself and stumbled on. The sound of the trees grew louder as she reached them. Only the alley to go, leading out by the off-licence, round the corner from the very pub she had come this way to avoid. Don't, said the trees, don't.

Before the dark alley entrance, she turned, teetered in a staggering circle, letting the PVC bag carry her so she became a whirling cudgel, with her eyes shut against whatever she might see or hit. Nothing. The bag stuck to her hand, making her overbalance, carrying her into the mouth of the alley, before it hit the wall with a crunch and the air was full of the caustic smell of bleach. A large hand, smelling of booze, grabbed at her hair, took a hold, hauled her back.

She came to a trembling halt, dizzy, her arms by her side, the right still holding the dripping bag she could not detach, her mind wondering irrelevantly what had happened to the safety cap, her head yanked backwards, exposing her throat. The skirt was fully bunched round her waist by now, the coat heavy, the sweat pouring from her armpits, she would smell; and he was not even breathing faster, perfectly calm. She could feel the light of a lamp, made skittish by the moving branches of the trees, flickering across her face. Do it now. I shall not scream and I do not bleed: my cunt is so dry, you'll have to push. Put the bleach down my throat, only do not use a knife: please do not use a knife, and make it quick.

The hand released the hold on her hair. The elbow round her neck drew her closer. She could feel a rough jaw graze painfully against her own soft skin.

'I want,' a whisper in a honeyed voice, 'I want . . .'

Slowly, she twisted towards him. 'Oh,' she said. 'It's you. Is it really you?'

'Me? Oh yes, it's me.'

The sound of his laughter rose into a shriek of hilarity. She knew that sound: he must have laughed in that same, uninhibited way since childhood. It went on and on and on, cutting across the sound of the trees and a distant yell of celebration from the pub. The diesel engine of a bus grunted in the near distance, and still the laughter went on.

The bleach from the bag dripped onto her shoes. She considered the waste of them and then, slowly, with all the repetitious obedience of passion and terror, she raised her mouth for the kiss.

PART ONE

CHAPTER ONE

I f it ain't broke, don't fix it. Don't mess with the system. Leave well alone. Etcetera.

When I am old, Helen told herself, I shall cease even trying to be good. I shall have no conscience, wear lavender, lace and false bosoms, and, in the meantime, I shall never learn to wield an electric drill.

She continued muttering and shaking her head as a substitute for obscenities while she stood in her kitchen and watched the dust settle. An old friend was dead on the floor after all these years, lying among a shower of mordant flies and the remnants of breakfast. Deceased, still twitching in the extremities, filthy in parts with her own sweaty fingerprints. Murderess.

She watched the butter dish teeter on the edge of the table before a delayed landing, greasy side up on the floor among the other detritus. Someone from a laboratory could examine the life cycle of the dead flies to give an estimate of how many summers it had been since the roller blind had refused to roll further than half mast and only then after gentle treatment. Helen had simply forgotten the habit of teasing rather than pulling. Carelessness so often led to death, but, with the fickleness which so horrified her, the wavering thoughts moved on to rejection. Why had the blind been there? Why mourn it? Because it hid three panes of glass, one cracked, two dirty, in a window where the sash-cord was uncertain; a state of affairs reminiscent of everything else in the place: the chest of drawers which demanded pushing and pulling, the toilet roll on one fragile nail, the wonky chairs on uneven floors, the windows which did not shut. Everything in her domain required concentrated co-ordination of hand and eye to make it work, but there was nothing so broke it needed fixing; the whole place was merely a kind of assault course requiring extensive training. Strangers would need to know how to pull the lavatory chain only with a certain force, kick the hall cupboard before trying to open it, ease the living-room door over the rug and not touch the kitchen blind without further instruction. If it ain't broke, don't.

Helen West, hot and sticky after a long day's work, sat and waited for the resentment to die. The only debate remaining was between the merits of gin against white wine, but even such decisions were academic in this house. There was no ice for gin; the fridge, panting like a dog in a desert, was capable of cooling, but not of making ice after all these years, so she held the wine while wandering from room to room, only four in all, excluding bathroom, suffering as she went the kind of discontent which felt like the rising damp she could detect in the bedroom. There were also a few summer beetles escaping garden predators in favour of a hostess who hoovered her basement floors as rarely as Miss West did. Helen thought, If I took down the wall between the dark hall and the living room, the place would be lighter, especially without a blind at the kitchen window. The legal mind which was her curse and her profession turned on complications such as planning permission, building regulations and other bureaucratic interference, before moving on to simpler ideas, such as new colour schemes, which required less fuss. Major alteration would only spawn a thousand minor problems; the hell with it.

The second glass of wine began to wane, and the mess from the kitchen floor was inside the rubbish bin when Bailey arrived. Her turn to cook. After three years of evasion she was finally learning how to overcome reluctance by buying only the best and simplest ingredients she could prepare inside ten minutes, but despite that, he usually came prepared for the eventuality of hunger, armed with a polythene bag, this time containing cheese, bread and a punnet of leaking strawberries. Usually she was grateful; sometimes irritated; today, simply neutral. The hug was perfunctory.

'What happened to that blind, then? Finally gave up?'

He was careful not to jeer. Most things in his place worked. He had one efficient floor on top of a warehouse, acquired before fashion knocked the prices out of sight and then knocked them down again. A distinguished flat, clean, clear and easy to keep. She liked it, never envied.

'Drink in the garden?'

'Fine.'

She hated him for knowing when to hold his tongue. Also for dusting an iron chair before sitting down, so that he would rise with the trousers of his dark grey summer suit clean enough for a man who did not like anyone to detect where he had been, while her cotton skirt would be striped with the dusty pattern of the seat. The garden always soothed her spirits, resembling, as it did, a warm, wet jungle in need of the kind of ferocious attention she could not apply indoors, but even while she was admiring the fresh sprung weeds, the controlled shambles of the kitchen remained disturbing.

'I was thinking of knocking down the living-room wall,' she volunteered. 'Or painting everything yellow. New curtains, new everything.'

He nodded wisely, sipped his lager. Two of these and he would feel the difference, but Bailey's diplomacy survived any amount of alcohol, while Helen simply became more talkative, more expansive with the wide-armed gestures which knocked things over.

'Expensive plans,' he murmured. 'You been taking bribes again?' She laughed, the bad mood lifting like a driven cloud.

'Oh yes, of course. Chance would be a fine thing, wouldn't it? Imagine anyone paying a prosecutor to lose a case. They'd have to be mad to think there was any need. They lose themselves. Anyway, I was thinking, yellow all over. Let the light in.'

Ah, my generous girl, he thought, with the dark hair, and the dark flat and a liking for light. Bailey thought of his own current work, more darkness than light, plenty of jokes. A solicitor for

17

the Crown and a senior police officer should never meet like this to discuss the décor of their lives. They had tried to keep their professional roles apart since their personal fortunes were inextricably mixed, half the week at her place, days off in between, half the week at his, in a muddled relationship, full of affection and argument, waiting for a better formula to occur to both of them at the same time. Bailey looked at Helen. If it ain't broke, don't fix.

'Hmm,' he said. 'Yellow's a nice colour. Some yellows, anyway.' The woman he had interviewed this morning had worn a yellow blouse, blood from her broken nose mottling the front. The whole effect had resembled rhubarb and custard. He could not remember the colour of her skirt, only that it was held in her fists as she spoke and her bare arms were patterned with bruises. She loved the man, she said. She did not know why he did this to her. Bailey did not understand why. Even less did he want Helen to understand why.

Bailey loved Helen. Helen loved Bailey. It was as complicated as that. The thought of either of them raising a hand against the other was as alien as the planet Mars. Making a simple suggestion was dangerous enough. The cat, fresh from a roll in damp grass, rubbed against his calves, leaving a green stain which Helen noticed with satisfaction.

'But,' he continued cautiously, 'whether you paint it yellow or not, you'll always have a downstairs flat, therefore dark. Won't you? Why don't you just get in an odd job man and a spring cleaner? Then you'll be able to judge what else you really need.'

She pulled a face and stroked the cat with a bare foot. Bailey had often offered his services as Mr Fixit, carpenter, and, latterly, been rebuffed. He had been hurt by this, sensing in retrospect some tribute to the doctrine of the self-sufficient, liberated woman Helen would never quite be.

'Are you suggesting my home is dirty?'

'No, of course not. Only that you don't have time to clean it. Not clean isn't the same as dirty. The place gets a lick and a promise at least once a month. Why should you clean it anyway? Liberated women get help.'

'From other, unliberated women, you mean?'

'There's nothing wrong with domestic labour. You never mind helping someone else scrub their house, you just don't like doing

18

your own. And if you were otherwise unemployed, you'd be glad of the going rate.'

'A pittance.'

'Regular employment, a mutually beneficial arrangement and clean windows.'

She went inside for more wine and another lager for him. The cat followed, licked up the traces of butter on the kitchen floor with noisy enthusiasm. Bailey's nonchalant figure in the garden was slightly blurred by the dust.

He was not ornamental. He was infuriating but consistent. He was still slightly more defensive than she was. There had never been a courtship, there had just been an event. If it ain't broke, celebrate.

The wine gleamed light golden through a slightly smeared glass; the lager was deep amber. In the evening light after summer rain, the red walls of the living room resembled a fresh bruise. Like the inside of a velvet cave in winter, with the firelight covering all the cracks, it was dull and garish now.

She could make it corn coloured, all over. Get some good old-fashioned, middle-class chintz. Clean up the cat; forget the blind. Start all over again. Make herself and her home both elegant and safe.

Cath's lampshade was yellow. A colour once parchment, a nice shade from a second-hand shop, faded even then, the fringes dark brown. A pig of a light for sewing, but Cath liked it. Not that she could sew here, anyway; she hadn't done such a thing for months. Perhaps it was years. She just sat by the lamp and waited.

The room around her bore traces of effort, now sustained on a less frequent basis. The walls were smudged from frequent cleaning and the patchy renewal of paint. She shuddered to think what was under there. Some of her blood, she supposed, a lot of her sweat and a bucket of tears.

Joe had offered to cook. Ready-made, frozen pancakes with something called chicken 'n' cheese in the middle, about as good for a man as they were for a small woman, accompanied by frozen peas, boiled to death, and the bread and butter which was better than the rest put together, her contribution. She sat listless although aware, ready to spring into an attitude of appreciation, her eyes tracking his progress in the kitchen, stage left, while her head was turned towards the TV screen. When the meal arrived, she knew she was supposed to murmur appreciation, ooh and aahh as if the man was a genius to find a plate; she was already rehearsing the lines, dreading what he might burn, unable to suggest a better method. So far, the mood augured well. Cath did not quite know the meaning of relaxation, but as far as she could, she allowed herself lethargy, listening to his movements and his voice as she slumped, forever guilty in the slumping.

'Anyway, this bloke says to me, Jack, you're a very fine chap. Know an ex-army chappie when I see one. Got discipline, knows how to mix a cocktail even better than I know how to get'em down, hah bloody hah. That's fine, I said, but the name is Joe, sir, not that it matters, much. And then, Cath, do you know what he did? Right in front of the bar at the Spoon, the bastard downs his drink in one and falls off his chair. Could not rouse the silly old sod. He was a picture, I tell you. Gets this look of surprise on his face, grinning all the time, trying to focus, just before he slides away. Laugh? I could have died.'

She tried to match the pitch of her own laughter to his shrill giggle, managed fairly well, encouraging him to continue. Surely, oh surely, there was a formula for managing her own tongue.

'What did you give him, Joe, to make him fall down like that?' Joe worked in the kind of pub which catered to what he called the gentry. And their ladies, haw, haw, haw. And their bloody sons, baying at one another and sticking crisps in the ear of the next person, all good clean fun with Daddy picking up the bills when they were sick or went outside to kick cars on their well-heeled way to somewhere else. Joe had a love–hate view of the officer class, mostly love, an adulation which also got a thrill from seeing them in the dust.

Cath, tired beyond even her own belief, which marvelled constantly at how exhausted and how hurt a person could be while still remaining conscious, sometimes pretended to share his prejudice. People's problems, she reckoned privately, were all the same, provided you liked them enough to listen.

'I said, what did you give the bloke to make him fall over, Joe?' There was a smell of burning from the kitchenette: the transformation from frozen to carbon, all too easy.

'Vermouth, gin, mostly gin. Oh, a touch of Campari to give it colour; a smidgeon of fruit juice. Mostly gin and French. He downed it in one. For the third time, would you believe?'

The smell of burning increased, a waft of smoke drifted in from the oven, bringing with it an end to relaxation.

'Can I help you, Joe?'

'No.'

Anger stirred. Because he would not let her salvage the food. Because of the vision of some poor, lonely old man, buoyed up to spend his money until he fell off his stool, poisoned by a barman he trusted.

'Joe, you shouldn't have done that . . .'

'Done what?'

He was struggling in the kitchen, couldn't find the thing to strain the peas: it made him mad. Cath could see the end result of all this; she should not carp at his cruel jokes on drunken customers, could not stop, either.

'Done that. What you did. Encouraged that bloke to drink that poison. He relied on you, didn't he? Poor old sod. Poor old Colonel Fogey. Shame.'

There was silence. She turned her head away towards the inanities on the TV screen, wondering too late if there was time to move. Then the food arrived in her lap. Without plate or tray. A heap of hot, burnt pancake and soft peas which burned through the fabric of her skirt into her thighs. She braced herself, with her hair hiding her face while he hit her in the ribs and bosom, finished his flurry with a punch towards the abdomen exposed by the futile defence of her arms across her chest. They were hard blows, repeated for emphasis, making the peas bounce and flutter among the folds of her skirt. The sound from her mouth was simply a grunt as he stopped.

'Pig,' he said, dismissively. 'That's what you are. You even sound like one.'

He retrieved his plate, sat back and ate with his eyes fixed on the screen. For a while she was quite still, then she got up and carried her skirt in front of her, like an apron, her movements silent and unsteady. He did not take his eyes off the television and she did not speak. On her return, five minutes later, she was carrying a plate of bread and butter. Cath ate more bread and butter than anything else.

'What did you do,' he demanded, 'with that food I cooked for you?'

21

'I ate it, of course. What did you think I would do?' she whispered.

'You might have thrown it away, or something.'

'No, it was lovely. Thanks.' She began to cough, stopped herself because it hurt and would annoy him. Coughing lead to vomiting and that annoyed him more. She had learned to control nausea, to use it as a last resort, since there was an element of fastidiousness about the man. He would not go on hitting while she was being sick, but the downside of that was the knowledge that the presence of regurgitated food always stopped him feeling sorry afterwards.

'They don't feed you,' he grumbled, still not taking his eyes off the screen.

'No they don't, Joe, you're right.'

She nibbled at the bread and margarine spread. Not the stuff of genteel sandwiches, nor the stuff of doorsteps. The sight of it sickened her: pallid dough, golden fat. At work she had another kind of sustenance: bread with nuts, rich brown stuff with real butter layered on with a trowel.

She could have eaten anything out of their fridge if she wanted. She could have told them she was in trouble, but then she was not really in trouble. As long as she was clever and he did not hit too hard or scar her face, and she was able to pretend that the cleaning job was as hateful as the gentry who employed her.

'Joe?' she asked, pleadingly. 'Joe, would you get me a drink? Tea, I mean?'

Joe only drank tea at home. He drank alcohol behind the bar where he worked, noon and evening, not that it showed until he came home, unless anyone could call the odd snarling a symptom. She could imagine what he was like, wondered why they put up with him, hoped that they always would since the thought of Joe without work was tantamount to a nightmare. If he did not work, he would stop her working, but as long as he stayed where he was and she pretended her job never involved any conversation, that was all right. Drinking alcohol at home was not. Together, they preserved the pretence that he never touched a drop; she acted now as if she believed he could not bear the stuff, which, in his way, he could not. His body could not. On a bad day, which meant a day when he had trouble crossing the road, an argument with a customer, or suffered any kind of assault on his pride, the alcohol combined with disillusion to make a poisonous cocktail. It was only the booze which turned him from saint to sinner. He was staring at the screen, his plate empty, his belly unsatisfied.

'Joe? Please? I hurt all over, Joe?'

He wavered, then hooked his right thumb inside his ear and used his whole large hand to cover his face. She watched him, hardening her heart without great success, even while her own fingers moved cautiously across her aching ribs. He always covered his face when he was ashamed.

She went to make tea, bending in the middle to ease the pain, wanting nothing more than her bed. He spoke in a small voice, at odds with his well-muscled frame, in keeping with his height.

'I love you, Cath. I'm sorry.'

She felt his left hand clutch at her skirt as she passed, feigned anger. Inside the kitchen, she tidied with long, slow, regretful movements, coughing, spewing into the sink. Carefully, she chose his favourite mug, put a tea bag inside, poured on the boiling water from the new kettle without a cord. The kitchen gleamed. After a deep breath, which caused as much pain as effort, she took the tea in to him.

He was asleep in the chair, his face wet with tears. She brought the duvet from the bedroom, covered him and left him.

Their own bed was new, with drawers in the base, from which she withdrew a spare duvet, as pristine as the one over his knees. There were other rooms, all of them bursting with goods.

Cath worked hard to achieve this daily promise of oblivion. In the bathroom, postponing the real bath until morning the way they both did unless there was blood, she forced herself to slosh cold water over her warm body and face, recognizing the nature and degree of this kind of pain and doing her best to ignore it. She averted her eyes from the puckered scar on her abdomen, washed carefully and estimated the size of tomorrow's bruises. He never hit her face. Never.

Nothing broken: nothing which quite needed fixing.

'Can anyone remember Cath's phone number? Oh, Christ, where have I put it?'

'Darling, why do you want to know? You don't need to phone her, surely? She'll be here in the morning; besides, she doesn't like being phoned at home, certainly not this late.'

'Late? Time for bed, then,' said Emily Eliot, roguishly, ruffling his hair, winking in the mirror which hung over his desk. He looked up from the papers across the surface in orderly confusion, caught her eye and smiled.

'Not tonight, Josephine. I need another hour on this. What on earth were you doing downstairs? Bit of a row.'

'Oh, sorry, playing Scrabble. Mark was winning, he crows when he's winning, frightful child. Have you really got to work?' By this time, her arms were draped round his neck, smiles meeting in the mirror.

'Yup. You know how it is.'

'Dreadful,' she said mockingly, the kiss placed on his cheek denying even the slightest hint of resentment. 'A wife refused her connubial rights in the interests of paying the mortgage. OK, I know my place, I'll simply warm the bed. Now, where's that number?'

'For the second time of asking, why?'

'Oh, Helen rang. Can you believe, she said she was asking me because we're such an organized household, little she knows.' Emily's laugh was loud, clear and genuine. 'Only she was looking for a cleaning lady. Our Cath was saying she wouldn't mind a bit extra, and knowing Helen, she'll pay the earth, so I wanted Cath's number.'

'At this time of night?'

'Oh, yes, it is, isn't it? Bedtime.'

She stood slightly perplexed, as if she had totally forgotten the urgency. Emily's hectic sense of priorities, her need to fulfil each task as soon as it was suggested, fuelled this house and made it work, with the effect of a huge and elegant boiler. The occasional irritation this caused a hard-working barrister on the up was more than compensated for by the very sight of her and every single one of their children. Emily shared their high energy and that sand-washed look which was pale, interesting, and fiery; a big-boned woman, dressed in an old dressing-gown patterned with dragons cavorting on a purple background. Her hair stood on end: her face was scrubbed and shiny. Alistair pulled her into his lap.

'Give me a hug. You smell gorgeous.'

She plumped herself down while he pretended to groan at the weight and, with her arms round his neck, she squeezed the breath out of him. Then she looked at the papers on the desk.

There were bundles of them, loosely undone, with the red tape which had bound them pushed to one side.

'What have you got here, my love? Murder and mayhem?'

'Bit of both. I told you about it.' He did; he told her all about his cases, including the most tedious ones, and, even in the middle of the night, she listened. 'Murder, of course. What else can you call it when you have a fight in a pub, one side loses, goes away, arm themselves and come back? One youth stabbed, but only one man caught. Someone else is getting off scot free.'

'Won't he say who?'

'Nope.'

'Is this one of Helen's briefs?'

'No, Bailey's. These are Helen's.' He waved his hand towards the white-taped bundles. 'Even worse. Domestic violence. Wife-bashers. She seems stuck on wife-bashers at the moment. I wonder if that's connected to wanting a cleaner?'

Emily rose and kissed the top of his head.

'You wouldn't ever bash me, would you? However aggravating I am?' He slapped her large behind gently as she moved away. His hand made a clapping sound against the fabric of the dressing-gown; she felt the caress without irritation. It had the sound of shy applause.

'Bash you? I couldn't, even if you begged. Perhaps, if it was strictly consensual. A long, slow collision. No-one's injured by a meeting of true minds.'

'Certainly they are, if the meeting of minds also involves skulls. And I think,' she added demurely, holding out her calloused hand, 'you could finish that work in the morning.'

They got as far as the door, leaning against each other lightly, the old familiar relief flooding through him. What did men do, if they did not have a partner like this who bullied, cajoled, seduced and led them to bed with the stealth of a courtesan? A chameleon she was, a sometime tigress, tolerant, fierce; she kept them safe.

It was an impractical house, full of nooks, crannies and the assembled possessions of five individuals of varying ages. On the first-floor landing stood Jane, the youngest child, with snot congealed on her nightdress. A plump nine-year-old, moist with sweat and tears, her face framed against her brother's surfboard which rested against the wall, her skin pale and pink in patches.

Older brother Mark was dark and handsome at fifteen, her twelve-year-old sister, serenely fair and sophisticated, but Jane's carroty hair grew in twisted, uneven curls about her face, the longest locks sticky with saliva from being sucked into her mouth. Jane was not lovely, although in the eyes of her parents and in the words of their constant praise, she was beauty incarnate.

'It's that thing in my room, again,' she said, trembling. 'That thing, Mummy. He's been there again.'

She flung herself into Emily's arms. Father had his arms round mother's waist; they stretched from there to tickle Jane's damp and curly head.

'Well, what a nerve he's got, coming back after all this while. You'd have thought once was enough,' Emily said indignantly. 'Some people have no consideration. Come on, we'd better go and fumigate the beast. You know he loves warm weather. Funny how he never visited when it was really cold.'

Jane snuffled, mollified.

'Cath cleaned my room today. I thought if it was clean, he wouldn't come back.'

'But Cath doesn't know about the perfume, and anyway, he's gone now. We'll just make sure, shall we? And then leave all the lights on, so you know to run upstairs to find Mark or us, OK?'

Emily's voice denied the right to winge. The child nodded, made a sound like a hiccup and then turned away from their tableau of hugging and set off downstairs, confident they would follow. Alistair marvelled, and occasionally worried, how it was that Jane had acquired her mother's authority and graceful, plodding tread. They pounded downstairs with maximum thumping of feet. One of these days they could get the kind of carpet which softened sound: school fees came first. Jane had detoured, with a swiftness which belied her weight, into their own bathroom, where children were forbidden most of the time. She was after her mother's cologne. There was plenty of perfume in this house. Alistair brought it from duty-free shops on those visits abroad which left him sick with longing for home. Then he would buy more whenever he saw it. Nothing extravagant, but always the largest size, a habit of his. The end result was a wife who always smelled sweet, even when knee deep in household dirt, and a daughter with such a passion for *eau-de-parfum* sprays, she used them to control her own childish demons.

26

The ghost who Jane insisted haunted her room on an intermittent basis – usually as the aftermath of either bad behaviour or greed on her part, her father noted wryly – only did so when the room was a mess. Tidiness and cleanliness deterred him. Perfume killed him off completely. Emily sprayed the room, liberally. It had the same effect as a charmed circle. Alistair laughed and supposed it was cheap at the price.

Helen West fell asleep with the grilles left undrawn across the basement windows, the way she did when Bailey slept alongside her but never dared otherwise, and never told him what he already knew, about her being tough and also constantly scared. The presence of the grilles induced a distinct sense of bitterness and a slighter sense of panic when they were closed. Supposing the threat was fire or flood, something from within rather than without, how would she escape when panic made her fumble? Why was it always assumed that the danger came from outside?

Because that was usually so. Certainly so for her. The memory of that violent intruder, faded by the passage of time, came back not only when she saw someone in a street who resembled him, but also at night, making her sweat. Sometimes she could smell his presence in this room, simply by brushing away her hair, from where it fell over the scar on her forehead.

She could taste the blood in her mouth, squirm at the memory of her own violent reaction and all the helplessness which followed. She turned restlessly, distracting herself with visions of daylight streaming in to a clean and sanitized room, washed bare of all reminders. Yellow. The colour of corn and cowardice; bright enough to exorcize the devil.

Bailey felt for her hand.

'You all right, love?'

'No.'

He drew her close. 'All right. Come in here then. I'll tell you a nice, long story. A good one. Happy endings.'

She wanted to stick her thumb in her mouth, wishing she could give up thinking about present, past or future. You do not need me as I need you, Helen thought, taking the hand gratefully, listening to the voice talking through some silly tale until she would fall asleep.

If it ain't broke, don't fix it.

CHAPTER TWO

M ary Secura stepped out of her car, in the clean light of a
summer morning, pretending to look as nonchalant as
a local authority official come to check on a broken window pane
or the defective lift in Bevan House. She realized as she saw her
own reflection, distorted in the driver's door, that she had slightly
overdone the disguise. Officials from the council's repair depart-
ment might have been in proud possession of identity cards
pinned to the lapel, but they did not generally look quite as tidy.
Mary had a weakness for handbags, too; and suspected that the
average council official might not possess the same good, worn
leather. It was big enough to hide a radio, the only weapon in her
armoury which did not depend on common sense.

The radio was heavy, not intended as a weapon although
sometimes used as such when it was quicker than calling for help.
Bevan House stretched above like a sheer cliff; her mission would
take her no further than the third floor.

She ran her fingers (bitten nails, indicative of something, she
was not quite sure what) through her short hair to make it appear
less groomed, and walked briskly along the walkway to flat
fifteen, steeling herself to be both brisk and reassuring against the
possible hysteria of the inmate. Shirley Rix might be as brave and

resolute this morning as she had sounded on the phone yesterday, but she might not. The two of them had spoken almost every day for the last six weeks and if it was not quite friendship, it passed as such. All Mary had to do was get Shirley to the door, and she'd be fine. Once she had introduced her to Miss West, who was good at her job, then, hey presto, the bastard husband would be committed for trial.

The one thing which bothered her, less obscurely than the nagging doubt which made her nervous, was the hope she carried like a torch for women like Shirley Rix. Plus the fact that when she, a police constable specializing in domestic violence, was finished with the case, Shirley Rix would realize that despite all the support, she was still on her own after all. Having a husband who tried to murder you with the regularity of Mr Rix did not exactly enhance your prospects, either, even if he remained, as Constable Secura hoped he would, in prison on his wife's evidence for a long time. Poor Shirley: she did not have much of a curriculum vitae.

Mary knocked at the door, amazed, as she always was, at how Shirley managed to keep this little flat as free from squalor as it was, not exactly clean but far from filthy. Once upon a time, using the standards of her own parents, Mary would have regarded the semi-cleanliness of the Rix household as intolerable. Now she saw it as the triumph of motherhood, which also saved the lives of half her witnesses since it was usually the kids who made the mothers either leave or give evidence, in the end. The day this violent daddy forced his three-year-old son to drink beer, made him sick, shoved him into bed and then beat his wife for remonstrating, was the day Shirley Rix decided to give evidence. Good girl, Shirl.

Mary knocked again, this time louder, the feeling of dread beginning to take hold. She checked the time: nine twenty, forty minutes before they were expected at court. Miss West would be early, she always was; there were still minutes to spare. The third knock was louder still; she had the absurd desire to use the radio in her bag to shatter the wired glass which took up a quarter of the door. Through the glass an electric light glowed in the hall. Mary had been cheered by the sight of that, now she knew it was ominous.

When the door to flat sixteen opened Mary supposed she was

halfway to acceptance, as close as cool Helen West always seemed to be with her bloody good manners. On the doorstep was a woman of indeterminate years, somewhere between thirty and fifty, short on speech and square against the kind of ill wind which blew no good.

'If you want Shirl, she's gone. Kid and all. 'Bout an hour ago. Not coming back.'

The door slammed. There was the sound of two bolts sliding into place.

Mary Secura looked at her watch again, then knocked on Shirley's door one more time, knowing it was useless. Inside, the light winked at her while the place reeked of emptiness. When she got back to the car, she found herself trembling with rage. Six weeks' work, hours of building trust; such was the nature of friendship.

The foyer outside court number five, North London Magistrates' Court, was almost deserted. There was none of the stink, smoke and grumblings of the waiting area outside courts one to four, which Helen could see as she leant over the balcony watching the human traffic ebb and flow. Court number one was remands; she was glad she was not down there with a hundred cases to shoot from the hip: the overnight arrests, the bind overs to keep the peace, the guilty pleas, the postponements for preparation or non-appearance; the whole thing an exercise in concentration. Better to be up here, with a single case listed for the whole morning, if it lasted that long. The prisoner was in the cells, the two police witnesses had booked in, everything was set to go. She looked downstairs again, in time to see Constable Secura coming through the main entrance and barging, rudely, through the crowds. Alone. Even as Mary made for the steps towards the comparative calm of court five, Helen could feel her own bile rising, the vomit of frustration.

Mary Secura reached her side, slightly out of breath, said nothing, simply shrugged her shoulders. The defection of a crucial witness was not a phenomenon requiring an announcement. Even one still recovering from her split lip, missing teeth, fractured skull and broken arm, all suffered in the name of obedience to the man in the cell downstairs. Helen felt a brief white rage against the victim who remained a victim.

'The stupid, stupid bitch,' Helen said. 'The silly cow. What does she think she's doing? Are you sure she knew the date?'

Something snapped in Mary Secura's brain. She leaned forward with her hands on her hips and her face inches from Miss West.

'Of course she knew the bloody date! We've been through it enough times. She knew the date, the place and the fact I was coming to pick her up. And don't you dare call her a bitch. You've seen the photographs, you know what she's like. I can call her what I fucking like, it's me who's got her this far, but you can't, you stupid ignorant cow. You've got no bloody idea . . .' And then to her own consternation, she was in tears, turning to one side to fumble in the good leather handbag for the sheaf of paper handkerchiefs she always carried, dropping the radio with a clatter on the stone-tiled floor.

'I think those things cost hundreds, don't they?' said Helen. She bent to retrieve it while Mary, blowing her nose, made the same movement. Their heads almost clashed. Helen held the radio to her ear, shook it, pulled a face.

'Receiving Radio One, I think. It'll do.'

Both started to talk at once, breaking off with a touch of awkward laughter. Helen breathed deeply, pulled another face and sat down. Mary Secura did the same.

'OK, so what do we do? This committal has been on the cards for four weeks, he's been in custody for six and we've given every reassurance it will go ahead. We've got outside evidence of a row, shrieks and screams, injuries found after the police were called. His admissions vary from saying she fell over a pushchair to saying she went ape shit and hit him first and he had to calm her down. We can put him there, but not tie him down. Whichever way you look at it, there just isn't enough evidence without her.'

'Nope.'

'So I don't have much choice about going in there and discontinuing the whole thing, do I?'

'Please,' said Mary Secura. 'Please. Just try for one more adjournment. Give me one more chance to find her. She'll have to come home sooner rather than later.'

'Why should she?'

'Because she hasn't got anywhere else to go.'

'And then she'll only skip again, next time. After another few hundred pounds of public money?'

'Please,' said Constable Secura. 'Please, Miss West. Next time he might kill her.'

The usher stood by the door, smug with sympathy and the prospect of a short morning.

The tea was cold, the service indifferent.

'Look, I apologize for calling you a stupid ignorant cow,' Mary Secura said with a touch of stiff formality an hour later as they sat in the canteen. They had bypassed the rows of cheese rolls, weary even this early in the day, ignored the bacon smell from the steamers, the rack of sad toast which no-one would eat now, the baskets with packets of biscuits and the plates holding forlorn scones. Court canteens always purveyed food to the lowest common denominator of taste, bland in the extreme. Helen imagined the custard for the lunchtime apple pie was made once a month and carved into slabs.

'Don't wrap it up, say what you really think,' she said cheerfully. 'I wouldn't be here if the occasional insult made me curl up and die, but I don't like them much from someone I respect. Which is why I should apologize too. Of course I knew you'd have done everything you possibly could to get that woman to court. I implied you hadn't, because I was irritated.'

'Irritated?' said Mary. 'I was furious. I like Shirley. And the child's just beautiful.'

They were silent for a moment.

'Anyway, you're halfway right,' said Helen. 'I am ignorant. I mean, after all this time and all these cases, I don't understand the pressures. Not really. I still don't quite know how a woman stays with a man who hits her.'

Constable Secura stirred her filthy coffee.

'Oh, I think I do, a bit. Which is why I'd like a change. Something simple. Like catching criminals and getting convictions.'

'You been reading fairy stories again?' Helen asked. 'Or do you want to join the robbery squad?'

Secura shrugged and smiled. 'You know what I mean. From where I sit, a stint on robbery or murder looks like a holiday. You don't get too many results with battered wives.'

'If I were you,' Helen said cautiously, aware of her own

frustration rather too freely expressed earlier, 'I'd sometimes want to hit them myself.'

'Well I don't, because you get to the point where you can't get angry, any more than you would with a child. I only get angry with the man. It's like treading on eggshells. The neighbours call us out more often than the victim, and off we go. Usually the drunken bastard gets arrested on a late-night domestic and we come in to collect the evidence next morning. By which time the victim with her limited knowledge – and I can't tell you how limited it often is – looks at us like a dog turd. And screams. So you get her to climb down and maybe make a statement. Then she sits at home with a couple of screaming kids, works out that the devil she knows isn't half as bad as the one she doesn't, especially if the feckless sod helps keep the roof up. Oh yes, and then there's this little complicating factor of love.'

'For someone who breaks your ribs?'

'Yes, ma'am,' said Mary, saluting Helen mockingly. 'C'mon. You've got Bailey, I've got mine, we know all about Love.'

'Not that way, we don't.'

Helen sensed that Mary did not want to go on in such a serious vein. She cared too much, Mary did, took all professional failures personally. They had got their temporary reprieve, Helen implying that Shirl's absence could well be the result of illness or kidnap rather than reluctance. She could lay on the guilt with a trowel, Mary thought: she could make the buggers think they had no choice in the matter at all; and I do wish she'd talk about something else.

'Tell me something,' said Helen, leaning forward in so confidential a manner, Mary recoiled as if this normally calm prosecutor were about to confess to a bizarre sexual deviancy, 'do you and your bloke agree about colour schemes? I know Bailey and I don't actually live together, but he does spend a lot of time at my place, and I suddenly want everything yellow, and he seems to think yellow is nothing more or less than the colour of, well, pee.'

Mary bridled. 'What the hell does his opinion matter? Yellow? Paint or wallpaper?' she went on, eyes alight with a fervour. It was an illumination Helen recognized, the single-minded devotion of a fellow shopping-addict. 'I've got a yellow bathroom. Big roses. Love it.' She was fumbling in that big bag with the radio and the mass of tissues. For the sixteenth time that day she looked at her watch. Helen had a fleeting image of Bailey who never looked at a watch, even in the middle of the night, he always knew the time. Strange that he should also be a man who was passionate about clocks, when he was the last person to need them.

'Well, I have to phone in again,' said Mary. 'In case anyone's seen Shirl. Otherwise, I've got an hour. There's an amazing do-it-yourself paint and wallpaper shop down the road. Why else do you think I like this court?'

Eyes met in mutual recognition. Despite the photograph of Shirley Rix, shown to the magistrates, despite the memory of serious common purpose, there was also that peculiar elation which followed the demise of adrenalin, the slow ebbing of tension which brought about a certain euphoria. Then they were out there, heels clacking on stone steps, moving with the guilty speed of children playing truant.

Superintendent Bailey could feel Detective Constable Ryan's reluctance to get out of the car.

'I dunno, sir. Can't we just look from here? This thing might be short a set of wheels by the time we get back.'

'It's got an alarm, hasn't it?'

'Sure, but I don't quite know who it would frighten. Nobody under fourteen anyway. School holidays, guv, nothing's safe.'

'I can see cars with wheels. Let's go. Your tyres wouldn't pass an MOT, anyhow. Just don't want to look, do you? You've lost the honourable art of walking, that's your problem.'

They set off across the road towards Bevan House, which towered above them. It was fronted by a scrubby green, once landscaped by non-surviving trees, now littered with cars, which dipped down into a concrete approach that led in turn to a central portico, also concrete, before deviating left and right to side entrances and stairwells. Three stairwells, three lifts, most defunct at any given time. There were open walkways along the first twelve floors; after that the remaining twelve rose like a monument, too high for the windows to be smashed by anything but a passing rocket.

'Would you believe', Ryan volunteered, interested despite his truculence and his resentment at being there at all, 'that they put families with children on the lower floors, well, as far as possible they do, the council, I mean. Unmarried mums and dads go further up, singles at the top, but no bugger wants to live at the top. Least, that's the plan; it all gets muddled, except for nobody wanting to live at the top. I mean, is that where you'd want to live on a pension? Half empty, the top. Little flats, cubbyholes, really. Council can't get rid.'

Bailey looked with indifference at the frontage. He felt a distant rage that anyone could ever design a building so alien to human beings, then repressed that familiar old-hat opinion and wondered instead how much it would cost to persuade the children who played around them, dusty as the concrete on which they moved, to get organized and burn the thing down. Heartless architecture did not cause a riot all by itself, but it certainly helped.

'Show me,' he commanded.

Ryan shrugged. 'Damien Flood lived on the top. Would you believe he could run up all those stairs, even when he was pissed, which was often? He had another place, too, always running away from women, but this was his main gaff.' Ryan turned abruptly, almost full circle, so that instead of pointing upwards towards the height which made him giddy, he pointed away.

'Over there, see it? Just poking out, that's the leisure centre, right? Kept that nice, they have, video cameras and bouncers all over the place. Got a park round the side. The park was there first, if you see what I mean. Got proper trees and stuff. Damien used to go to the centre to work out: a lot of boxers did, though really they've got their own places. He wasn't so regular since he went to seed a bit, but he was still a fit bloke.' Ryan turned back, looked upwards again and shielded his eyes.

'I mean, anyone who could run up all them stairs, he must have been fit.'

Bailey squatted down. He was wearing a jacket over slacks, had had the sense to take off his tie. His thin knees stuck out: Ryan hoped his trousers would bag and knew they wouldn't. Nor would his voice stop.

'It was your job, Ryan. I gave it to you and said get on with it.'

'I did, too. We got a result, didn't we? Committed for trial. And if you've been too fucking busy to worry until we have to go and see some fucking barrister about it, why the hell are you on my back now?'

A child came up to them, dirty faced and full of cunning, trailing a skateboard. He stood with his powerful ten-year-old body full of challenge.

'See that car?' Bailey said, pressing two pound coins into a grubby palm. The child nodded. 'Go and look after it, will you? Got a man here worried about his wheels.' As the boy rushed away, Ryan felt the old, familiar humiliation spreading through him like his mother's hot flushes.

'I done what I could. We got a body, like I said. All right, they were all of them in that pub over there.' He gestured again. 'Near the leisure centre. Well-run pub. Damien Flood was in there with his mates. He won too much money at pool. The losing team came back for a fight. Damien got separated from his mates and then got stabbed. All right, I didn't get the three lads on that team, but I did get one. And you know I didn't force him to talk; I done every rule in the book to stop him talking, but he sang like a budgie. Lot of budgies, in these flats. They aren't supposed to keep pets.'

Bailey sat back on the grass. His silence was never a relief, even when he lay, squinting at the sun with his face red from the heat.

'What you got was a skinny little boy. You didn't look any further. You made no enquiries in the pub itself.'

'So what?' said Ryan, trying to hide his own irritation and all the guilt Bailey's nonchalance induced. It was all compounded by the man's ability to rise to his feet without a helping hand, like a dog bounding up to play. There was a sound of breaking glass. Ryan supposed it came from the prominent rubbish bins which flanked the main entrance, and marked the only attempt at architectural grandeur. Bailey heard it only as a normal sound.

'I hope that little sod isn't doing in the windows of your car.'

'Not yet. Why can't you get stuffed, sir?'

'Because I like to needle you, that's why. And you didn't try with this one, did you?' Ryan could have sworn that one of them spat, but Bailey, when next he looked, was as impervious as ever, kicking the dry ground with the toe of his shoe.

'Only I've seen the photos,' Bailey was saying as they walked back to Ryan's car. 'Seen better, seen worse, but Damien Flood wasn't killed by any nineteen-year-old kid who lost at pool. Or his friends. Come on, Ryan, come on.'

'All I could find,' Ryan said.

Bailey did not sigh any more than he ever looked at his watch or opened his mouth without purpose.

'Shame,' was all he said as they pulled away from the cliff face of Bevan House. 'Bloody shame.' Ryan knew at least the half of what he meant.

His footsteps padded down the corridor, tripped on the curled edges of carpet tile and moved on with less assurance. He opened the door, sidled his way inside, closed it behind him and breathed deeply. Now he had her. Half-past lunch and not back at work. Bull's-eye. Brian Redwood, Branch Crown Prosecutor, Helen West's boss, among other problems, a man of ferocious timidity, lowered his large behind into her chair, puffed out his chest, shook his head, drummed his fingers on the table and still looked like a man who bore the imprint of the last person who had sat on him. Then he began to prowl.

Mess was what he found. No evidence whatever of the clear-desk policy he advocated, less evidence still of respect for rules. A towering in-tray, nothing in the out, two dead plants and a packet of sticky mints in the top desk drawer. Redwood huffed, ate one absent-mindedly while continuing his researches. Old birthday cards, a shopping list, a pair of shoes requiring mending, nothing more personal than that. Perhaps she hid things, these days. His eyes fell on the paper sack in the corner of the room. Confidential waste, the place to put litter with no destination other than the shredder, cleared once a fortnight. Hmm. The brown paper crackled at his touch accusingly, and the contents were revealing. Policy manuals, vital memos from himself, delivered daily, part of his own attempt to rule by written words. It was faintly shocking to find that in Helen's case, his efforts represented nothing but the shortest route between the in-tray and the bin.

Redwood gazed out of the window and found, to his horror, someone gazing back. The office was separated by the mere width of a narrow street from other offices over the road, where a comely woman stared, and then waved. Redwood, a guilty thing surprised, felt as if he had just lost his trousers, and ducked out of sight still clutching a bunch of paper. He was on his hands and knees with his bottom pointing towards the door when Helen opened it. Just as she always did, he reflected later, she turned the tables on him.

'Something you wanted, sir?'

She dropped the file she carried under one arm. The paper spilled out and the photo of Shirley Rix's injured features lay uppermost on the floor. While Redwood looked at it without interest, Helen neatly hid her shopping bag behind the desk.

'You're late,' he barked, scrambling to his feet. 'Where have you been?'

'You should know. North London Court. Battered wives society. You've had me doing nothing but battered women for six months. Another no-show this morning.'

She was thinking of the contents of her bag. Of how she had substituted the vexed question of whether it had been right to ask for a witness summons for the woman in the photo with the search for yellow paint. Thinking of the various hues of silk emulsion paint, so delicious looking in little sample pots, she could have grasped them out of the hidden bag, peeled off the plastic lid and eaten one like a fruit yoghurt.

'We need a policy', Redwood barked, 'about what to do when these women don't turn up. When to give up and when to carry on. Write it.'

'Write what? What's wrong with deciding what to do in each case as it comes? Each one's different. Sometimes you should give up, sometimes not.'

'You might get it wrong.'

'Yes,' she said patiently. 'I might, you might, we might. And so might an inflexible set of rules. We don't have a policy written in stone for other kinds of reluctant witnesses; why have one for victimized women? We just have to listen to the police.'

'Helen, we're supposed to be independent of police opinion.' Redwood regarded her warily, waiting to see if she would take such remarks personally. He had a deep suspicion of all policemen and supposed her own view was jaundiced as a result of her misguided, miraculously long-running affair with one of them. Redwood was waiting for Miss West to recover from her strange infatuation with Superintendent Bailey with the same weary patience he had experienced when his daughter was recovering from measles. Partnerships like that were not against the rules, but they were not comfortably within them either.

'We can't be independent of their judgement when they've met the victim and we haven't,' she was saying calmly. 'Besides, there's hardly much scope for bribery and corruption in a Domestic Violence Unit.'

He was silent, then shrugged. 'I don't know,' he said. 'I really don't know how it happens. I thought this was the age of equality. If I hit my wife, it would be the very last thing I'd do.'

Visualizing the bulk of Mrs Redwood, Helen privately agreed.

'Think about the policy,' Redwood urged as he found himself, without knowing quite how, being shown out like a visiting window-cleaner.

'Sir,' she said sweetly, 'I think of nothing else.'

The sun had flattened itself behind their own building. New offices, nasty furnishings which would not outlive the lease. Men like Redwood promulgated bureaucratic nonsense in the hope of saving their seats from the encroachment of younger, even greyer men. Helen felt a quiet despair, suppressed by the dancing visions of yellow paint now hidden in the bottom drawer along with a supply of make-up, biscuits past their sell-by date, books loaned or borrowed and the ashtray Redwood had failed to discover. Sunshine reflected off the glass frontage of the offices across the way, obscuring her daily surreptitious examination of their lives. She buried her head in work.

The light faded, gracefully. The out-tray grew. Shouts of laughter echoed in the corridor outside. Someone ran past her door, yelling, 'Wait for me!' in a long and eerie wail. Someone else tripped on the carpet, and then there was only the disturbing descent of silence, penetrating slowly until, with a stab of disappointment, she looked up through the window to find that all the workers in the opposite block had gone. Alas, no chance this evening to see who had lingered and finally left with whom; no chance of an update on the fate of the opposite office Lothario.

The phone bleeped. A new phone, anchored to the revolving desk.

'Go home, Helen West. Go home now. Stop whatever you are doing and go.'

Her heart stopped for a moment: the silence of the building was suddenly oppressive, until the distant sound of traffic restored sanity.

'Emily, you scared me. What time is it?'

'Half six, you ninny. Don't you have a watch, for Gawd's sake?'

Somehow those strident patrician tones never struck a discord: hers was a voice inspiring pleasure and confidence; artlessly kind Emily, enviably efficient and, in truth, a bit of a bully.

'Two things. First, I left the number of the cleaning lady on your answerphone, but I doubted you'd ever get around to organizing a meeting, so I did. You're halfway down the fifty-nine bus route between where she lives and here, and she says it's no bother. OK? Be with you in an hour, so get your skates on.' Skates, bikes, Emily drew metaphors from all the impedimenta of her children. 'And the other thing is, she's here so late, helping me, because I've got people coming to supper. They don't include you and Bailey by any chance, do they?'

'Nope. Soon, I hope.'

'Christ. I wish I could remember who's coming. Isn't that awful? They could be a posse of vegetarian judges. Oh, by the way, she smells of carbolic soap or disinfectant, or something. And she does tend to eat with her mouth open, but that's nothing. Really. Helen? Don't forget to go home, will you?'

Home. With the dusty windows and the wild garden and the floors in need of a clean and the bees at the window. The thought made her shiver with pleasure. Halfway down the corridor, she remembered the little snack pots of paint in her desk drawer. She would not have trudged back for anything less, but these had the innate value of contraband. She was the only person she knew who had left a chicken defrosting on the office floor for a weekend. She boasted about that one, but not about the fish left under the top deck seat of the number 59.

She avoided the bus in the interests of speed. Below the hot streets, the Underground was tolerable with the mad work exodus an hour old. The street where Helen lived seemed fresh, dignified, safe, adorned by large Victorian houses with white stucco frontages, elegant in whatever state of repair, built for affluent families, currently subdivided, the basement flats like hers, euphemistically known as garden apartments, were sunny at the back, darker at the front. Helen walked down her own road with familiar pleasure, noting the age of the trees, the clematis on the black railings, the emergence of blood-red geraniums and startling blue lobelia in window-boxes. Then she did as she did with shameful frequency: stopped, looked in windows to see what people did with their rooms.

On the doorstep was a woman, waiting with preternatural patience, as if she never needed to move, would wait for ever, like a piece of garden sculpture.

'Yes?' Helen queried abruptly. 'Are you selling something?'

The sculpture stood up from the step and smiled. 'I'm Cath,' she said. 'I've come to clean. If you want me.'

'Cath?' Helen echoed. 'Cath? Oh, yes!'

She unlocked the door, turned back, smiling apologies for her own gross delay, muttering how she was usually early; forgive me, she was murmuring. She wanted to apologize for her own house, suddenly spotlit as they went into the kitchen, which caught the full blaze of the sinking sun from the south-facing garden; and it was then, catching in the absent smile of the other woman a signal of nothing, that the cat came in and Cath lifted her off the floor in a crow of delight. For one split second, hers were the same hurt, brown eyes which had stared from the photographs of Shirley Rix, defying the world to say that her own fate was her own fault. Helen shook herself.

No-one had identical eyes, any more than the same voices or fingerprints.

Aside from that, Cath had the face of a madonna.

CHAPTER THREE

I f it ain't broke, don't fix it. Which raised in his mind the strict definition of 'broke'. For 'broke' read broken, not penniless. Bailey could hear some pedantic judge translating the phrase for the benefit of a jury. 'Ladies and gentlemen, this means, if an object is not broken, it should on no account be repaired.'

Somehow that did not sound quite the same. Lacked a certain *je ne sais quoi*. Bailey looked at the clock in his hands which had sent him off on this tangent. Not broken as such, M'lud, but working overtime, with the hour hand racing round at the same speed as the one counting seconds. He set the clock down on the work surface. 'Just let me know which hour of the day I'm in,' he murmured, 'and I'll phone up the speaking clock to check the week.'

The repair of this old timepiece could wait until Helen had seen it. 'Look,' he would say. 'That's what happens when you see your life passing in front of your eyes. At the last glance, you are now fifty-six.' Maybe it wasn't so funny after all.

Bailey, long and thin, with his slightly cadaverous features, did not look like a man who smiled easily, although he could and did, frequently, if sometimes shyly, like a man amazed by his own amusement. Helen made him smile: he could catch himself watching her from a distance and grinning. He supposed he was lucky. Not many men could have these ups and downs, these swings of mood, these black days and this unfair ambivalence in the face of commitment to a rather beautiful woman, and still find themselves loved and tolerated, albeit with a degree of exasperation. As an old-fashioned man, raised to regard marriage as the desirable norm, Bailey was ashamed of his lack of formal commitment; sometimes, he realized that Helen had reached the point in their relationship when that was what she wanted. If you don't want to make a lifetime of it, he told himself sternly, you should let go and make space for some other bugger to do better, but he did not want that either. Nor did he want anyone else, not even the freedom to search for a relationship less complex, although he had flirted with the idea, as had she, both retreating from the brink. And he had proposed marriage, repeatedly, in the early days, to be met by her uncertainty, hurtful at the time, like someone refusing a gift he had taken the trouble to wrap. The tables had turned in the last few months: he supposed he was getting some small revenge.

According to the clock, one hour had passed in one minute. Helen was late. They were currently in one of their tranquil phases, a celebration of the hazy days of summer, but despite his silent insistence that their relationship remain as it was, the uncommitted, nevertheless exclusive kind, he had to admit that all this talk about tearing down walls in her flat disturbed him a little. He wanted her independent, of course, but not so independent that she built a life without reference to him at all. You're getting your cake and eating it, said Ryan, ever jealous of the bachelor state. Bailey supposed he was. He hadn't said to Ryan that even eating cake took effort.

Nor did he confide in Ryan that Helen and he had hardly made a good job of living together the one time they had tried, although the choice of place, which both of them loathed, had been less than fortunate. And their tastes did not coincide. She was all for deep colours, dozens of pictures, warm fires, dark old curtains, so that her red-walled living room resembled a gentleman's club. Bailey's huge single floor, with not one curtain, contained less colour than her bathroom. There was wood and more wood. Shelves rather than cupboards, the pastel work surfaces of the integral kitchen where he placed the clock all cleaned with a spray and wipe. The only dirty thing around here was the cat which came and went and remained missing for days at a time. Cats are like women, Bailey told himself with the cynicism of a policeman; they stay if they want to.

Eight thirty, supper simmering and no-one to share it. If all else failed, he would read a book. He had been thinking of going further than his LL B, acquired at night school; he might even read a law book. Pity, though: it was one of those evenings when he really needed to talk. There were not many couples, he reflected, who could discuss murder while eating lamb chops. Nor those who study post-mortem photographs for dessert. He wanted to share his current moral dilemma: a trial in which he knew they had not arrested the right man. If not exactly the wrong man, not the right one either.

The flat was clean: he was clean. Only his conscience was like a dirty windscreen.

Helen did not know what to do with a cleaning lady. The confrontation made her awkward. It struck her as a rather lonely and boring job; and, for that reason, she hated to ask anyone to do it, even though as a Crown Prosecutor, not rich like her City and commercial cousins, there was enough for a good standard of living. Including someone to clean the house, if only she could suppress the guilt which came with asking.

'And this is the living room. And this is the bathroom,' she heard herself saying, sounding to her own ears like a condescending estate agent to an idiot client. Cath nodded. Of course she would see what they were, she wasn't blind, Helen told herself furiously, her own embarrassment made worse by Cath's passivity. She was a strong-looking young woman, but she walked with a slight stoop, as if she carried something heavy round her waist, and instead of speaking, she inclined her head. But she showed no sign of recoiling from the scattered clothes in the bedroom, or the gritty feel to the kitchen floor.

'I'm sorry about the mess,' Helen was saying, 'only I don't have much time . . .'

'I wouldn't call this mess,' Cath said neutrally. 'It isn't even really dirty. You've got a nice place.'

Helen was instantly charmed.

'And of course,' Cath continued, 'I could help you with the

44

garden.' That made Helen defensive again. The garden was hers.

'I like doing the garden,' she said. 'It's the housework I can't stand.'

'That's all right then,' said the woman mildly, in a quiet, almost whispering voice. 'I was only suggesting it because Mrs Eliot said I should.' She was suddenly disconcertingly chatty, as if she now knew the worst and could cope with anything else. 'Now, when it comes to dirt, you should see what Mrs Eliot's lot can do. Amazing. Bathroom and kitchen look like bomb sites most mornings. And what those kids take to bed is anyone's guess.' She spoke of them with a kind of urgent fondness and reverence, shaking her head. Helen felt a guilty treachery to find herself so avidly curious about the true state of Emily's house. It was like looking in windows: she could not suppress it.

'Tell me more,' she demanded.

Mark sometimes went to bed in his wellington boots, could she believe that? Yes, she could. Jane had learned to make pastry recently, then thrown a lump of it at the old-fashioned extractor fan in Emily's kitchen, there were still clods of it stuck to the ceiling and probably getting mouldy in corners. Along with the fragments of boiled egg which Mrs Eliot had left on the stove while she got embroiled in one of her incessant phone conversations. Boiled eggs go off like bombs, Cath remarked. And then there was the grill pan with fat in the bottom, set alight when Mr Eliot had forgotten his bacon; the marks of that joined all the others. Helen was secretly delighted. It was a relief to know that Emily's fine house also carried scars.

'Well, do you want me to come or not?' Cath asked.

Helen did, very much.

'I can do Tuesdays and Thursdays, say two hours in the afternoon. You're a long way from Mrs Eliot, but it's halfway home for me, same bus route. Number fifty-nine.'

Her voice was peculiarly flat when she stopped talking about the Eliot's. She seemed in no hurry to leave, but stood looking round the walls of Helen's living room with slow pleasure. 'I do like it here,' she said.

On her way to Bailey's, driving with careless abandon, Helen felt as if she had passed some kind of test. And, as far as the Eliots were concerned, achieved some kind of equality. The Eliots were a couple of very few friends she and Bailey could call mutual to them both. Usually, it was difficult to share friends with Bailey. He was not a sociable animal, despite his great and diffident charm, and there were hazards in taking him out and about among friends who thought policemen were dangerous freaks. He would find himself attacked for a parking fine, sneered at for the release of a terrorist, forced to defend himself for the latest police scandal, cross-examined for ancient miscarriages of justice; and although he ignored it all, she could not. Many a supper party had ended in awkward silence, with the pair of them relieved to depart. He was too proud a creature to be baited like a bear. But with Alistair Eliot there was the firm foundation of professional experience and mutual respect. They had all shared the same cases and similar concerns, while Emily shared gossip. The charismatic Eliots had no preconceptions about whom they should and should not know. Alistair's father was a bishop: Bailey had suggested there was something loosely Christian in their ever-open door.

When we next go there, Helen was thinking, I must remember to look at the kitchen ceiling. And ask Em why she thinks Cath smells of soap.

The number 59 bus route rose like a sluggish wave in the depths of north-east London, where Cath lived, and moved with the speed of a canal boat right through the centre; it dawdled around the glories of South Kensington, where the Eliots lived, and then over to the depressed south. The depot, into which she had often ridden on the top deck, remaining where she was until the bus turned back again, always saying, if asked, how she had gone to sleep or there was something she had forgotten to buy, was a place she loved for the serried rows of buses, coaches and double-deckers standing under the high roof like so many Thomas the Tank Engines. The fumes filled her nostrils, but the place was cool in summer. There was something immutable about the number 59. They were all such old buses with conductors and drivers, never the newer, one-man-operated type which she hated for their impersonality and the rude noise of their brakes audible from her bedroom on a quiet night. When the number 59 had gone in for a cream and maroon livery, she had simply sat up straighter in her seat, as proud as any shareholder. If anyone got on the bus and refused to pay, Cath was incensed, even if their inability was accidental or their condition clearly wretched. Cath despised people who did not pay their way. She did not think she was poorly paid, abhorring those who were poorer still.

Joe was well paid, he had not wanted her to get a job. Between you and me girl, they would show 'them', a thing or two, the bastards. She thought of 'them' whenever the bus took her into Kensington where Joe worked. Not really a public house, more of a hybrid between that and a wine-and-cocktail bar, standing in a mews and, at this time of year, obscured by blooming window-boxes, flowering tubs and trailing plants which covered the white walls in a blaze of pink, blue, white and green. Busy Lizzie and ivy added an air of discreet and tasteful attraction, underlining the promise of privacy.

By this point in its journey, the number 59 had lumbered into the undisputed territory of 'them', Joe's adopted territory and that of his enemies. Part of her was infected by his formless class hatred as the bus turned through Sloane Square and shot up Sloane Street to Knightsbridge. It was as though it traversed foreign territory, littered with women shaped like horses or greyhounds, wearing a uniform of smart cotton shirts embellished with pearls. They got on the bus for jolly short hops, braying at children called Justin or Hugo. The children were all rather like Emily's, Cath had reflected with a shock as the bus had lurched round the corner, taking her to Islington and Helen West. Cath had never thought of Emily as one of this alien breed. She was just Mrs Eliot with a face full of freckles, husband and family, the epitome of everything Cath admired.

Thinking of Emily and her brood made Cath wince with longing. It was the hot love for the children she would never have, the love for a family who asked her to belong, poured praise and gifts upon her head, said, come in, come in! and seemed to mean it, whereas she knew she couldn't come in. Not ever. Not even close.

Twenty minutes north from Helen's, forty minutes from Emily's, accelerating as if scenting home territory, the 59 bus lurched level with the leisure centre. It could have been a million miles from Harrods. This was where she lived, in the maisonette with attics which Joe had wangled from some army connection, next to the park where Damien had died. She was now in the land of the 'us', where never a 'them' was seen, but the local community had forged a similar version. 'Them' was those with houses worth burglary; 'us' was those who did it. She felt light hearted, almost light headed, as she took the longer route to the late-night supermarket, avoiding the leisure centre grounds. She had found another place to love, if not a person. Another set of keys, belonging to a voice which did not have the same high, light tone of enquiry that Emily's did. And a place to clean which was, to Cath's mind, safer than houses.

Dark and secret and safe, with a cat and a garden. Down there, without a view, where she could make everything shine, and Joe would never know where she was.

When Emily phoned Alistair in a slight state of panic at seven to say, darling, could you possibly remember exactly who the hell is coming to supper, he consulted his diary and said he did not know.

'Where did they come from?' Emily asked, wildly.

'I really don't know. Are they friends of mine, or friends of yours?'

'I don't know. Listen, darling, are you ready to come home?'

'Not quite. Need to talk to the other junior in Monday's thing. Matter of fact, I'd arranged to meet him for a drink. Is that all right with you?' he added, anxiously.

Emily was glad to have a husband as uxorious as this, but there were times when his delays irritated, even though she did not really want him home yet. She did not care whether he met a colleague in a pub or a playground. It was a different sense of anger, fuelled by the fact that although Cath had been there, labouring all day, the house remained doggedly out of control, with Emily, as usual, inexplicably relieved to be rid of her. Emily stood on the first-floor landing and yelled, her voice drowning the racket of a fight below.

'Quiet, you upstairs, just bloody shut it, will you?' Then on a lower scale, no less authoritative, in a voice sounding more like a growl, she abandoned the subtle approach.

'Help required here, you bunch of little sods! All hands to the mast! Those who do as they're told get to stay up watching this perfectly wonderful video I've got. Loads of sex and violence. Those who don't, go to bed. And that means you, Jane. Mark, your surfboard is going out of the window, now. Jane, do you hear me?'

It was a long, skinny house where voices echoed. Three children, fifteen, twelve and nine, stood in the hall looking up as their mother came down.

'Ah, there you all are,' she said in mock surprise. 'Dad's in the pub,' she announced, casually. They looked at her, wide-eyed, expectant, suspicious, trusting.

'So will someone lay the tables, please. For eight. I want the knives and forks, one big knife, one little one, not from the kitchen drawer, all in straight lines. Two wine glasses each. And I want both bathrooms tidy. If you please. Oh, and while we're at it, can anyone remember if I wrote down the names of the people who are coming?' There was the sound of a small stampede as they disappeared. She had, after all, taught them everything they knew about bribes. She had not really needed the help; simply needed to look at them, check they were still there.

The oh so busy Lizzies and the vivid, purple lobelia, balm to the spirit, bloomed on a preternaturally hot July evening, when the light seemed endless. Outside the Spoon and Fiddle, a title hidden by greenery, Alistair Eliot sat and regretted the lie he had told his wife. He was not meeting anyone: he had simply wanted to stop and nurse half a pint of lager the way he did once in a while in summer, and even then he agonized about deceit. Last summer, during the reign of a super-efficient, albeit slightly sluttish nanny, alas, now departed, Emily and he escaped their progeny to sit for an hour as he sat now when the house seemed fit to burst and Em had to admit she was going mad. They needed to be somewhere else to discuss their domestic concerns and the show of flowers here was better than any left remaining in their own little garden after the stamp of juvenile feet and the constant cry of 'Catch this!'

Emily had brief but intense flirtations with places outside home, and for this one in particular, they had cause to be grateful. It was the barman here who had listened to them talking a year ago about what Em described as the rising tide of scum in their house. He introduced them to Cath. Excuse me, he had said

49

with a careful swipe of the table, I couldn't help listening. I happen to know of someone who's rated highly. You hear things in here, you see? Shall I tell her to call? Cath had been a godsend, but it did not follow that the Eliots both went back to the Spoon. Emily alone had surmised Mr Fixit the barman was married to Cath, but, apart from that, they did not know quite from whence she came, and cared even less. She was Cath, the Treasure, with no surname and a telephone number only for emergencies.

Alistair sat, early in the evening, fiddling with his half pint and his good fortune. Raising his right fist level with his mouth in order to sip the drink, he noticed his cuff smelt of perfume, a lingering smell, which had been with him all day, competing with the window-box flowers, irritating and refreshing by turns. It had been pleasant to smell the blossom among the disinfectant fumes of the cells where he had been first thing this morning, but not so pleasant now. The scent of it seemed to have grown stronger as the day wore on. Alistair smiled. He need have no conscience about his wife. He carried her with him, wherever he went. Or it might have been Jane, with her arms round his neck this morning, her nightie soaked with *eau de parfum*.

Quite aside from the need to have an interval, however short, between the circus of court and the more stimulating circus of home, Alistair stopped at the Spoon and Fiddle to nod to the barman. There were refinements to Alistair's conscience which Emily did not share. She did not see that once you were bored with a place, you did anything other than simply stop going there, even if the service had been excellent and the memories delightful, and in this wide, pragmatic sweep of temporary patronage she included hairdressers, butchers, bakers and restaurants in the constant search for something new if not necessarily better. Alistair, on the other hand, would have gone to the same small rat-run of entertainments and services, year in year out if left to his own devices. To do otherwise made him feel slightly guilty. Objectively, he was well aware that he owed nothing to the Spoon, with its strange décor of flowers outside and an odd assortment of military memorabilia above the bar inside, either for good times had or for the respite it had given during the difficulties of last summer, nor was there any real debt to a barman because he was so pleasant and married to the cleaning lady. He simply felt a kind of duty to call in from time to time, just in case Joe felt unfairly abandoned. There was another feature, too, in this strange refinement of manners. For all that he was born of patrician stock with a lineage in Debrett, Alistair was secretly more at home with the little people of his world than he was with the great, the rich and the good.

In any event, the motives did not matter, since Joe the barman (known as nothing but) seemed to appreciate the effort. When Alistair had walked into the miniature saloon during the slack hour between the end of post-working-hour sippers and the start of serious evening drinkers, the smile on the barman's face lit the dim interior. Joe knew everyone by name and with minimal supervision from the owner, he ruled this little roost with all the efficiency of a quartermaster. The cocktails, along with the military memorabilia, were only an optional extra to attract those seeking either novelty or the quickest road to oblivion. Alistair wished they would take down all those regimental badges on the wall, as well as the ceremonial sword and the crossed bayonets which did not go with the immaculate chintz: He drank like someone who has never really learned the habit, ordered the usual half.

'Ah, Mr Eliot! What a pleasure. No need to come into the dark. Sit outside, I'll bring you the usual. I feel like one myself. Get into the sun, will you. Tomorrow it'll rain . . .'

The man never showed sign of drink. He looked like the ex-soldier he was (ex-barman, officers' mess, sir, he had told Alistair once), so the latter supposed he had long since overcome the alcoholic hazards of his profession. Alistair did not mind the chattiness, he liked it, in fact. It was a change from the taciturnity of many of his clients, and once he got home he was in for a long evening of holding several conversations at once.

'Family well, Mr Eliot?'

Alistair was a literally minded and humble man. If anyone asked him a question, he answered it fully. Joe Boyce thus knew quite a lot about his family.

'Well, Jane and her brother have been fighting like cat and dog. Funny that, they used to play like puppies and in between bouts of scrapping and when they aren't leaving marks all over one another, they still do. Strange, isn't it? I don't understand these relationships, really, do you? I was a one and only. I would have loved a brother.'

51

'Well, you say that, Mr Eliot, but they can be a mixed blessing, you know.' It was one of Joe's virtues, Alistair decided, that he not only spoke softly, but also expansively. Alistair loved to listen. Part of him did not want to be a barrister at all: he was sick of talking.

'Me, I'm like yourself, the only one. They got rid of me into the army as soon as they could, don't blame them. But my wife, now, she had a brother and he was a real trial to her. Needed looking after every day of his life. Always on the scrounge for money, always in trouble with the law, drunk as a skunk. I tell you, Mr Eliot, he nearly had us divorced. Because you can't turn away your brother, can you? You have to let him into your house, come what may, even if he is a disgrace.'

'Yes, I suppose you do,' Alistair agreed, genuinely curious. 'And then how do you get rid of him?' He had a sudden vision of how Emily might deal with a relcalcitrant relative of his own. The thought was not comforting.

'Well, this one, Mr Eliot, he got rid of himself. After I'd tried to befriend him and everything. Got him a job, even, but no, he wasn't having anything, that one. You can't stop a man if he wants to kill himself, can you?'

'Is that what he did?'

'Yes, you could put it like that, in a manner of speaking. Got himself killed in a fight.'

'Sad,' Alistair murmured, the lager suddenly sour on his tongue, even though Joe spoke airily, as if the incident were many moons ago and a hundred miles from here. Pub brawls, affray, the spontaneous formation of little gangs to exact petty revenges were all part of his stock in trade. He had dabbled in more cases of manslaughter than he could count, and suddenly did not want to talk about it. As usual, Joe Boyce sensed the need to move the conversation aside, in the same way he knew how to move a chair for a customer who was only on the brink of deciding they needed to sit.

'Now, Mr Eliot, here's a joke for your daughter. We're down at the bottom of the sea, sharks swimming about all over the place. One shark is a moneylender shark, and another one in debt, so the second one he goes off and catches a poorly old octopus, brings it back to the other one, for breakfast. So what does the moneylending shark say?'

'I don't know.'

'He says, Hallo there. Have you got that sick squid you owe me?' Alistair, who loved such childish and ghoulish wit even more than his youngest daughter, laughed immoderately.

There were times when even Joe Boyce forgot the distinctions between them and us.

'So how was your day really?' Bailey asked, rolling the clichéd question on his tongue, turning it into a drawl.

He did not think of himself as a detective, nor had he ever invested his own job with a scintilla of romance. He was simply a functionary who had to mop up trouble and sometimes go searching for it, but there were times when he could resemble a machiavellian private eye with the looks of a seedy lounge lizard. He even had a silk dressing-gown, provided by Helen, which had seen not only better days, but better years.

'Which day are we talking about?' she asked, looking at the clock with the speeding hands. 'Oh, today. Well, I told you about Cath, the cleaning lady who is going to revolutionize my life. She might even oversee the revolutionizing of my flat. The nicest thing about today is the comforting discovery that Emily Eliot is not quite the domestic paragon I thought she was.'

'Are you being bitchy?'

'No. It doesn't count as bitchiness when you're talking about someone you like.'

'First I heard. I'll never understand women.'

He was teasing. Helen thought of the vacant eyes in the photograph of Shirley Rix, and the tragedies of wilfully wasted lives. Of Mary Secura's passion for her job and of Cath with her apparent passion for cleaning.

'You don't understand women? I'm not sure anyone does, even other women.'

She had not mentioned Shirley Rix to Bailey. It made her too sombre, and her lingering guilt would have to fade before she could speak of it. Instead, they had talked long and late about Bailey's case, never thinking it was wrong to talk shop, since neither of them did so with anyone else. It re-established sanity in his mind to tell her why he was worried, although he was often economical with the harsher facts, wanting to protect her; she did not exhort him to get on with it and forget moral self-indulgence in the interests of results. So Helen knew all about the pub murder, nicely far away from her patch, so that she would never have a professional hand in it, to Bailey's relief. She knew about a group of men going out drinking, an argument with others in a pub. Three of the visiting team went away, see, coming back armed to the teeth, ready for the fight which ensued, leaving one of the home team injured, the other two in pursuit of the assailants, who had run soon after the first exchange of blows. The home team thought their injured friend was merely winded or scratched; when they came back to find him, he was dead. Brutal, foolish, wasteful and bloody. It was the drink which did it, said the one assailant who had been caught soon after, knife in back pocket. He had gone to the scene deliberately armed, ready to do serious injury. He would not name his companions. Death had been the result of his part in this loose conspiracy and since he had contributed, he was charged with murder. Although he had not intended to kill, struck once, he said, and ran as soon as blood was let.

'And who'll care?' Bailey had said over supper. 'The three who were armed were all yobs. They couldn't have won against three men. Only the one we've got is less of a yob and stupidly loyal.' They had wandered from that theme to others, to weekend plans, to the speeding clock which told them a month of their lives had passed in one evening, until Helen's thoughts returned to Bailey's laconic narrative of pavement death.

'What was his name, the dead man?'

'Damien Flood. Ex-boxer. Pool player. Handsome man.'

'I don't understand men,' she said. 'Why do they always want to fight?'

'Hormones, I'm told. I wouldn't know. I don't want to fight any more.'

'No, you don't.'

Not for me or against me, she added to herself. Not for anything. You sidestep, like a dancer. You would fight for your own version of justice, but you will not fight to keep me.

54

CHAPTER FOUR

S he could hear the thump, imagine the silence which would
follow; then the chorus of voices. Then the screaming. Mary
Secura played it like a video in her mind, first fast, then slower,
until the frames were frozen. A slow wash of blood came down
over the scene, like the crimson curtain in a theatre. End of Act
Three. Time to go home. Act One: Shirley Rix, pretty child,
bruised by her dad. Act Two: pretty woman, battered by her
husband; devoted mother. Act Three: on the run, for reasons she
wouldn't begin to define for herself. She tries to cross the road on
the way to her sister's at nine thirty in the morning. She has an old
suitcase in one hand, the child is being dragged along by the
other. Shirley has to adjust the suitcase: it is heavy. She loses hold
of the child who wants to go home. He runs into the road; she
runs too, screaming at him, unable to see where he has gone
before someone grabs him as the bus grunts to a halt. And as all
the passengers lurch forward in their seats, Shirley gets a sidelong
blow from the lumbering beast, enough to send her spinning into
the path of the car which is late for work, impatiently overtaking
the number 59. Shirley Rix, crashing against the windscreen,
teeth bared, arms and legs waving like the obedient puppet she
was, sliding out of sight, her fingers clawing the bonnet, leaving

marks. The driver, numb, the whole scenario falling into silence apart from the boom of sound from his stereo, until, with the actions of an automaton, he turns it off. Other sounds, then. The wailing of a car horn, a woman's scream which turns into a chorus, the drumming of heels on the road as the body with the broken neck jerks without control. Someone at the side is hugging a child to an ample stomach, pushing his head into her skirt while he protests at the embrace of a stranger, but the stranger will not let him go.

They all watch, paralysed. Someone else moves forward, treading carefully.

Mary Secura waited in the Unit in case someone rang. However pointless and aimless it seemed, she needed to remain where she was, to play with paperwork, and compensate her own nagging sense of failure. She had often suggested, to blank stares of amazement, that if they wanted to be more effective than they were, there should be someone on duty at night. It was the drink, so most of the victims said, which meant someone should be sitting in this office beyond the witching hour when public houses closed and men went home to beat their wives. Poor Shirley Rix had denied her husband the chance to kill her. Mary had no business being here. No-one was paid overtime to wait for a call when the answerphone worked and victims of any kind had universal recourse to dialing 999. The sergeant at the front desk had asked, didn't she have a home to go to? Mary resolved to use the back way out.

She had what her employers described as a stable existence, particulars of which had been added discreetly to her annual reports for the last two years. Officer resides with PC Dave Inglewood (nice lad: should go far), attached to traffic, 'A' division; joint mortgage on maisonette. There was no mention of her hunger for achievement which he did not share, or the relief she felt when the patterns of his duty rosters meant they scarcely saw each other for weeks on end. Her parents, regretting the absence so far of a wedding ring, looked with pride at the photos, dusted daily, of their daughter in a starched white shirt and blue uniform. Hadn't the girl done well?

The office nested in the nether regions of the police station: second floor, through two fireproof doors, turn left, right and straight ahead. No-one rang while Mary fixed a photo of Shirley Rix to the wall. It showed Shirley's bruised profile hidden behind the smiling face of her fair-haired baby. The picture had been taken merely to make her relax, c'mon Shirl, let's have one of Jason, oh, isn't he gorgeous. Pride made Shirley turn to the camera. This mother-and-child picture was not part of the case which, like all good prosecutions for domestic warfare, lumbered off the ground with all the speed and efficiency of a crippled jumbo jet. They had given Shirley a copy of the picture: Mary supposed Mr Rix would find it amongst her things on his release, flourish it in indignation while he sued for false imprisonment.

Finishing the careful pinning of the photo to the notice board, Mary realized she was being stupid. Each additional minute here achieved nothing more than compounding a reputation for eccentricity, hardly a virtue in police circles, especially for a woman.

She had reached the first set of heavy fire doors when she heard the phone behind her. She turned back in a hurry, but there was always the wrong decision to make with these double doors, whether to pull or push, which one to shove first, what to drop in order to use both hands, and by the time she was back inside the tidy office, with the files ranged against the wall and the empty computer screen staring at her, the ghostly, cheerful message on the answerphone was halfway through its reassuring recitation, ending abruptly with a click and purr as she grabbed the receiver and listened to nothing else.

That was the point when Mary Secura sat down and wept for Shirley Rix, who had died while her one protector had gone hunting wallpaper with a solicitor. She would never be able to forgive Helen West for distracting her. She hit the double doors with her fist on the way back out, stopped, winced, then used her palm to push the door in the right direction. Outside in the car park, someone whistled, slow but loud.

Mary was thinking, there must be another way. She was still thinking it when she slammed through her own front door to a clean house with a yellow bathroom.

Is this all? she was asking herself. Is this really all?

Home, sweet home. Cath put down the phone and giggled. Joe had an answerphone; they had everything. They had the top two floors and the attics of this creaking house for next to nothing. Home, sweet home. There was a landing at the top of the stairs, living room and kitchenette on one small floor, bedroom and bathroom on the next, then three attic rooms above, each with a brown stained ceiling, and in one a hole in the plaster through which she could see the stars. Someone owned the place, Cath supposed. Some poor old fart who had forgotten about the rent and the legal action long after Joe had ceased to pay and said it was now their own, since no-one had bothered them for a year, and let's face it, Cath, it was cheap at the price even before then. Yes, even though she felt they lived here through some kind of theft. Spacious, yes, but it leaked, was cold, and probably condemned.

'Oh, Joe.' She had been hot with pleasure. Now she blushed at the memory of her first sight of those bare dark walls, the stains, the lino floors, the dripping kitchen tap, everything else taken except for the stains and the stairs.

'I said I'd look after you, didn't I?'

He could not have a wife of his in a council house, even if they could have got one, and he hadn't tried. Got to be black or lesbian, he had said, and oddly, she had believed him. Council houses were for poor people, he had added, and we're gonna be rich. Cath had risen to the challenge like air bubbling out of water. She was already an expert at what could be lifted from skips and second-hand shops, the dirtier the better; a keen bargainer at the kind of auction where no-one looking for valuables would bother, fought over pennies for things worth their weight in gold. Cath knew to walk down a street the night before a weekly rubbish collection, finding treasures; she could knock on doors where someone had left a square of carpet, a three-legged chair, a kitchen cupboard. She could make shelves using good wood and breeze blocks, and find the posters with the daisies on and the tea towels to match. She was built for work: she had no embarrassment in her quest for a home.

Needs must as the devil drives, she had said cheerfully, although Joe was not the devil then. Cath had been homeless once, and that was the memory which drove her. But Joe's pride was a different animal, one which could not feed on leftovers. The more she did, the quieter he grew. When the walls were painted, and the floors more or less covered with something or other to hide the scratched and broken boards, and the kitchenette had recycled taps which did not drip and a cooker which was free along with a fridge, he was so pleased he beat her black and blue. All round the body, leaving buttocks and thighs a patchwork of bruises. Had she possessed the ability to speak to anyone at all, she might have confessed that the beating took the edge off her décor, since she never quite lost her sense of irony, but the voice had gone the way of two broken ribs, and she did not have any friends. In his insidious fashion, he had seen to that.

No friends between them, either, except her brother, Damien.

The light on the answerphone maintained a steady glare, which Cath liked when she came home to a dark room; it had the same effect as a night-light, although to all other intents and purposes, it was redundant. The light indicating a message never meant more than a wrong number, an occasional call from Joe's employer, big Mickey Gat, or someone selling double glazing. The latter struck in the early evening (Hallo, my name's Lucy, have you got a minute?), and Cath always found she had enough minutes to make them run through the gamut of their wares before putting down the receiver. There, she would say to the wall, that's stopped YOU bothering anyone else, although she had liked being bothered. When Damien was alive, there had been more phone calls, of course, and even if his voice had been so slurred that he sounded as if he was on the other side of the world, he was always an improvement on a salesman. These days, without the occasional illumination of his voice, Cath used the phone to gain access to other answer machines, listening to the messages, sometimes leaving one of her own, slamming back the receiver as if it was hot should anyone real happen to speak. There were all kinds of company to be had this way; all kinds of dreams. For instance, the girl on the Domestic Violence Unit message had a nice voice. Friendly. It could have belonged to the girl the neighbours sent round one morning after a worse than usual row. The one who had not believed Cath when she had said, no, nothing's wrong, will you please go away? The old couple downstairs who had done the reporting did not live here any more. Instead, there were new people: kids, who made enough row themselves to cover Joe at his worst.

It was nine in the evening. The day was beginning to die, and through the sparsely covered floorboards of Cath's living room, the steady thump of the base rhythm entered her feet without a tune, and echoed in her ears.

She took a plate of bread and butter and a cup of tea one floor up and ate it, perched on the side of the bed, careful of the crumbs. Sometimes, if it was not too cold, she took her snacks in the attics, unbearable though they were. She loathed these rooms not for the temperature, or the dampness which dried out over each successive summer, but for the objects the rooms contained. Boxes from mail-order firms. Joe's dreams of a better life, drawn from the imagination of his which was as fat and one dimensional as the catalogues he regarded with such reverence. Joe's storage dump, the warehouse of his dreams, lovingly acquired against the day when they would move into their palace. She had said to him once, in the days when she still teased him, that if he ever went near a court of law and they offered him a bible to take the oath, he would ask for a mail-order catalogue rather than scripture, on the basis that there was not a word or promise in there which he could bring himself to disbelieve. Better than all that military stuff he'd had once, though, even though Damien had liked it. At least she'd made Joe get rid of that, once he realized that it too was second hand.

Cath ate the bread and butter, still hungry. He would not want her going out for chips. Once she was indoors, she remained there. It was an aspect of him she had loved, the big man guarding the small woman. Lovable Joe. Even if she shrank from the man in his living room; even if she despaired and ran away again; even if their mutual entertainments outside these walls consisted of no more than yet another visit to yet another pub, she was proud when it happened. At least she had her man, and her home was spotless, which was more than that poor Helen West. If it ain't broke, don't fix it.

The attics seemed to sway with the sound of traffic. She hated the height, thought lovingly of living below stairs, hurried down again to the same pulsating noise from below. The phone rang when her mouth was still full. Cath looked at it in amazement, her jaw drooping before she clamped it shut with her fist and winced. He never rang, not Joe. Cath remained paralysed and then started to chew furiously as the phone spewed out Joe's cheerful message – 'Hallo! We aren't here at the minute . . .' – a message which made it sound as if he and his spouse were constantly out at parties. If he was not behind a bar working, he would be in front of one drinking, and still Cath found herself looking over her shoulder, chewing even faster in case he was in the doorway, commenting on her manners for not acknowledging his presence and eating like an animal. As she stood, head turned, limbs immobile, all she could hear was the warm and hesitant voice of Helen West, beginning as if she too was thrown by the sound of Joe's pretty speech. The voice grew more confident and assured as it went on. Without putting her conclusions into words (a pastime Cath found dangerous and deeply suspicious), Cath sensed someone who was not entirely at home with a machine and not nearly as confident as she looked.

'Oh, er, hallo, message for Cath. Christ, I've just realized it's a bit late to be phoning, but did I actually give you the keys? Anyway, tell Mrs Eliot if I didn't, I'm so stupid. Look forward to seeing you next time. Take care, Helen.'

The voice hurried towards the end, as if the very sound of it made the speaker nervous. I'm so stupid, it said. Cath rocked on her heels, surprised into a sudden snort of laughter and a sudden, delirious sense of pity. Fancy, this other woman was really a bit pathetic, looking the way she did and being the age she was, ten years or so older than Cath, and not having a man who looked after her.

Cath washed up her plate and knife, used them again to make sandwiches for Joe, then went round the kitchen with a damp cloth and a weary touch. She thought of Helen West, weaving a romance to explain the inexplicable phenomenon of a pretty woman without a man. And there was something else. Helen West verged on the beautiful, but she had a great big scar in the middle of her forehead which showed when she swiped away the long, almost black hair which was held back in a slide that could not quite contain the mass of it. Cath knew about scars. The scar alone was sufficient reason to tolerate the woman.

Cath found herself standing over the machine, looking for a way to play back the message so she could hear it again. She had liked the sound of insecurity and her own luxurious feeling of pity, and she had not thought of Damien for at least an hour.

*

61

Joe Boyce walked towards the number 59. He had a satchel in which he carried some of the tools of his trade. He did not want them stolen, such as they were. A small knife with a comfortable handle, a shiny Thermos flask for mixing and shaking, a chamois leather, soft as silk, for polishing glasses to a high shine. Last month, someone had broken and entered the Spoon and removed all the spirits from behind the bar. Joe had only shrugged. He had told Mickey Gat more times than he could count that the back of the place was insecure and, besides, the loss of the spirits was not the end of the world. Cocktails were out of fashion; the buggers only wanted beer and wine in summer, apart from the strange old school from the jungles of Chelsea, living on pensions and borrowed time, who bundled themselves into a corner to drink one whisky sour after another. It was the younger varieties, throwing money around while they yawed in those dreadful voices, who got so far up Joe's nose and down his throat he wanted to hit them, but they were the kind big Mickey wanted in the pub. Big Mickey knew nothing about fine wines, but was not a fool. Don't encourage these slow, steady drinkers, Joe was told; nor the ones who come in for half a pint and stay for ever. Joe was respectful to the boss. Mickey Gat was an outstanding and unusual member of the British working class and Joe had plenty of time for those, even those coasting round the edges. Mickey may have been a wolf in sheep's clothing, but still a wolf. If Mickey, born Michaela, had been a mere male, instead of a creature of male mannerisms and attitudes, that male would have been intimidating. As it was, Mickey the woman, with all the strengths of a man plus all the subtleties of her own sex, presented a combination fit to terrify.

''Ere's a little something for your lady wife,' patting Joe on the shoulder with a power which made him wince, one broad-built person to another. 'She'll like this. You could put yourself in luck, old son.'

Mickey was all East End charm, laid on with a trowel, half of it genuine, half of it borrowed from a childhood fascination with the Kray brothers. She had little enough in common with Joe. Mickey's sporting career had been successful for a start: she had been women's weightlifting champion, and had dabbled with wrestling until it ruined her make-up. The muscles still showed. Joe's inglorious boxing career had been monitored by Mr Gat,

Mickey's old man, once famous in the ring himself, wily enough to turn triumph into promotion and management, a good gambler, clever enough to diversify the business in all directions, make a pile and a retinue of friends; while Joe's small stature and lack of discipline both inside and outside the army boxing ring had cost him a disgrace. Mr Gat (Harry to his friends) was now 'him indoors', wreathed in the cigarette smoke which had curtailed his career, and, without spite, Mickey liked it best that way. She wore the mantle of his local fame, the business of boxing and pool, the pubs, the merchandise, with the ease of a cloak. It was not anything she told anyone, Harry least of all, but it had always been she who had the brains.

Takes one good bloke to know another. Mickey winked like some amateur comic performer about to tell a lewd joke, adding to the most innocuous exchanges an air of harmless conspiracy. What else Mickey did for a living, except own this pub and two more in Clapton to augment the market stalls, Joe did not know and made it his business not to ask. Mickey rarely came near the place at opening times, unless early or late when the bulk of customers were gone. The morning uniform of shiny shell suit was replaced in the evening by more glamorous gear. Even without the colours, the sheer size of Mickey would have terrified the regulars with their elbow patches. Despite the soft voice, her body seemed to have been poured into the mould of a muscle-bound character from a comic. Superwoman expanded into a mountain range without too many valleys. In comparison, Joe was only a miniature, just as he had been with his brother-in-law, Damien, Mickey's best friend. When the takings were particularly good, Mickey would slip a paw into a capacious pocket and hand Joe perfume. From the outset of their acquaintance, Joe had been left in no doubt, without a word on the subject being spoken, that if his own hands extracted anything from the till of the Spoon, he would find his knuckles mashed to a pulp.

Mickey had manicured nails, a curious affectation for such a masculine female.

'Here, take it,' thrusting the perfume again. 'She'll love it, I promise.' A shiny fingernail with a half-sovereign ring tapped a sharp nose, knowingly.

There was a small living area behind the bar, a bathroom and kitchen, full of boxes left by Mickey, all preserved in exactly the same state in which they had arrived. If you were loyal to Mickey, loyalty was returned, but what Mickey did not know was that the only occasion when Joe was ever tempted to laugh, was when that paw with the bright nails extended itself with a boxed bottle of perfume held in the palm.

'Go on, Joe. You'd think I was giving you an f'ing bribe. Take it!'

'Thanks.'

Joe half adored Mickey, except for the sweet smell which accompanied all her gestures, and the scent in the back room, from the boxes.

Present for Cath, just like Damien had done.

Eleven thirty and all quiet tonight. He locked up, heady from the smell of the window-boxes, satisfied with a day's work, soberly conducted, untroubled by the perfume in his satchel. The pretty mews, all low houses, solid doors and cheerful lights, was softly silent as he walked towards the main road for the bus. He had encountered nothing all day but open politeness and sweet-mannered customers, no drunks, no wrecks, no-one drowning sorrows and no aggression. Until that motley crew who had arrived just on closing: kids, already drunk and wanting to make it worse. He shut the door in their faces, listened to them banging on the windows for a while, took no notice, apart from sticking up two fingers in between wiping the bar. They had barked and sworn in upper-class voices, summer holiday kids. Leave them. That's what Mickey said. No after-hours stuff, Joe, not ever. I'm the licensee, right? It just ain't fucking worth it.

He hit Sloane Avenue, walking with a lilt to his step, and it was there they began to follow him. It was not as if he ever aped Mickey's appearance, not consciously at least, but he was a small, well-groomed man with fashionable baggy trousers, the short back and sides of his haircut artfully trendy; he was thirty-three and a man has to look to his youth. Even if he never could have looked a patch on Damien.

'Wanker,' someone said out of the darkness, three feet behind.

'Fucking queer,' said another.

'Naa, just can't get it up,' said a third, and that last remark, intended to do no more than insult, but loaded with a horrible element of truth, made him turn. He saw there were five of them:

64

one fat, bare chested, belly hanging down like a sumo wrestler; one thin as a rake, so the hand holding something in his pocket stood out from his skinny thigh like a growth; two others, middle sized, shifting and sniggering; one more little one, hanging back, as if in need of his mother. He eyed them for a minute, weighed the chances, his mind clear. One fat slob, three others more drunk than sober and a little frightened fairy. Enough, in terms of weight, but his legs could not move. He had a terrifying sense of *déjà vu*, as if he had been in the same place, same time, again and again. The whole scenario assumed a sickening familiarity: he should have braced himself to find that old aggression, the adrenalin sending heat waves to beat against his temples and make him mad, but instead he looked at their faces and heard the music of a siren in the distance. The faces were implacable. They all looked like Cath's brother, features masked in a kind of genial malevolence, all of them twitching. He shut his eyes for a minute, blinking to blot out the presence of that dead man. When he opened his eyes again, the predators were that much closer, only a few feet away, circling with the inhuman technique of animals surrounding prey.

Joe acted instinctively. He screamed at the top of his voice, a shrill shriek, like the high-pitched wailing of a baby. Then he fell to the ground, clutching his satchel to his chest. 'Oh! My heart, my heart! Help me please, help me please!' The words stuck in his throat with their own indigestible hypocrisy, rising like bile along with the peanuts he had consumed behind the bar, with water, in lieu of drink. The effect was the one he desired. With his head turned south, he could look towards Knightsbridge, the bus stop and the presence of taxis. To the left, and a hundred yards away, there was Mr Eliot's house, where he had once peered through the window and frightened a child; he could not stumble towards that source. He writhed in the dust of the pavement, moaning and twisting, not all of it feigned.

They ran. He looked like he was dying, so they ran. Except the last, the little fairy who had hung back in the first place. He paused, then he stopped and then he kicked with remarkable precision. One to the head, his training shoe connecting with the swell of bone just below the left eye. Joe tried to shield his ears, crossing his arms across his face. The little fucker was not out of breath as his boot connected with Joe's ribs, casual kicks which

65

carried the whole weight of the body behind them. An agile body, bending to whisper in his ear. 'Get you next time, sonny. Here's one for luck.'

One final kick which made him scream. He could not meet the eyes.

Damien's eyes, to the life. It was all so bloodless, so shameful.

The conductor on the number 59 had an ebony face, stretched across beautiful bones, and soulful brown eyes which refused to connect. It was the distant expression of a man who has learned to see no evil. Joe stared at him, challenging him to say something as he got aboard, the only passenger clambering upstairs as the bus moved away, using his hands so that he practically climbed on all fours, clinging to the satchel like a lifeline. When he began to fumble inside it with trembling hands for his travel card, he started to feel the first sensations of sheer relief and the enormity of what he had missed. Christ, they might have got the keys to the pub, and what would Mickey have done about that? He dreaded to think: he would have had to go back and stay there all night, waiting for them to come back. There would have been no question of calling the police, that much was understood. The relief made him tremble more, so that when he held his card up for the conductor, it danced in front of his eyes. He was aware of the black man standing there, swaying slightly instead of moving away.

'Hey, man, where have you been?'

Joe thought the conductor must have noticed the mark on his cheek, the dirt on his clothes. He looked at him but the man was not looking back. He was simply standing there, wrinkling his nose.

'You smelling real sweet, man,' was all he said with a twisted smile, lumbering away to the only other passengers on the top deck, three girls, huddled together giggling at the front.

Joe delved back into the bag. The smell was overpowering. Perfume, the box mashed where he had rolled on it, the liquid sending out fumes which seared his nostrils, made him close the bag and push it away from him.

The shame of it. To lie down and scream like a baby, and come up smelling of roses.

Joe hated perfume. He walked down the road to the place he

66

called home. Perfume made him feel as though he should be followed by cats; it assailed his senses like the smell of manure; it reminded him of being clutched to the bosom of his mother, his grandmother, his aunts, and all those who had left him somewhere along the line. He never gave Mickey's perfume to Cath. He could buy his own gifts for his own wife.

He could not bear to fumble in the bag again, to contaminate his hands by looking for the key. He rang the bell and waited, imagined its throaty and croaking sound upstairs, another thing to be fixed. There was no answer. He rang again, started shouting, Cath, Cath! Let me in. He knew where she would be, up in the attic rooms, staring at photos of Damien, lighting a candle to his memory. The hands around the keys were unsteady: he thundered upstairs.

She was there at the top, holding the door open, anticipating him with her timid brown eyes, dressed in nothing but a towel which she clutched to herself. He could see the faint shadow of bruises on her arms, and another wave of sickening shame swept over him. She saw his face, the bruise grown swollen and livid on the journey home.

'I bought you some perfume, Cath,' was all he said as he stepped inside.

'Joke from Joe,' he added. She looked at the bruise, without touching him, still holding the towel across her chest. Then she wrinkled her nose, slightly, smiled with the smile of a sphinx.

He had no idea from where the blow came, only that it was he who had administered it. She went reeling back, into the living room, hitting the wall. He followed, feeling for his belt, panting. And then he was pinning her to the floor, pushing himself inside her, oblivious to the dryness, pumping his seed in there, quickly shouting as he came. Then he lay across her on the rough carpet, sobbing.

'I love you, Cath. I love you.'

She stroked his head.

'I know you do.'

One hand stroked his hair against her chest. The other fingered the scar on her abdomen which made her so impossible to love. There had been the promise of a child, long, long since. She had not wanted it then, not while she was a child herself, and now, in her arms, she cradled this other.

CHAPTER FIVE

'Why is it, Bailey, we offer you administrative jobs, suited to the rank you've somehow managed to achieve, God knows how, and you sidestep the issue? We send you for management training and you go straight back to the street. Like some bloody homing pigeon.'

The blank face before him showed no glimmer of emotion, less of humour, a face carved from granite. It reminded Bailey of a gargoyle, weathered by centuries into something almost beyond further decay: not the face the divisional commander showed to his grandchildren.

'I suppose I like nicking people, sir.'

'You've got a degree, haven't you? We need brains like yours in think-tanks, Bailey. We need you at the top.'

'I don't think so, sir. With respect,' he added thoughtfully, to make it look as if serious thought was a habit, 'I think you need me at the bottom.'

'Of which heap, Bailey?'

'The dung heap,' said Bailey. 'The septic tank, not the think-tank.' The commander's smile did not alter the gargoyle effect. They would speak again soon, he said, and to Bailey's ears, the words contained more threat than promise.

He walked down the corridors of New Scotland Yard towards the lift. Each floor was the same, built round the central shaft, with minor alterations to the layout. The gents lavatory was always in the same place, the senior command offices had similar styles, and on one floor, the number of which he could never remember by some Freudian convenience, there was a foyer of portraits of old commissioners and a dining room reserved for those *en route* to becoming the next. Bailey had indeed managed to skip his way up the ranks without ever resorting to politics or policy. All he had done was remain industrious and effective, but inconspicuous, making no complaints and telling no tales. For useful loose cannons like Ryan he had simply rearranged their duties; in the case of men with a propensity to violence or light fingers, he sidestepped the whole paraphernalia of discipline proceedings by telling them exactly what he was prepared to do to them should they fail to reconsider their careers. Turnover could be high under Bailey's command. He could exert more quiet terror than a hanging judge and inspire the kind of loyalty reserved for the Queen. Ryan said he was a secretive bastard, who never caused embarrassment: that was all there was to it.

Which meant those on high should let him alone to perform where he excelled: trouble-shooting, organizing an investigation wherever he was asked, a humble, only ostensibly obedient maverick, rolling with the punch of being landed with teams of inadequates. Some learned to take responsibility; others, like Ryan, would always be the second lieutenant in need of a leader. Most police officers were eminently adaptable. Except himself. He could no more live and breathe in this ivory tower than he could have flown above it. Senior officers mess, waitress dining in cosy style, a corridor of portraits and committees, advancement beyond the stratosphere; speak now, the commander said with his forked tongue, and all this could be yours.

Outside, there was another bomb scare. Bailey had to wait to get out from the underground car park while someone stuck a mirror beneath his car. Girls in skirts were asked to consent to the same examination on their way in to work, and he wanted to suggest to the man on duty that if he had brought in a bomb, it would have been gift wrapped.

The sun shone, melting the irritation and sense of impending doom. Bailey might have lost that capacity for fury which had made him want to hit walls, but he could not shed his contempt for ambition, any more than he could rid himself of the far more corrupting force of pity; he looked to his own demise without a sense of tragedy. At forty-seven he was old, for a policeman. The equivalent of an honourable discharge would not leave him penniless. He just wished he had reached the age when he was really pragmatic enough to leave alone a delegated quick-result case like the murder of Damien Flood.

He chuckled with a sense of freedom as he rounded Parliament Square, saw the traffic jam, stopped and ran his tongue behind his top teeth, executed a U-turn with the satisfying ease of a taxi driver diving towards the prospect of a fare and then found that the change of direction left him, suddenly, directionless. He was pointing towards Victoria when he wanted to go north-east to his own happy hunting grounds. There was no other immediate reason for Bailey to go for a drink at the Spoon and Fiddle. Owned by Mickey Gat from Whitechapel. Run by the brother-in-law of a four-month-dead, one-time athlete, pool player turned drunk, killed in the aftermath of a pub fight. Bailey could recall, word for word, the statement made by this brother-in-law, Joe Boyce, background material only.

'I get one day off a week from being a barman,' the statement said, 'and when I do, I go to a different kind of place to drink. If Damien was around, I would go with him. To tell the truth, he wasn't the best companion, since he could not hold his drink, always picked a fight, while me, I get quiet and sleepy. Anyway, he did pick an argument with someone in the pub, the Lamb it's called, only round the corner from where I live, as a matter of fact, and it all ended up in threats, you come outside with me, all that stuff. Damien loved it of course, Damien would. He had three friends with him, big blokes, like himself, all ex-boxers, they could handle anything. I dunno why it is when blokes are big, they seem to attract trouble. One of them wanted to go home, so Damien said go then, but he didn't, and then Damien says to me, stay, will you? And I said, the hell I will, if this lot are coming back for a fight, I've your sister to look after and I'm not getting hurt for anyone. Fine, he says, fine, and we get another drink. I don't drink much myself; you can't when you run a bar, but when I'm not at work, I take anything offered. They're a good laugh, that crew of Damien's, when they get together. That other team were long gone, I forgot about them.'

Ryan had taken this statement. He had an ear for the vernacular and an ability to make people talk, something to do with his deceptively friendly face.

'Anyway, I hardly noticed that the crowd had left and I forgot the fact they threatened to come back. I can't, for the life of me, remember what the argument was about. Damien was good at pool; the pub has five tables; he'd won some money off a bloke who thought he was better; Damien had fleeced the poor kid on a bet, that was it, I think. Oh, maybe three or four games. What was lost? I've no idea. Maybe fifty, more like a hundred, but Damien was so shambling and so clever, they couldn't see him coming. He was more than good at pool: he was brilliant.'

There would have been a pause in the statement, for tea, Bailey guessed, rehearsing it all in his mind. The man was not a defendant, merely a witness. He would have been afforded all the luxury the police station could allow. Which was tea or coffee in a smoke-filled interview room, not quite far enough away from the sobbing and grunting in the cells.

'Anyway, the place closed and out we went. Damien wanted to go to some other place, I said, no, not me, I must get home, your sister has an early start. He nodded, he never thought much of me, to tell the truth, and you were either with Damien or against him. So I didn't wait to see if there was anyone there in the shadows, if you see what I mean. He had more than enough going for him with his friends around him. I was only ever asked along for the ride because my wife wanted Damien and me to be friends; he's a bit flash for me. If he wanted a fight he had one. Boys will be boys and there never was any stopping my brother-in-law. I never dreamt it would go so far.'

Not a bad bloke, that Joe Boyce, Ryan had said to Bailey. Bailey had never seen the man whose evidence had been agreed as part of the setting; it would provide nothing of great interest to either prosecution or defence at the forthcoming trial. Pleasant Mr Joseph Boyce had helped with descriptions, that was all, leaving before the action, as Damien's friends had confirmed in their own, sorrowful evidence. Since they too had failed to prevent the death, they could not afford contempt, although one of them suggested it. Joe was nothing but a hanger-on, adopted

71

by Damien and Mickey Gat because he was wed to Damien's sister, Mary Catherine Boyce: there was a statement from her too.

Bailey could not have said why he wanted to cast his eyes over Mr Boyce, some little trace element of bitterness in the statement, perhaps, but with his car accidentally pointing west instead of east, the time was as good as any. Ryan was a fine investigator. He got on the wavelength and spoke as he was spoken to, but his judgement, well, that varied.

Bailey always knew the exact time of day, and as long as it was greater London, exactly where he was without reference to anything or anybody. The map and the minutes past the hour always seemed to tally with his preconceptions. The talent was one he dismissed as no more than accident; you walk round streets, he said, you get to know which way is south and how long it is since last you slept.

The Spoon and Fiddle surprised him, first for its diminutive size, then for the luxuriance of the flowers, third for its signs of taste and privacy, and lastly, as an afterthought, its proximity to the Eliots.

'Mr Boyce?'

The man turned from an assiduous polishing of glasses at the bar, responded with an almost stagy deference, clicking his heels.

'At your service, sir!' A small man, Bailey noted, muscular; soft round the chin.

He produced his warrant card. 'About the Donovan trial. Can I have a word?' It sounded such a clichéd way to begin but Bailey knew life was full of clichés; most people understood little else and expected a policeman to talk like his TV equivalent. What he had not expected was for Joseph Boyce to respond in the same clichéd terms, by looking visibly shocked, turning white, so that the livid bruise on his cheekbone and round the left eye burned in a pale skin like the mark of a branding iron. The reaction was quickly controlled. Boyce shook himself, looked resigned, then smiled with a sigh and extended his hand.

Bailey did not want to take it, did so reluctantly. The pressure was dry and firm.

'My, but you gave me a shock. I thought all that was over, bar

72

the shouting. I hope they hang the bastard, but you can't these days, can you?'

'You seem to have been in a fight, Mr Boyce.' Bailey pointed at the bruise, somewhat rudely.

'Kids. Followed me home last evening after I wouldn't serve them a drink. It's nothing. I got away lightly.'

'Did you report it?'

'C'mon, sir, you know better than that. When I couldn't begin to tell you what they looked like? I just wanted to get home. How else can I help you?'

There was a hidden truculence behind the easy manner. The man was clean, but Bailey could sense fear.

'I just wanted to check a few points on your statement. About your brother-in-law and the evening he died. I'm sorry if it upsets you, but if I dot the Ts and cross the Is, there's less chance you'll be needed at the trial.'

The light of hope sprang into Joe's eyes. 'That would be great,' he said firmly. 'I don't want to go anywhere near a court if I can help it. Upsets the wife, see? What do you want to know? Thought I said it all.'

Bailey hoiked his long frame onto a bar stool. He had not quite thought what to ask, an investigator without portfolio and a car pointed in the wrong direction, but he was rarely at a total loss for words.

'Were you fond of your brother-in-law, Mr Boyce?'

'Oh yes, of course, even though he could be a problem. Anyone who knew Damien loved him. You should have seen the turnout for his funeral. I've never seen flowers like it. Never.'

Bailey nodded, without adding that he had been present himself on the edges of the same funeral, taking in the appearance of Damien's friends and looking out for signs of his family. There had been one woman sobbing, only one. The flowers had been repellent; Bailey's experience showed that the amount of floral tributes at funerals was often in inverse proportion to the grief, indeed they were sometimes a last revenge.

'Is your wife the only relative?'

'There's a cousin or two somewhere, but otherwise, yes. The parents died when they were kids; Damien and she grew up together. Like peas in a pod. Very close.'

'What does your wife do, Mr Boyce?'

73

Boyce turned from friendly to angry.

'Leave her out of it, will you? She's had quite enough, what with having to identify her only kith and kin and then being asked to confirm what time I came home that night, as if it was me who needed the alibi! What does it matter what she does for a living?'

Bailey could picture the statement of Mary Catherine Boyce. Short and to the point. Identifying her brother. Saying what time her husband had gone out and come in. Cleaning lady, he remembered suddenly, as if that mattered.

He got up. 'I'd only want to ask her a few questions about Damien's background. I know there was a fight, but we're still, well, how can I put it, short on the motive.'

'Anyone can get killed in a fight,' said Boyce, pointing to the bruise. 'Happens every day in this God-forsaken place. You could work hard all your life without ever putting a foot wrong and still go that way. What difference does your background make?' He was becoming increasingly agitated.

'Where could I find her, Mr Boyce? I'll do my best not to cause any upset.'

'I believe you. Others wouldn't. Why don't you send that other bloke? I liked him.'

Because Ryan is so often blind, Bailey thought, watching the other man struggling for control. Boyce was working out how to minimize the inevitable, a primitive, Bailey concluded: a body responsive to orders and not so stupid as to imagine he could hide his wife for ever. Nothing unusual in that: there were not many men who wanted police officers calling on their wives, especially a spouse unlikely to declare her meagre income or pay tax on it. But it was not this aspect of the black economy which worried Boyce. He was weighing up the pros and cons of where such an interview with Cath should take place. Should he invite this interference home some afternoon when he could insist on being present, or could he ensure Bailey saw Cath somewhere where she would be equally awkward, embarrassed and taciturn? He smiled. There was no malice in the smile, Bailey noticed, merely satisfaction.

'All right, if you must. No time like the present. She's working round the corner here. Chantry Street. You might know it. Big houses. Number seven.'

Then it was Bailey's turn to mask surprise. Declining the now effusive offer of a drink, something Ryan rarely did, he left with a nod of acknowledgement.

As he reached his own car, Bailey saw a large, silver-coloured Jaguar, old but perfectly preserved, moving with all the grace of an ageing ballerina as it rolled over the cobblestones of the mews. It stopped outside the flowers of the Spoon with scarcely a sound, while Bailey looked on, enviously. There were few materialistic ambitions which moved him much, outside the clocks he collected, but the sight of this elegant vehicle inspired an acquisitive admiration. The very best vintage, he thought, I would love one of those, a car which was more than a car. He was thinking, as an antidote, how such a motor would not last five minutes in his neck of the woods without a garage built like a fortress, when a figure rose out of the driving seat, yawned, stretched and executed three karate kicks, before ambling into the Spoon. A huge creature, dressed in a vivid shell suit, with a walk both languid and energetic, the sun catching pale hair and a face tanned by sunbeds. Bailey smiled to himself, envy of the car dispelled. Awesomely gorgeous Mickey Gat. A legend in her own time, except for lazy investigators like Ryan who never listened to important gossip and never kept their eyes open wide enough. Feminism incarnate, in one sense, that was Mickey Gat; big enough to make jelly of a man. One of a dying breed, lawless, but law-enforcing. Like the Jag, Bailey reflected: they were both in their way the very best of British. The sight of Mickey, looking like a bull in a china shop amid the discreet wealth of the mews, somehow made Bailey feel at home. He smiled after the retreating figure with affection, almost with desire, which was only in part for the car.

Mickey had attended the Damien funeral, probably contributed some of the flowers of which Joe had boasted, but it had never been part of Ryan's narrow mandate to explore any closer link. It made no odds, surely, who the murdered man knew; he was killed in a pub brawl and no single witness had suggested it was more complicated than that. Bailey shrugged. Neither had the ripples of the investigation turned up the fact that the sister of the deceased worked for a family Bailey knew. Why should it? Mary Catherine Boyce working for the Eliots; the fact did indeed stretch the long arm of coincidence. Bailey had learned never to be surprised by the elastic length of that particular limb. He decided, all the same, not to go to the Eliots' number seven Chantry Street. Something told him that was a move which could embarrass Emily Eliot, and her Treasure. Let well alone. If the woman the Eliots called Cath, and her statement called Mary, had not told them anything about her family, least of all the death of a brother, it was not for Bailey to invade her privacy; after all, he had no real purpose, even less official blessing for these formless, further enquiries. He was only here because he had turned his car in the wrong direction. Mary Catherine, known as Cath. The woman who had also turned Helen's flat into a different version of itself over the last week or two. If Bailey vowed to keep diplomatic silence with the Eliots, should he then use Helen in pursuit of his own curiosity? She would not like that.

Emily Eliot sang as she worked. Occasionally, when her usual reserve deserted her, Cath would croon a little too, stopping if she thought she was heard. For some reason Emily could not discern, Cath rarely seemed to get further than 'Onward Christian Soldiers', and only the first verse of that. 'With the blood of Jesus, going on before!' The words would emerge in the midst of a barely recognizable tune, half grunted, half sung. She and Emily rarely sang in unison, although that was often the way they worked. There was never a shortage of tasks in the long mornings Cath spent in the house. One day a week, they would tackle something specific. Today it was a large dressing room attached to the main bedroom. Emily was sure it had moths in it. One of Alistair's suits had been eaten to death. She did not enjoy these joint tasks: they made her loud.

'Little sods,' Emily yelled. 'Look at that! Why the hell can't they go for cheap old sweaters? Why concentrate on the one thing which costs money? Mohair and something, this was once. Nice and soft for them to get their little teeth into, they can't even make an effort. Look at it.'

'He didn't wear it once, last winter,' Cath pointed out. Emily beamed, her rage subsiding. Put Cath in here, with her awful disinfectant smell, the moths would die anyway.

'He never really liked it, that's why.' She emerged from the depths with an armful of clothes on hangers.

'In fact, most of the things in the back of here no-one really likes. I just hate the thought of the bloody moths chomping away without asking permission first. Most of this belongs on the rubbish heap. Unless there's anything you want, of course.'

'I'll think about it, can I?'

Emily nodded, suppressing the irritation which so often beset her when she and Cath worked in close proximity. It was a reluctance to touch her, no more than that, which Emily translated into a slight aversion to one who was at once so passive and deferential, and at other times as stubborn as a mule. She knew Cath would take the clothes as soon as her back was turned. She just could not do it while she was being watched, and that was irritating too. If Cath felt the slightest insult at the idea that she was a fitting recipient for old garments otherwise unfit to wear, she did not show it and knew no such insult was intended. There were features of the upper middle class which made Cath marvel. The money they had never seemed to go on new things: people like Emily could bargain like a trader in an Eastern market, she was always making do. The children wore hand-me-downs without complaint since they had long since realized there was no choice; the cars were far from streamlined and the furniture was old. Cath could see the value of the furniture she treated with such care, but although she admired the taste, she wondered why Emily would not give her the second-hand rug with the faded colours and get herself a new one. If their positions were reversed, she was quite sure that Emily herself would take home the contents of her employer's wardrobe without turning a hair.

'Coffee,' said Emily firmly. Cleaning ladies were supposed to have a reputation for time-wasting gossip, talking when they should be working, or so she heard, but here, the situation was reversed. Emily talked, at length, about nothing and everything, and it was usually Cath who rose and said, time to get on. Emily sometimes talked to avoid the challenge of silence and a sense of intimacy she resented, but she did not admit that, even to herself. It seemed ungrateful. Instead, she loathed, without comment, the way Cath ate wholemeal bread with open-mouthed hunger, never closing her mouth until it was finished. They went downstairs, Cath last, Emily singing and shouting for Jane. Cath watched her.

On the first landing, Jane appeared, with one finger over her lips in a request for Cath to say nothing, then took her hand. She was an affectionate child; they all were, even Mark, the surly teenage son home from school. He would greet Cath with a bear hug; she would pretend to protest, giddy with the sensation of outrageous affection. She bent towards Jane. 'What is it? A game? Are you hiding?'

'No. I got something for you. Quick.' She darted away into her father's study. Cath shook her head. Mr Eliot's study was strictly taboo: no child was allowed inside; even Cath herself was forbidden to enter Alistair's domain which remained more or less orderly, the way he was himself. Cath made a warning tut, tut.

'Lovey, you know you shouldn't be in here. What if Mum catches you?'

'I know,' Jane whispered. 'But I wanted to draw you a picture and I didn't have any paper. Not the right kind.'

The child loved the perforated listing paper which spilled out of the old and faithful printer in the study. Her own supplies were never as good as those she stole, and Cath could see the point. Jane held up a banner of three pages, waving it like a flimsy flag. The multicoloured drawing began with a large head, wearing a hat with flowers. A stalk-like neck led on to the next sheet, containing a thin torso with the suggestion of a bosom, dressed in a black dress with straps over the shoulders. The waist led on to curvy hips and the final sheet depicted a pair of inordinately slender legs ending in high heels, and the name CATH.

'It's a picture of you,' Jane said, urgently, impatient at the lack of comprehension. 'You. Going to a party. In Mummy's clothes. Can't you tell? Here,' She thrust the fluttering paper, already creased, towards Cath's calloused hands and Cath wanted to weep. Emily's voice came from the kitchen, faint but definite from this level.

'Thank you,' said Cath gravely. 'Thank you very much indeed. I shall keep it for ever.'

They grinned. Cath pointed towards the desk.

'Is that how it looked when you came in?'

Jane nodded.

'Are you sure?'

The nod became more definite. Cath shut the door very quietly behind them and, rolling her extraordinary portrait with great care, led the way downstairs, the first line of 'Onward Christian Soldiers' bubbling in her throat. She put the gift in her bag which lay on the hall floor, felt a moment of happiness. They love me, she thought, they really do. They think I'm lovely. Like Damien thought I was lovely. She caught hold of Jane's hair as they approached the kitchen at the back, pretended to drag her in.

'Look who I found, playing all by herself in her room like a good girl,' she said.

'Hmmm,' said Emily, tearing at the cellophane covering of a packet of biscuits with her teeth. 'Not the last time I looked.' And then with the sudden change of subject which often took Cath's breath away, she asked, 'Cath, what's that bruise on your arm? You didn't have that yesterday, did you? It looks jolly sore.'

Cath glanced quickly to the point of her right arm where she had pushed up the sleeve of her blouse well beyond the elbow. Casually, without showing the hot flush of guilt which crept across her, she pulled the sleeve down.

'Oh, that? Oh, I'm not too sure.'

'You must know,' said Emily, equally casual.

Cath pretended to think, taking the proffered cup of coffee, sitting down slowly. The kitchen table still held remnants of breakfast, a movable feast in this house. Her brow cleared.

'Now I have it, I do remember, yes I do. You know I go to your friend, Helen, on Tuesdays? Well, I was doing out her bathroom, yesterday afternoon, leaning in to do that big bath of hers, you know, and I sort of fell in. Bang, with my arm right against the taps. Stupid, wasn't it? Doesn't hurt,' she finished, addressing her remarks to Jane who sat pressed so close to her, the warmth of her skin passed into her own.

'You fell in a bath?' Jane chortled. 'Silly!'

Emily laughed too. 'Really, Cath! Listen, you must tell Helen. She'll have to pay you danger money. Are you sure it doesn't hurt? Only I've got all sorts of liniment, stuff like that . . .'

'No,' said Cath, firmly. 'No, it really doesn't hurt at all.' Not here, it didn't. Not in this house, in this sun-filled kitchen where a child drew a picture showing the cleaning lady as a glamour queen; where people really cared for her. At that moment, nothing hurt. Nothing needed fixing.

'Tell me,' said Emily, still casual but consumed with curiosity, 'is Helen's flat really as dirty as she claims?'

*

Sometimes Joe went home in the afternoon. If the lunchtime trade had been rich and the afternoon trade promised nothing, Mickey told him to use his sense and shut up shop for a while. It took almost an hour with the number 59 crawling through daytime traffic, so that he never had time to stop for long before turning back in time to open again at half-past five. He never quite knew why he bothered, unless to see if Cath was in; he hated the sight of his own front door with the peeling paint in the bright and unforgiving light of a fine summer's afternoon. Walking away from it in the morning, he did not look back; coming home after dark, he did not notice the outside either, but in the afternoon he did. He looked at it with disgust, and considered what a raw deal his life had given him. Nothing was fair; nothing ever had been, not since he had been a little kid with parents who gave him everything and promised him the earth.

His bedroom had been full of toys, anything he wanted, and their new house full of new things, until Dad disappeared and Mother found a grateful widower who had no room for a spoiled son. Joe had left them as soon as he could, and never gone back. He did not think of his parents with gratitude, he remembered only the bitterness of their defection.

A new house in the place where he grew up was what he knew he deserved in life, if only he could fight his way through the conspirators who combined to keep it from him. It was never his own fault that he had failed to become a First Division football player or a champion boxer, that he managed to leave the Army after seven years without the beginnings of a trade, that he could not concentrate, had a problem with drink, relationships and, unless motivated by the fear he had for Mickey Gat, laziness. Nothing to do with him: it was them; they were gunning for him.

Afternoon journeys on the bus could render him incoherent with self-pity, especially if he was forced into a seat next to someone who smelt. Bus people hardly entered the conspiracy against him, but he hated them anyway. Not as much as he had hated his brother-in-law Damien; a different kind of hate, a fearful, envious loathing of someone who, drunk or sober, remained the epitome of everything he was not. Joe unlocked the door and trod upstairs. The heat was stuffy, stuffier still when he went up to the attics. It was not true that he had secured this substandard flat through an army friend as he had told Cath;

Damien had got it for them. Just as Damien had got him the job with Mickey Gat. Damien had been a fixer. Everyone loved Damien, including his sister. His sister loved the sod 100 per cent, he could not do wrong in her eyes.

It took a person who hid things in his own house to know when someone else did the same. When he had come home last night, he had heard her hurried footsteps descending from the attics as he opened the door and met her bright, guilt-tinged smile of welcome. Cath did not much like the attic rooms; he knew she did not. She would watch him receive yet another parcel from the mail-order firm with tight-lipped disapproval, murmuring nice, very nice, then buttoning her lip, as the package was all wrapped up again and consigned to one of the rooms. She would not willingly go upstairs, he thought, as he often did, to gloat over the colour TV, the camcorder, the three-piece luggage set, the patio furniture, the barbecue, the tool boxes and the wealth of smart kitchen equipment they somehow never used. Knives in a block, a fish kettle when they never ate fish, the blender, the coffee maker, the gadget for scooping ice cream; she just could not think the same way about these things. She simply did not see that they were the way to a better life.

Joe forgot how these goods made him feel rich, as well as safe. The first room was gloomy, with three boxes obscuring the light from the window, and yes, he was right, something had been moved: they had not been there before. He moved to one side a telephone, a twenty-four-piece dinner service, a set of casserole dishes, all encased in packing. There, beneath the window, was the shrine in all its obscenity. He almost expected to see a lighted candle, but found only three photographs of Damien, covered in clear polythene bags, sitting on a tray among three small vases of dying flowers.

For a moment, he wanted to tear at the flowers with his teeth. He plucked them from their containers and crushed them underfoot, for fear of contamination. He picked up the first photograph, gazed at it briefly and tore it in half, put the two pieces together neatly and tore it again. Then he took a lighter from his pocket and holding the other photographs together, held the flame to the corners. They were slow to ignite, the polythene melting rather than burning, the photos inside curling grey then brown. It took a matter of minutes to create a pile of slightly sticky ash, and in that time the trembling of his own limbs did not improve. The lighter flame scorched his thumb, but he ignored the pain until it was done.

Oh Cath, with all she owed him, would she ever learn how to love him best?

CHAPTER SIX

Thou shalt be cured, brother. The course of justice ran as smooth as a saloon car over boulders. More like an engine heated beyond endurance in a summer's-day traffic jam. The courtroom faced south at the back of an old building with a view of railway lines, there were blinds across the windows, diffusing a sulky light as the heat poured in. Air-conditioning had been abandoned: it was louder than the trains.

Helen's allotted place was uncomfortably close to the witness-box, so that when the woman inside it made her nervous gestures, Helen could feel the drops of perspiration, gathered from the armpits into the palms, flick across her own face, like a kind of spittle she could not avoid. The pages she turned were damp.

'Fifteenth of March, this year. Can you recall that date?'

'Yes.' Voice no more than a whisper, fingers moving uncertainly, looking for something to hold.

'Speak up a little, if you would. Questions come from me, answers to the magistrates. You don't have to look at the defendant. Please.'

Her voice barked the series of orders, plaintive to her own ears, brisk to others, merely compelling to the witness. The defendant looked harmless.

'We've established you live with the defendant. What time did he come home that evening?'

'About eleven thirty.'

'Normal time?'

'More or less.'

'Did you have any conversation?'

'Yes. He said he wanted something to eat and I said there wasn't anything. He got angry.' She was gaining confidence now, going faster.

'What happened next?' (Oh for a pound sterling in the bank to mark every occasion she had prompted a witness with such a neutral question.)

'He hit me.'

'Can you give us a bit more detail?'

'He . . . he head-butted me. You know, bashed his head into my face. I felt my nose go, there was blood everywhere, I started screaming and the baby woke up and . . .'

'Could we take this just a little bit slower? You see that lady writing down what you're saying. If you could just watch her pen.'

Phrase by phrase. The words, the blows, the crying of the baby, the decisions, should she go first to the child or to the bathroom for fear the blood would touch him. Helen's hair was piled neatly over a crawling scalp.

She leant towards her opponent. 'No argument about calling the police, is there? Can I lead on that?' She turned over another damp page, as if she did not know it by heart. Behind her, she could feel Mary Secura relaxing slightly.

'You called the police. What time was that?'

'A bit later. About half an hour.'

'Why delay? Why not do that at once?'

The skin on the girl's face was flushed a dull red, swollen with the first signs of anger.

'I only called them when I saw what he'd done.'

'Do you mean your injury?' There was an impatient gesture of denial; another flicker of moisture landed on Helen's hair.

'No. He'd only gone into the kitchen and eaten the baby's food. Two jars of baby food, and he'd drunk all the milk. I didn't have any left for the morning. That's when I phoned.'

The cut-off point varies every time, Mary Secura said. No

84

telling what will make them crack, the smell of another woman; the drinking of the baby's milk. Presto.

Summer had grown into a stultifying incubus of grey skies and humid life. Later, cooler, Helen was attempting to explain to Emily Eliot not only the wonder she was feeling two weeks after the arrival of Cath to clean the house, but also the mixture of emotions she felt at the end of a case she had managed to win. How it should have been a sense of triumph, justice done: a man waiting sentence of imprisonment, Mary Secura grimly pleased, witness weeping. There was no sense of triumph at all. Nothing but the sensation that all her manoeuvring, posturing, bullying and flirting in cross-examination could ever reveal was simply a pale and inaccurate version of the truth. Emily did not really want to listen; no-one wanted to listen to this, not if they came from the foreign realms of normal family life. No-one wanted to hear her expound on the frustration of playing justice by the rules, not for the sake of actually doing any good, but simply because that was the only way of doing the best possible. Emily did not want philosophical conversation.

'I think your lifestyle is perfect, you know,' Emily was saying, mournfully. 'A virile man visiting a couple of days a week, no kids, double income, all that,' she added in the wine-and-coffee bar next to Peter Jones, late-night shopping, Wednesdays. For the first time ever, Helen was irritated with Emily, which was why it was important to put the record straight. A friend was a friend. A friend with kids was one you always had to cross London to see, since your convenience was always subject to theirs, your time infinitely less important, your own commitments to keeping yourself alive, apparently, nil.

'You make it sound as if I do nothing for the rest of the time,' she said. 'And I don't have access to Bailey's income, don't want it either. Pity, he earns far more than me.'

Emily looked crestfallen. 'Oh, I'm sorry,' she said, defusing any misunderstanding before it grew into discomfort. 'I'm not being very sensitive or realistic, am I? Only there are times when I envy you.'

'You joke,' said Helen. 'All I'm saying is you wouldn't have envied me this morning in court. And, as it happens, I often envy you.'

Her own words came back at her like little arrows. Envy for another was anathema. Even if they did have healthy children, faithful husband, wonderful house and a vision of life Helen found increasingly appealing. Castle walls, she told herself. Just build them.

'No, I don't joke,' said Emily pulling a face. 'I know you work hard, and it isn't easy, but keeping a family like mine often makes me feel like the clothes in the tumble dryer, all mashed up, even if they come out all right in the end. I don't know how long it is since I read a book.'

'Well, tough,' said Helen, crossly. 'I read them to stop having nightmares.'

They had only come out to make the final choice on the blues and yellows which had haunted Helen for a fortnight and now made her see double. Helen loved to shop; Emily Eliot knew how. Emily turned shopping into a mission with measurable targets; Helen treated it as an excuse for glorious indecision.

'You wouldn't like a conventional family life, Helen, you really wouldn't.'

Funny how people go on protesting that their own fortune is not as good as it looks, Helen thought. Samples of the chosen curtain material lay on the table in front of them; Helen had a dozen others at home. She slightly regretted the finality of choice, still agonized, reeling at the shock and the cost, wondering if there was still time to change her mind before Emily's needle-woman did her worst.

'How could you say I wouldn't like married life with 2.2 kids? I could just about do it if I got a move on, even though I'd be an elderly primagravida and I could save precious time by having twins.'

'Yes, well, you'd better decide before you redecorate the house. Don't think you know it all just because you've got a cat.'

Helen said nothing, feeling the stirring of a depression which often arose, like the beginnings of a headache, when she subjected her life to scrutiny. Emily watched her closely, then picked up a small piece of golden coloured cloth with blue woven into the fabric in thin stripes.

'You were right about this one,' she said. 'Listen, H, am I right in thinking you've got to the stage of wishing dear old Bailey would make an honest woman of you? Do I detect faint yearnings towards the joint mortgage and the patter of tiny feet?'

'Put like that, I don't know.'

'Well, just in case you were, let me suggest the primitive approach. You know how they dislike upheaval, poor darlings, and adore their creature comforts? Well, once your three or four rooms are revamped, beckon him in to an oasis of domestic bliss, nice food smells and all that. Works a charm.'

Helen laughed out loud. 'Is that what you did with Alistair?'

'You'd better believe it. Even the nicest men are ambivalent, you know. You have to lead them to it.'

'And now,' Helen said, 'even if it crossed his mind to want to go, which it wouldn't, of course, your darling Alistair couldn't possibly leave, could he?'

'Over my dead body,' Emily said, with a grim determination Helen found slightly disconcerting. 'I'd fleece him,' she added, 'then kill him. Another glass?'

'You only have to go round the corner. I have to get the 59.'

'Oh Gawd, never mind.' A hand was waved. Emily shuffled forward on the small table, arms across bosom, confidential. 'Now, never mind men. How are you getting on with Cath?'

'What?' Helen was thinking of nest-building, a spider making a web to catch a big, ungainly fly. Emily drummed her fingers on the table, then snapped them in front of Helen's eyes.

'Look, I need gossip. Cath, our cleaning lady. Listen, I never mentioned it, because she is such a treasure, and I trust her absolutely round the kids, but she can irritate. A bit clumsy here and there. Sometimes she's so careful I want to scream. Then she goes off into a different world. Must be why she's got the most frightful bruise from falling into your bath.' She bit her tongue, in memory of Cath's habit of open-mouthed eating.

Cath never cleaned the bathroom. Helen had been specific in saying leave the bathroom, that is the only bit I never mind doing and besides, I just can't ask anyone to clean my lavatory. The bathroom was the only thing pristine in the first place. Helen felt defensive and evasive.

'I've scarcely seen Cath since the first time,' she said, carefully. 'I don't have to. She's usually going out as I'm coming in. Otherwise, I've only seen what she can do. Oh, by the way, who came to dinner the other week?'

Emily put her head in her hands.

'Vegetarian judges. Three. With their wives. I'd cooked a leg of lamb.'

The sultry day had transformed itself into an evening of treacherous splendour after a shower. The light was perfect, and the stillness made the trees flanking Helen's street and Helen's garden droop with graceful relief, the leaves green and luscious from the earlier rain. There was the pretence of a fickle greeting in the languid movement of the branches, like a hapless crowd of tired schoolchildren hired to greet a late-arriving celebrity.

Curtain material bought, paint purchased. Renew the house; there was nothing more important.

No Bailey tonight, no hand and body held in the dark. Helen let herself in through the basement door, noticing as she did so how clean the windows were, reflecting her pale face and long dark hair, distorted into greater untidiness. And then when the door swung inwards, she noticed the smell, the first, now familiar and pleasant scent of Cath's ministrations. Lavender polish, a whiff of bleach, an absence of dust and the removal of any other odour. Helen revelled in this smell, liked it enough to mitigate her own reluctance to give away keys, an aspect of the arrangement she detested. She was not like Emily Eliot: she did not really like an open house.

But there was more than a smell; there was someone else there. She could sense the breeze which wafted down the long corridor and threatened to slam shut the front door when the French windows were left open in the bedroom. As her hands fell to her sides, nerveless with a sudden fear, the door slammed behind her. There was a momentary return to throat-constricting panic, but as her eyes adjusted to the light, the fear refused to emerge. In the gloom of the hall, she saw the hoover crouching like a sleeping animal, a duster on the floor, and from the bedroom, the strange grunting sound of someone humming 'Onward Christian Soldiers'. Burglars did not clean; Cath did that. The slow development of relief turned to anger.

'What the hell do you think you're doing here?'

It was a stupid question, and even in the phrasing of it her anger ebbed away. Cath was cleaning the French windows, standing with her mouth open in mid-verse, the cat curled at her feet, the woman herself smelling of work, blouse abandoned and wearing nothing but a T-shirt, modestly ill fitting. They gazed at one another in mutual shock.

'I'm cleaning the windows, aren't I?' Cath mumbled defensively. The light was bright, the way it was at the back of the house. Helen squinted, eyes adjusting yet again, still taking in what they had to see: the upper part of Cath's arms covered in bruises which extended across her chest. Cath followed her glance, then deliberately turned away.

'You frightened the life out of me,' Helen said, moving towards the bed which was central to the room. She took off her jacket and laid it down over Cath's white blouse. The other woman did not speak, did not resume the singing either.

'Working late?'

'Yes.'

'I'll make us some tea, then.'

It was cruel, she supposed, to make a woman sit in the light of the south-facing room where clean windows spared neither her exposure nor the aggression which suffused her face, as she sat with her arms hugged across her chest, a picture of defiance and misery combined. Sweating, just like the witness. Wary eyes, like Shirley Rix.

'I thought you cleaned for me between three and five.' She looked at her watch. 'Seven thirty now.'

There was a mumbled response and a violent shaking of the head. She has lovely hair, Helen thought. Rich and curly. Instinctively she felt for her own head, the hair lank from the effect of the courtroom.

'What did you say, Cath? Didn't hear you, sorry.'

'I said, it was so hot, I couldn't stand the thought of that bus.'

'Did you sit in the garden, then? Fall asleep or something?'

Helen wanted to relinquish the simple art of cross-examination, to rid herself of the habit of incessant questions, and make herself turn a blind eye when the woman's eyes pleaded with her to do just that. She put the tea on the table. It seemed quite inappropriate to offer wine, especially since she remembered her own embarrassment at the thought of Cath finding so many empty bottles in the bin. Helen leant towards her, biting the bullet reluctantly.

'Listen, Cath, you don't know me and I don't know you.

Perhaps that makes it easier. Only you aren't going anywhere until you tell me about those bruises. Is that understood?'

'Is that understood?' said Bailey to Ryan. 'No wisecracks with this lot. We've got to be sober and reasonable.'

'I'm always reasonable,' Ryan objected.

'So said the fox in the chicken run. We want to look like two coppers out having a drink and a chat.'

'They won't expect us to be sober, then.' Ryan was slightly mutinous, he hated drinking halves, almost as much as he detested combining work with pleasure.

'What was it you said we were here for?' he asked. 'I thought you just said we'd go out for a drink. I haven't been out for a proper drink since—'

'Last week,' Bailey interrupted drily. 'I saw the state you were in Friday morning. You think I'm blind? Your eyes were like candy floss.'

'Never touch the stuff. Tell me again. That Damien Flood murder is all wrapped up. So what the fuck are we doing here?'

'Oh, nothing much. Mickey Gat, maybe. Having a word with anyone who might like to come over and chat with us.'

'Who is this Mickey Gat? Not much chance of anyone chatting in here, is there?'

Bailey sighed. Ryan's ignorance of Mickey Gat summed up exactly how much effort he had made with this case.

'Oh, I don't know. That's Dave Jones' cousin over there, giving us the glad eye. Surprised they let him in.'

It was not such a bad pub. There was none of the sensation of danger Ryan secretly enjoyed in half the East End pubs, where a policeman was as obvious as a flag and as much loved as a black beetle; where you could feel the boots aching to crush, smell the mood and taste the hatred on the tongue. Not here, it was a well-run place, a drinking parlour sure, catering for old lags and young blood, of all races, but its real *raison d'être* was the pool tables. Most of the custom played pool, which made for an atmosphere in which any other kind of contest was irrelevant. Equally *de trop*, most of the time, were wives, girlfriends and anyone who did not play.

'They must earn a fortune off them tables,' Ryan remarked. 'Fancy a game?' Bailey shook his head.

The bar was a stark contrast to a place like the Spoon and Fiddle. This was the kind of place where Mickey Gat would be at home, full of highly domesticated drinkers. Mickey would not risk a fight. Risks for money were a different matter, because in Mickey's book dishonesty was not even antisocial. Which was why it was so odd that the place where they sat should be the scene of a violent argument leading to death. Not here. There was never any blood on Mickey Gat's floors, only in the little park round the corner, next to the leisure centre.

'I still don't understand why.' Ryan had a complaint in his voice, which, however irritating, still acted on Bailey's conscience. God alone knew why: Ryan owed Bailey more favours than either could count. The two men never acted in accordance with the irrational affection between them. They did little but joke. Ryan was sulking because the atmosphere made it impossible even to do that. He looked down at his feet, moodily examining a new pair of shoes which were too hot and too heavy for summer. He wriggled his toes inside the unyielding leather. Nothing doing. No more new shoes either, what with the kids going to school and his wife talking about feeding him on sandwiches. A bit like Bailey's bird, although the occasional remark from sir seemed to indicate that she had improved. He bent to adjust the laces, froze.

Mickey had changed into evening gear. The feet were squashed into white high heels. There was a gold chain round one ankle. Black leggings extended over huge calves and gargantuan thighs, disappearing beneath a brilliant white shirt, on which the legend 'Michaela' was stitched in lurid gold thread over the straining bosom which merged into the stomach to form a massive trunk. A series of chins ascended into a wide face. Pale blond hair danced in fat, salon-disciplined curls. The lips were coral coloured, the eye-shadow piercing blue, and the age of the vision indeterminate. Ryan's eyes landed back at the level of an enormous pair of hands, manicured nails held delicately at waist level, cradling an orange juice.

'Can I get you boys anything?' asked Mickey Gat. Ryan was petrified. So that was why Bailey had brought him here on the pretext of a treat. He had needed a minder, or, perhaps, bait to throw to the lions.

'Only I don't seem to have seen you recently, Mr Bailey,'

Mickey's voice continued in a good natured rumble. 'And I need to know to what I owe the pleasure. What are you drinking?'

She was the largest woman Ryan had ever seen, six foot all round. He would rather have tried to stop an oil-tanker. Ryan could feel the earth move with each breath. He raised his eyes further towards Mickey Gat's vast, squashed face and found it was wreathed in smiles, and even Ryan could tell a grin which was not quite a preface to a threat. It meant either she would play with them first or she was pleased to see them. The slap to Bailey's shoulder would have knocked a lesser man to the floor. As it was, only the table shifted position by an inch. The legs of a chair creaked ominously as Mickey sat, heavily.

'How you doing, Michaela? No, haven't seen you in a while.'

'More's the pity, Mr Bailey, because I haven't been doing so good. Oh, I mean the kids are fine, so's the old man, and business isn't bad. I take it you aren't here to check up on the licence or anything like that, 'cos if so, hop it. Otherwise . . .'

'No, Mickey, nothing like that. You know me better.'

She sighed. 'Well I thought I did, but you never can tell.' She let out a roar of laughter which shook the hanging light above her head. At the bar, where drinkers had paused to listen, heads turned back and normal conversation was resumed. Ryan began to breathe normally.

'I'm always pleased to see you, Mickey. Better luck than I expected. I'd have stopped to chat outside the Spoon, nice pub that, but it didn't seem right, you were busy. About Damien.'

'They got him, didn't they? That poxy kid who did it? Little bastard.'

'We got one of them, Mickey. Only one.'

Mickey shook her head slowly. It reminded Ryan of a bull shaking away the irritation of flies.

'That was a bad business, Mr Bailey. A bad business. They were strangers in here. We shouldn't have let 'em in.'

Same could apply to us, Ryan thought, vowing to keep his own mouth firmly shut, unless to drink.

'Anything I ought to know, Mickey? I mean, we'd like to mop it up a bit better than we have. The boy came back armed, sure, but he says he didn't use his knife for more than a scratch.'

Mickey snorted. 'He would say that, wouldn't he?'

'And this Damien,' Bailey continued, sliding his cigarettes off the table and into his pocket, 'he was a bit special, wasn't he? I mean no enemies you'd know about?'

Mickey nodded approval at the disappearance of the cigarettes. She could drink the tank dry, but never had much tolerance for smoking; bad for sport. She shook her head, smiling sadly. The fags reminded her of little Harry at home, coughing his guts up.

'No, Mr Bailey, no enemies and I wouldn't tell you a lie. He was magic at pool; let's face it, Damien was magic, full stop. Full of laughs, could have been a great boxer if he hadn't liked life better. Oh, there was some people got ratty when he took their money at the end of a game, but that never lasted. He'd give it back if they asked nicely. Everyone loved Damien. Naa, it was a bunch of kids from another pub, what a bloody waste.'

Sentiment was Mickey's second nature; Ryan noticed she was near to tears. The spectre of that was terrifying. The arm of an average man would only go halfway round those shoulders.

'Family?' Bailey asked, tentatively.

'Only his sister. He used to take her everywhere when he first started, till she met Joe Boyce. Think they was orphans or something, close, anyway. Nice, innit? Family sticking together. Well, they were all they had, that's why. I owed Damien a few favours, Mr Bailey. That's why I gave Joe the job at the Spoon. He's another one drinks too much, but not so's you'd notice.' There was a slight element of caution. Two pints appeared on the table. Ryan restrained himself from seizing the glass, stared at it hungrily, nodded thanks.

'Well, this Joe Boyce, he wasn't much help, was he?' Bailey suggested. He was boxing in the dark, Ryan could tell by the voice. He couldn't understand the man, really he couldn't. They'd got a result on a two-bit murder, hadn't they? Or they would, after the trial. Why this time-wasting when it was time to move on? Plenty more bodies out there. Mickey spread her hands, and rumbled with laughter again.

'C'mon, Mr Bailey. Wee Joe Boyce is just a hanger-on. Trails after heroes, thinks he's hard, but couldn't hurt a fly. I mean, I can't hold it against him. Damien was good to him, sure, but he would never have expected Joe to act as his minder. Joe had his wife to look after, and besides, he'd be fucking useless. They'd often go for a drink together, then Damien would give Joe a present, perfume or something to take home to Cath, and off he would go like a good boy. That's Joe Boyce all over. He does what he's told.'

'He's like this one, then,' said Bailey, nodding in Ryan's direction. 'Ever-obedient and full of respect, aren't you, Ryan?' Ryan nodded back, dumbly, followed Bailey's lead and got to his feet.

'Which is why I've got to get him home to his wife,' Bailey continued. 'You know what you married women are like.'

'I do, too, Mr Bailey,' said Mickey, moving a manicured paw in and out of the side pocket of her shirt, extending it towards Ryan. 'We're like cats, us women, you know. We only stay if we're fed.'

'Why do you stay?' Helen felt she should have known, but she could not keep the incomprehension out of her voice.

Cath succeeded in keeping the amazement out of hers. 'Oh, I wouldn't want to go. He's good to me, really. I dunno why he is the way he is, but he is. It's only the drink, without the drink he's not so bad. He can be lovely, my Joe.' Cath could not keep a note of pride out of her voice.

'Have you ever told Emily about this?'

'Course not. Why should I? She's a respectable married woman.' Meaning of course, that Helen was not. There were enough signs of Bailey's presence about the place, second-best shirts in wardrobes, the odd pair of shoes which would only be worn by a male, items of underwear, which indicated an alien presence. Cath's obvious discovery of these, and the sentiments it evoked – either pity or disapproval – affected Helen, just a little. She had lived her own life far too long to sink beneath the weight of other opinion, but how she lived remained private territory. She shook herself. It had been a good idea to offer wine, after all. It loosened Cath's tongue.

'What brings it on, though, the violence? Not just drink?'

'Mixture of things, I s'pose,' Cath muttered. 'Like I've bought something second hand. He only likes new stuff. He can't stand the idea of someone else having used it first. Unless it's army stuff. Me, I'm the opposite. There doesn't seem any point in getting new things if you can get old ones with wear in them. Except a bed, of course. I couldn't stand a second-hand bed.'

Suddenly Cath was weeping, a guttural series of sobs, more like

94

a fit of sneezing, ugly. Helen did not move. The air in the garden into which they had moved, grew colder; the perfect evening had waned away into a red sunset. She did not know, or, for that matter, like Cath Boyce enough to offer comfort, and somehow sympathizing with Emily's irritation with Cath, did not quite want to touch her. Or maybe it was Mary Secura, teaching her, by adverse example, how to keep her distance. Cath did not try to control her tears, as if she knew it would be a vain attempt. She let them flow without the slightest effort to dab her eyes, blow her nose or control her face, before the storm passed as abruptly as it began.

'I like your house and Mrs Eliot's. I couldn't tell Mrs E. because I need my job.'

'She wouldn't sack you because . . . because you were having a rough time at home.'

Cath raised one eyebrow, shrugged, and then spoke carefully.

'No, she wouldn't. Anyway, Joe gets the hump, sometimes. He's never quite worked out what he ought to do, you know? Apart from marrying me. I'd been working in one of them big hotels, chambermaid, he'd been in the Army. I think he met my brother through boxing or it might have been pool but anyway one night I go to meet Damien, and there he was. My man Joe.' She suddenly leaned forward and clutched her stomach. 'Got anything to eat?' she demanded.

Helen found the three packets of peanuts she had earmarked for a typical supper in Bailey's absence. Cath launched herself towards them with sufficient hunger to scatter the contents far and wide as she tore the packet. She did not seem to notice, chewed loudly and swiftly. Helen turned her head away.

'Well, I just loved him. Damien always said he'd find someone for me. He's my brother. We were always together since we ran away. Almost always, anyway. Joe was living in a hostel. Wasn't no good, nowhere for us to go, see? We got married anyway, Damien had a lot of money then. Joe loved Damien, everyone did. He knew Mickey Gat, Harry, and all the boys. I don't suppose I could have one of your cigarettes?'

'Of course.'

'Joe got us our flat, Damien got Joe his job with Mickey Gat. I think it was round about then he started.' She took a drag of an extra-mild Silk Cut, looked at it, puzzled. It was quite clear to

Helen that it made her feel nauseous. Lunch was a forgotten memory, half a sandwich somewhere. She felt equally, vicariously, sick.

'What's he going to be like tonight?'

Cath waved a hand in an airy gesture. 'Oh, he'll be fine. He's usually fine on Thursdays. He's OK as long as I don't criticize.' And then with an abruptness which belied the fey gesture of the sweaty hand a moment before, she was on her feet, her face suffused with embarrassment.

'Got to go,' she announced. 'Where'd I put my shirt?'

'On the bed.'

'Got to go,' Cath repeated. 'Got to go.'

'Sit down,' Helen commanded. 'I can drive you there or get you a cab. Which would you rather?'

'The bus,' Cath said.

'You told me you stayed late today because you couldn't stand the number 59.'

'I live on that route. Damien and me had a place on that route. I met Joe in a pub on that route. I go to work on that route, so does Joe. I'm sick of the sight of that route. Not all the time. Now.' She had grown. She seemed to expand before Helen's eyes into something she had never seen, then shrink again, back into the folds of Cath.

'Your brother? Can't he help?'

Cath looked at her with hatred. 'Of course not. He's dead.'

There was a silence which defied words.

'I'm sorry,' Helen mumbled. 'Should have kept my mouth shut. Will you do something about it? About Joe?'

'No, and you can't make me.'

'No, I can't.' Helen remembered Mary Secura. You can't make them; they have to volunteer.

'You won't tell Mrs Eliot, either?'

'Why? You haven't done anything wrong.'

'No,' said Cath, uncertainly. 'I haven't, have I?'

When the front door closed, Helen felt only relief, tinged with guilt. She knew what they all meant now, the Mary Securas and the judges and the great British public. In her heart of hearts, she did not want to know either.

She did not want to know: she had too much knowledge of guilt and misery already. She did not want to be sensitive, compassionate or an ally. If she could not have a dull life, she could have a secure one, behind walls, where all problems could be postponed unless they were her own. A life without a cleaning lady who brought in garbage instead of taking it out, in a place where there was no-one to pity or ask her to treat what could not be cured. She did that all day, already.

While Bailey and Ryan, in their sobriety, drove away from Mickey Gat's bar to venues more convivial, Helen West began, first half-heartedly, then with increasing energy, to wash the surfaces of the red-painted room. She removed all the pictures first, then scrubbed. Ready to paint. Revamp, renew, building walls.

PART TWO

CHAPTER SEVEN

I t was raining outside. Too warm for central heating, too chill for the window to be open, they huddled in a fug, windows misted, adding to the sense of claustrophobia in an office already too small. The photo of Shirley Rix was no longer on the wall. Instead, there was a series of postcards, bright blue seas, golden sands, legends of absent colleagues having a good time. Only the childless remained at work in August. If you can't take a joke, Sylvia had been saying to Mary Secura for the fifteenth time that week, you shouldn't have joined.

'All right, Mike Ryan, if you want to be useful, get a mop and bucket and clean up here. We've got rain coming in these brand-new windows. If you don't shift your bum from off my desk, I'll scream harassment.'

'You're so lovely when you're roused,' he murmured. 'I shan't fight, I'll take the compensation. You reading dirty magazines again, Mary?'

Ryan shifted his weight from the edge of Mary's desk, picked up her copy of *Good Housekeeping* and flicked through it. He was a frequent visitor to the Domestic Violence Unit of his neighbouring station, which had the added attraction of an all-female staff. Besides, he had a soft spot for Mary. Ryan liked females between sixteen and fifty, full stop, but Mary could see beyond the winking, sledgehammer humour, into his odd dependability, while all the time, there was that little *frisson* of mutual attraction, heavily disguised.

'You don't want to talk to her. She's in the doghouse, she is,' said Sylvia, shoving her bag over her shoulder, preparing to leave.

Ryan took no notice. 'The things you girls read,' he was murmuring, looking at an illustration of the perfect bathroom, offset by a bath full of foam with toes pointing coyly out of the water. 'And are you?' he continued, without looking up as the door closed. 'In the doghouse?'

'Yup,' said Mary.

'What did you do, then?'

Mary leant back in her chair, eyed the no smoking sign on the wall and lit up a cigarette with an air of nervy abandon.

'Well, you know that Shirley Rix case? No, you don't, but I told you about it. We'd got this bastard husband dead centre, in custody, court date fixed, perfect. Only the wife skipped on the day of the case and the CPS got it put off for a month. Clever, yes? But on the same day Shirley gets run over. Won't be giving evidence, except in heaven. And I don't tell anyone, right? I'm so frigging mad because this bastard's going to get away with it, I reckon he may as well stop where he is for another couple of weeks.'

'Didn't tell anyone? No-one at all?'

Mary shrugged. 'Oh, I told his solicitor, who informed the ever-loving spouse he was a widower, before going on holiday himself. But I should have told the CPS, shouldn't I? So they could go to court and discontinue and get the little rat out. But I didn't. I left him to run up the walls and now I'm in deep shit. So's the woman from the CPS, though God alone knows what she was supposed to do. She's been quite good about it really. Phoned me this morning as if nothing had happened, but then she wanted a favour. Do you think I'll get the sack?'

'Naa,' said Ryan. 'They should give you a medal.' He reached for one of her cigarettes. 'Poor innocent languishing in jail, is it?'

'Innocent, my eye. He's going to get his kid back and turn him into a drunken little yob.'

'Look,' said Ryan, not quite the expert since Bailey had saved him from all but three disciplinary proceedings. 'What you've got to do is plead mistake and overwork. Blame the solicitor. Say you put the memo in the out tray. Just don't let on it was deliberate, right? You'll be fine, honest. Wear a short skirt and loads of perfume.'

She looked at him, a shade wearily. 'Right,' she said. 'Right. That'll make all the difference.'

The silence was heavy; the rain dripped, making a mockery of summer.

'How's home, anyway?' he asked casually, eyeing the magazine. 'You decorating, or what? Preparing for the patter of tiny feet?'

Mary gave a strangled laugh. 'Preparing to split up, more like.' Then she sat up, dragged her bitten nails through her hair in a gesture he always found endearing. 'No,' she added, 'forget I said that, I didn't mean it. He wants the patter of tiny feet. I can't stand the idea. Working here doesn't just put you off men, it puts you off the whole idea.'

'If you two split up,' Ryan said with his melting smile, 'there might be a chance for me.'

She laughed this time, stood up and shoved him off the desk. 'C'mon, Mike, what do you really want?'

He sighed, theatrically. 'Your body. And a favour. Not necessarily in that order.'

It took less than a minute to turn up the name in the card-index. Mary Catherine Boyce. One negative visit, nine months before. Police called by neighbours, Mary taken to hospital, discharged herself the same evening, follow-up visit next morning by domestic violence personnel. Further assistance refused.

'We keep all these,' Mary explained slowly to Ryan, 'for future reference. In case they come up again, which they usually do. And we leave them a number to call us direct. Some of them do, months later.'

'Not her, though,' said Ryan. 'Just a one-off. Not even a breach of the bloody peace.'

'Funny thing with her, though,' Mary mused, 'she was half stripped when they took her to hospital. That's what made everyone panic, made the lads think it was a whole lot worse than it was, a few bruises, not nice, not too nasty. She had this massive scar, see, puckering her stomach, a real corker. Looked as if the old man really tried to kill her once. But when we went round, she explained it was a scar from a caesarian operation. In her teens, she said, nothing to do with her husband. Doctor must have been a butcher in training. Yeah, I remember. She wasn't like the others, I mean not frightened. You going to tell me the connection?'

'Nope. My guvnor's idea, not mine. Not enough to do.'

'I'd like to work for Bailey,' said Mary, 'if and when they push me out of this.'

'Play your cards right, why not?' Ryan squinted at the card, waiting for inspiration, shrugged. 'Bailey wanted to know if he had any violent tendencies, God alone knows why. Personally, I don't think a single fight with the nearest and dearest counts.'

'Speak for yourself. Anyway, what makes you think it's like that?'

Ryan tapped the card with his finger. ''Cos it says here, file dormant, stupid.'

Mary leant forward.

'You know I told you about the CPS solicitor asking for a favour this morning? All a bit vague, hypothetical. Well, it was about her cleaning lady. Cath, no surname known, but telephone number same as on this card. Covered with bruises, and what should she do? Nothing, I said, there's nothing she can do. But it looks like your Mr Boyce is still at it.'

Ryan sat down heavily, knocking *Good Housekeeping* off the desk.

'Oh, my lovely Mary,' he said. 'In the interests of your career, do you think you could see your way to another favour?'

'What do I have to do?'

This time his leer was more pronounced. He leant forward and kissed her on the lips, so briefly it was a peck. Then sat back.

'No,' he sighed. 'Not that. Just go and make a follow-up visit, will you?'

The rain stuttered against Helen's windows in the afternoon. She pressed her nose to the glass, transfixed. Those in the offices opposite, full of personnel so much better dressed, weaving their way through banks of office machinery the CPS did not have, achieving goals of which no government agency would dream, also had cleaner windows.

There was one middle-aged supervisor who held her attention. He had receding hair and glasses, was slim, trim and busy, and equipped with his own room and secretary, while his opposite number occupied another room at the far end of the floor, which Helen could see if she craned her neck. The two men were almost identical, so were their secretaries. Man number two (without specs), never stirred from his little sanctuary, but man number one (with the specs) was certainly flirting heavily not only with his own typist but also with her equivalent, six rooms away, while nobody in the open-plan area in the middle seemed to realize. From the distance of a narrow street, Helen could see it all clearly and toyed with several ideas. The first was to stick a notice in her own window; then there was another, more complicated scenario of blackmail. She would collar Mr number one, tell him how she had rumbled his little game and offer silence provided he kept his eyes peeled and returned the compliment by delivering her a weekly video record of Redwood. Redwood poking around offices and writing policy was not an exciting prospect, but catching him doing his exercises or changing his trousers, that would be fine.

I could show it at this afternoon's meeting, she thought, wake us all up.

She was pretending not to be shocked by Mary Secura's omissions, acting as if she did not believe they were deliberate, murmuring about communication problems, while all the time she knew it was utterly wrong to leave a man inside any kind of prison, even a remand prison, when there was no longer evidence to present of his crime. Rough justice surely, but too many lies had been excused on such a basis. Justice, about which she was quietly passionate, hence her constant frustration, was not a deity ever served by pathetic revenge. Justice was only achieved by laborious attention to the long-winded method and process of the Law, however deficient that was, since nothing, in the end, worked better. Truth and rules were the only workable formula. She knew that. Creating justice was putting yourself above it, a wilful and destructive arrogance.

Look at him now, over there. Man with specs is on the patrol. He dips into offices, saying hello, bowing himself out, making sure he knows where they all are, having a word, passing by, leaving them all frightened to move. Then he makes sure, when he reaches the other end, that man number two is hopelessly entangled in a long phone call which necessitates his waving his hands about, obviously stuck on the line for at least ten minutes. Seen through the clarifying blur of two sets of windows, the little Romeo embraces number two's secretary passionately, having just kissed his own. He was sitting on her knee, and she, heaven help her, looked grateful.

The phone rang. 'Convene now, you're late,' Redwood barked. Helen sighed into the receiver. Trust a man like that to spoil the film.

'We need to know,' he was saying to the assembled group as she entered his room and took a seat at the back, 'why we have these failures.' He held his hands in front of his face, looking at them as if they were his only inspiration, and Helen thought of a very old lady, following a knitting pattern.

'We need a system,' he added, looking in Helen's direction, 'to monitor at least those most conspicuous failures in our communication with the police. That means, of course, building up relationships whereby we trust them and they trust us.'

A few silent heads nodded wisely, no-one noticing such public inconsistency from a man who found any kind of trust anathema and thrived in an atmosphere of mutual uncertainty. Helen drew sketches on her pad and did not raise her eyes. Once the walls in her flat were painted, supposing the paint would cover all the lumps and bumps, then the windows would be ready for new curtains, and would Cath come this week, and what would she think of the mess?

'We must impress upon police personnel the need to tell us everything. Everything,' Redwood repeated for effect. 'Such as when a witness is never actually going to turn up.'

'Like when they die,' Helen said, audible without being loud.

'Did you say something, Miss West?'

'Nothing.'

'Good.'

Pardon me for being alive. Insolence would be her downfall. All this was about poor Shirley Rix, with those great big eyes, staring out of a photo, a nameless, numberless person she had seen depicted but never met, to be remembered as another notch on the bedpost of guilt, one more tick in the record of personal failures. Mourned by Redwood like any other source of embarrassment. Helen sat at the back of the room, mulish. Even from that distance, he could feel her bitter impatience.

'We've had a bit of a débâcle,' Redwood went on. 'In a case which should have been dropped at a far earlier stage. Ladies and gentlemen, please, if it is clear that a witness is not going to give evidence, make the clean decision sooner rather than later. Don't seek adjournments simply for the sake of saving face. And then don't just put it back on the pile for someone else.'

Helen cringed. She watched the others, nodding, puzzled, sensing that someone in their midst was in disgrace for disgracing Redwood's service, wondering which of them it was.

She drew on the pad a rough sketch of rearranged furniture in her living room, slapped her own hand as if receiving a reprimand, and tried to suppress tears. Regret less for her own humiliation than for Shirley Rix and the failure to survive. Also for her own reserve, which would prevent her from tapping on the window of her office and waving at someone in the building across the street. It was that same reserve which had made her hesitate this morning before phoning Mary Secura for advice, suddenly suffused with shame both for doing nothing and for not knowing Cath's surname. What a fool was conscience, so effective in restraint, so weak in the spur to positive action.

She was grateful for the protection of home.

To call this place a mess, Bailey thought later as he squeezed himself in, is the understatement of the year. He recognized Helen's present mood although he had rarely seen it in such an extreme. There was nowhere to sit. Furniture from the living room was in the hall and in the kitchen; he was forced to insert himself round the door with indrawn breath and clamber over a chest of drawers until the dying wheeze of the Hoover stopped him in his tracks. From the small room she used as study and dining room, he could hear a theatrical sigh, before she appeared, dishevelled.

'Who was it you were trying to keep out?' he asked, pointing to the chest. 'Or is there someone you were trying to keep in?'

'I'm cleaning cupboards,' she said, with dignity. 'And yes, I know that may seem strange, but I've got a man, painting ceilings only, tomorrow. Decorator had a cancellation. Isn't that lucky?'

Bailey did not look as if this counted as luck. In fact, he looked acutely disturbed. It had been a long, wet day. He had brought no provisions with him and it did not look as if the kitchen was fit for use in any event. The floor had become a dumping ground for plants and ornaments; the surfaces were littered with books. She followed the direction of his eyes, and looked a little crestfallen.

'How about a drink?' she suggested brightly. He smiled at her.

'Don't worry, I'll get it. Don't look so guilty. You're not a wee wifey who has to warm my slippers, you know.'

She could sense the irritation behind the light words, and countered it with a rising irritation of her own. No, she was no wee wifey, or even a *grande dame* with a gin and tonic waiting for her hero and provider to come home. She was a working woman, gritty with the residue of the day's guilt.

'I thought the wonderful Cath would do all this kind of thing,' he said.

'You've seen what she does. She cleans everything which moves. She doesn't wash walls and make the place fit for painting. I do that.'

Helen followed him into the kitchen and adjusted herself into a leaning position next to the fridge, where a dusty bowl held a selection of meaningless keys, none of which she could identify but she preserved them all the same.

'Listen, Bailey, I want to ask you something about Cath . . .'

Bailey shifted in immediate discomfort and kept his back to her. He had deliberated whether to reveal Cath's connection to the dead Damien Flood, and, after a day or so, found the decision to remain silent easier than the alternative. This was always Bailey's way when in doubt, although when Helen copied his secrecy he could quiet see how infuriating it was. There was no reason why his professional knowledge should impinge on Helen's life, or the Eliots' for that matter. What would it achieve apart from unease, if either of them knew that the woman wielding their dusters had a brother who had died by the knife and a barman husband with a dubious boss? He shrugged. Silence was not always golden.

'What about Cath?'

'Only that she's being beaten up by her husband.'

'Yes, I know.'

'You what?' She was furious. 'You knew, and didn't tell me?' She handed him a glass of beer with an expression which made it clear she would rather have thrown it.

'Whoah, now, climb off that high horse. I only knew recently and because of something else entirely. Background material. Remember me talking about that murder a week or so ago? The brawl? The victim was Cath's brother.'

'Well sod you, Bailey. Aren't you good with a secret? I suppose you would have told me if I'd given my keys to a homicidal maniac?'

'Look, don't be stupid. If you or I handle confidential information because of what we do for a living, that's what it's supposed to remain: confidential. Of course I would have told you if I'd known before you hired her, but she hasn't done anything wrong, has she? She didn't confide her family history to you or Emily Eliot, why should I? What difference does it make?'

'The whole bloody difference between knowing something and not knowing. And the fact that you seem to assume I'd broadcast the information on a loudspeaker, along with details of where I'd heard it.'

'I never said that. I didn't even think it, either.'

'Christ, Bailey, I sometimes wonder if you're hiding a clandestine wife and a tribe of kids. Anything else you'd like to tell me, such as you're leaving for Timbuctoo in the morning and it slipped your mind?'

'OK, OK. I'm sorry.'

He was not sorry: he was angry; and the fact that it was an anger without rhyme or reason only made it worse.

'What should I do to help her?' Helen demanded.

'Nothing. There's nothing you can do. Besides, your friend and Ryan's friend, PC Mary Secura, might call on her. I just want someone to get inside that house. Don't ask me why either, because I don't really know. Do you think we could drop this conversation?'

He had finished a glass of the amber liquid, still in the jacket he had worn against the rain. In the shambles of the flat, he had no desire to take it off. The cleanliness and order of his own home was suddenly appealing.

'Do you want some help?' he asked diffidently.

'No, thanks,' she replied with equal diffidence.

'What shall I do, then?'

'Sit and read the paper, but since you're itching to go home, perhaps that's an option you'd like to consider. I was going to get cleaned up and take you out for supper.'

'But you're not quite ready yet, and you'd really rather clean your house?'

They stood glaring at one another for a minute. Then he nodded and turned to leave, the dignity of his exit marred by the chest of drawers and the need to breathe in to get by. That small idiocy made her smile for a minute, but only until his footsteps died.

Oh, shit. The understated disagreement was worse than any row. She wandered into the red-walled living room, still fuelled by anger, and stood there listening for his car, while a small voice told her, You know him by now, you might also know he keeps things from you, and in all fairness you do the same to him. But she had looked forward to seeing him, she always did, and there had been a particular desire to talk to him this evening: he was a fair, kind and honourable man and he would have made suggestions to soothe her sense of inadequacy even if the advice in the last resort was simply to live with it. And if she was honest, the bit about not being a wee wifey had gone home like a well-aimed arrow. What was she supposed to do for the pleasure of his company? Comb her hair, paint her face, recline in négligé with Vivaldi in the background and a kitchen smelling of coffee?

The steam had gone out of the cleaning. She looked at the emptiness of the living room, the marks on the walls where the pictures had been, the gouging of the nails making it resemble a gangsters' hideaway where the walls were peppered with shot. When Bailey finally went, which surely he would in the absence of either the commitment or the support which were the vital plant food to any kind of relationship, would he leave his mark? Would there be rectangles of faded patches in her life, imprints all over her body, like a rash, to indicate where he had been? Would she just carry on? Should she fight the inevitable, become an Emily? For the moment, she could only follow instinct. Clean the walls. Offer practical help to Cath. In that order.

Blue and yellow curtains, this time next week. Ceilings, tomorrow.

Joe was not the only one good at hiding things. He had been quiet last night, home late, hunched over the TV, refusing the sandwich she had made, so silent she hadn't dared speak. It was often thus after conflict, a complete withdrawal by them both until finally one reached toward the other in shy desperation. A cold reaching out; a brush on the arm, a cup of tea accepted with mumbled thanks, a comment ventured on the weather. And then a few halcyon days of sweet normality until the whole cycle began again. It was only the drink, plus the terrible fact that he seemed to require a level of fury to complete the act of love with her. She supposed it was the scar, it put him off; he liked to touch it but then he was repelled. On that one time the policewoman in the plain skirt came round, the one whose voice she occasionally ordered by phone when she played with the answer machine, well that girl had not made a lot of sense, but on the other hand, Cath could still remember everything she said. Don't say he only hits you because of drink, she had announced. It's him AND the drink, don't you see? Other people drink and simply go to sleep, or buy their wives perfume, or cuddle the cat. Against her better judgement Cath had laughed, explaining irrelevantly that the man could not stand cats and as for perfume, he was allergic to that and, really, he was a good man most of the time. Your choice, the woman had said. Yes, it is, Cath had replied. My choice. Everyone has a cut-off point, the woman had said, let us know when you get to yours.

Cath would never have cut off from Joe. Unless Damien had asked. Until now.

They both hid things from each other: the small objects which would cause trouble. It began with his army memorabilia, preserved against the call to arms he would always crave, since, despite the disappointments, he had loved military life and dreamed of it still. Like everything he did, the memorabilia collection was half-hearted: uniforms, caps, badges, in the main, bayonets, all cheap to buy, cheap to sharpen into usefulness, until, of course, Joe's horror of the second-hand and the discovery of how many thousands of others did it, made him desist and hide the small collection with a suggestion of shame, since she had always loathed it. Most of it had long since gone over to the Spoon. There had been days when he did as she asked. She did not know whence that syndrome had fled, only that it was long gone. Gone even before Damien died.

Cath never said 'killed'. She only said 'died'.

She breathed deeply. In the attics sound was muted: reduced to a steady thump from downstairs and the steadier drip from the residue of the rain through a point in the ceiling. Boxes had been moved from the floor beneath. Nothing could be allowed to happen to Joe's hammock until they had two trees, or the grass strimmer until they had a hedge, and Oh, the waste of it all. She had placed the shrine by the window, on a dry space on the floor surrounded by Joe's goods, in the hope it would lie undisturbed. Now the flowers, admittedly dying when last she had tended them, bore the imprint of a foot; there were stains on the wooden floor indicating the colour of the pansies taken from Helen West's garden. The photos had gone. The candle she had lit in the hope of bringing Damien back, like a moth to a bright flame, lay on the window ledge. Cath touched a fresh set of livid bruises on her thigh. They were not important. It was the desecration of memory which was the cut-off point.

From far down below came the cracked sound of the doorbell. Cath did not panic. She moved downstairs out of the attics, slowly and demurely. It no longer mattered who it was.

I'm mad, said Mary Secura to herself. And I wish that meant I was bad and dangerous to know. She had the good leather handbag slung across her chest, and was oddly grateful for the raucous beat emanating from the ground floor. The door sprang open; a voice shouted from upstairs. Mary followed the sound, away from the life below, fishing in her bag for a card, a leaflet and the radio which would signal help into a well-deserved silence.

The door at the top was open. 'Hello?' she called with a false gaiety, looking into a hall and the room beyond, both impeccably clean. The woman appeared, long curly hair round her shoulders, surprisingly smiling. She was dressed in a dull skirt and long-sleeved white blouse; no sign of neglect, perfectly normal, but stooping.

'Don't mind me if you're busy,' Mary said, extending her warrant card. 'Only I'm from the Domestic Violence Unit. For a chat, if that's all right. Any chance of a cup of coffee?'

This neat little person showed no symptom of alarm. Cath thought she had guessed the reason for this call. It was all down to that Miss West, and while yesterday she would have resented this breach of promise not to tell, this manifest interference in her life, today she did not mind such an act of fate. Her smile grew. Mary was confused, taken aback by such docility.

'I don't have any coffee,' Cath said, 'only tea. What time is it?'

'Nine thirty.'

'Well, I suppose we've got time. Only he comes back around midnight, and I've still got to pack.'

'Fine,' said Mary, 'I mean fine. What do you want me to do?'

'Put the kettle on, I suppose, since you wanted a drink. Then give me a lift to my brother's place. I've always kept the key, you see.'

'You're leaving?' said Mary. 'Now?'

'What do you think I said?'

'Where will you go?' Mary was nonplussed, awkward, wondering just what situation she seemed to have precipitated and whether the woman was sick in the head.

Cath was impatient, she seemed to imagine Mary had come armed with an agenda in perfect accord with her own.

'I've got a place to go, I told you. My brother's.'

'Look,' said Mary.

'Oh, all right then,' said Cath, turning away. 'I'll walk or get the bus. It's only one stop, but I've got a few things to take.'

'Listen,' said Mary desperately. 'Do you want to make a complaint against your husband?'

'What would I want to do that for?'

'Then why are you leaving?'

'That's none of your business. Are you going to help or not?'

Mary thought of Shirley Rix. Shirley had been slow with explanations and the help had still come too late.

'I'll help,' she said. 'Forget the tea.'

The Eliots' small garden had become scrubland, resembling a poor football pitch after a long season without rain. Now it was swampy, the way Jane Eliot liked it best. She had added to the demise of the remaining flower-beds by jumping out of her bedroom window, conveniently on the ground floor at her own insistence. The route out of her window and round to the back door which led, via a corridor, back into the house, was one she could repeat again and again, flinging herself out from the edge of her bed, running back, doing it again, for no purpose other than a slight thrill. This evening, dressed in nightie, she paused in the twilight to rescue a remaining flower, without apology for having crushed the rest in weeks of indifference.

People dug in the ground and hid things. Her friend Susan had a dog which hid bones in their garden. Jane was in possession of stolen goods herself and, while the theft had been easy (from the bottom drawer of Daddy's desk, where he kept small surprises for them all, especially for Mummy), conscience had this way of creeping up. Jane loved perfume, always had to beg for it, as well as other grown-up indulgences, and she did not see why. So she had taken the biggest boxes she could find. The earth seemed a good enough place to preserve the contraband, ready for transfer to school at the end of these long holidays. While Mark and the others shouted over a game in the kitchen, Jane scrabbled with her hands at the soil below her window. Just as it was occurring to her that she would find it impossible to disguise all this dirt on her front and would have to invent something to explain it, she struck gold.

Not gold exactly, but a golden justification of very base metal. An old something or other; she could say she had been mining. Perhaps it was worth a fortune, and ugghh! Worms! She pulled the thing out of the hole she had made, dropped it and stood back, squinting in the dying light. It was a dagger, something like that, it had a handle like a sword and a metal sheath, rusty, unpleasant to the touch. Jane looked round, then moved three yards away and quickly dug another hole, a shallower grave for the Givenchy.

Then she carried the bayonet indoors and found she was wrong. Neither parent thought it was anything special and in no way did the discovery excuse the dirt. So she went to bed in mild disgrace and clean clothes. The bayonet remained in the kitchen. They were not alarmed: it could have been there for ever, although Emily remarked that the blade had been sharpened once.

Alistair suggested they could use it to poke the fire in winter. His parents had done the same. They did not listen to Jane when she said maybe it came from the man who had crept into the garden. The one who was scared of perfume.

It was a good tale to tell, raising the spectre of the bogeyman who no longer gained her the attention he had, but it was like all good tales. No-one believed you.

CHAPTER EIGHT

P re-trial conferences. Ryan hated them. Going over old ground with a new barrister who pretends he understands it. Bailey, looking both aggressive and uncertain, and a timid young man from the CPS taking notes.

'This is the way I see it,' Bailey announced. 'No, more like the way I smell it. Feel it, if you like,' he added, noticing the expression on Ryan's face at the mere mention of intuition. 'Like I feel egg coming down all over my face.'

'Well I understand why you find it so unsatisfactory,' Alistair Eliot remarked. 'But it's too late, isn't it? I mean the way it's been delivered to me, your investigation is complete. Trial date set, only a month away. Trail gone cold and hardly time for further enquiries now. Of course it isn't entirely fair. There were three men involved in the fight, on either side. The three who came back to collect the money they'd lost had weapons: pool cues, a knife or two. The other three, including the dead man, Damien Flood, weren't armed, unfairly disadvantaged, you might say.'

Ryan considered the relative sizes of the men and the boys, and shook his head. Fights between drunks were never equal.

'Damien Flood doesn't seem to mind the disadvantage,

according to one of his friends. He wades in, gets into a close scuffle with our defendant, who manages to hit him on the side of the head, and he reels back. His friends are so big that they've frightened one youth and disarmed another. They leave Damien, take up the chase. They catch the one who grappled with the deceased. With remarkable restraint, they merely slap him, find out where he lives and let him go. Then they go back and look for Mr Flood, who seems to have gone home. He is not where they have left him, slightly hurt, as they thought. They go to Damien's bedsit. No sign. They back-track through the leisure centre. Find him there. Call the police.'

Alistair shook his head. He was in formal role, sitting in chambers: a small room, shared with three others, crammed with books. Ryan considered a barrister ludicrous without wig and gown, found himself shocked at the sight of an obvious scorch mark on a shirt, noticed how the man's hair lay flat against his skull as though waiting for the headpiece. Then Alistair caught Ryan's scrutiny and smiled with such unfeigned sweetness that the other man blushed.

'Anyway,' Alistair continued, 'because Damien's friends knew where the youth they had pursued actually lived, he was arrested. He has always refused to say who the other two of his gang were and is adamant none of them, bar himself, carried a knife. He's also adamant he only used it to inflict a scratch, but the evidence,' he glanced at a lurid photograph on the desk, blenched slightly, 'is clearly to the contrary.'

'A little flick knife,' Bailey murmured.

'Not enough to do damage like this, you mean?' Alistair asked gently.

'The pathologist says possibly, but only with considerable force. Since we don't have the actual knife, only one identical to the one the boy describes, who can say?'

We should have found that knife, Bailey thought. The boy said he chucked it away, can't remember where, but showed us an identical one he kept at home.

'In any event,' Alistair continued, 'it makes little enough difference. We aren't putting the case on the basis that this boy was totally responsible. We're putting it on the basis that our defendant went away and armed himself, on his own admission. He came back to the scene intending to do serious bodily harm.

117

In the ensuing fight, a man was killed. We do not need to prove anything else, but the *intention* to do serious injury. If death results, even by recklessness, it is murder. That's the law. Murder does not necessarily involve an intention to kill. Even if his *compadres* were equally guilty, it does not make this one innocent of murder. What egg on face do you mean, Mr Bailey? It seems to me you have done the best you can.'

Surnames here. No first-name terms in this set of chambers, not like at home, laughing over the Eliots' kitchen table.

Alistair spread his hands. 'But,' he said, 'having told you I don't see this case as anything other than straightforward, albeit stuffed with dissatisfaction, leaving the defendant free to blame his absent friends, I must now tell you that I am walking away from it. The CPS agrees someone else should take over. We juniors are easily interchangeable, you know,' he added, noting Ryan's look of disgust. Fickle bunch of bastards, Ryan thought. They take on a brief and all that money, then they dump you in the shit almost at the door of the court.

'Yes, I understand,' Bailey was saying, giving Ryan a stern glance before relenting and explaining. 'Didn't I tell you, Ryan? Damien Flood's sister works for Mr Eliot's wife. It all gets a bit personal, see?'

All Ryan could see, from his position of discomfort, crowded up against the third desk in this room, was the top photo on the desk. Taken at the scene by flashlight. Damien Flood, sprawled against a tree, trousers undone, belly exposed. Not the belly, the contents, spilling out on the ground. Not a stabbing, an evisceration. Lights and liver like his granny used to boil for their pets, and for the first time in a case he had never really cared about, Ryan could see why Bailey was worried. That little punk on remand could not have done this, not without help. Could he?

A fly landed on the lurid colours of the photograph. Out of some kind of respect for the dead, Bailey flicked it away.

'I'm sorry about this,' Alistair Eliot said after the others had gone and they were left alone in the crowded room, sunlight streaming through. 'I didn't feel I had a choice. I've sat down outside a local pub and talked to a man who's a witness in the case, the dead man's sister is in my house every day . . . Can you imagine doing the trial, even as the junior, with Quinn doing all the talking and me the homework? I'd have to explain to poor Cath what was going on, wouldn't I, and then either she, or I, or Emily, would feel about as comfortable as a hair shirt.'

'There's no need to apologize,' said Bailey. 'Ignore my sergeant's sulking. Nothing lost. You only opened the damn file a few weeks ago and there's plenty of time for someone else to absorb it.'

'I need advice,' Alistair said suddenly, 'of a domestic nature.'

Bailey grinned. 'You're asking me? Why not try an expert?'

'You'll do. You know more about women. So far, I haven't breathed a word of this to Emily. I adore my wife, Bailey, you know I do, but I've got the feeling she'd smother Cath with kindness, counselling, etc. She'd be knocking on the door of the Spoon and Fiddle and dragging the husband out by his hair. You see, Emily always believes something can be done. About everything and everyone. I don't.'

'Nor do I. Is that your answer?'

'I hate keeping things from her, but how can it help? Would it be worthwhile, do you think, if I popped into the pub, I do quite often anyway, and just dropped a hint to Joe Boyce, I mean, something just to let him know I knew that he hits his wife? I don't know much about these things, more Helen's line, isn't it, but I've always imagined that if a chap knows someone else knows he's hitting his wife, it may limit him. For shame.'

'Or it may make him stop her coming to work for you.'

'Oh,' said Alistair, confused. 'I didn't think of that possibility. Dear God, what a privileged, sheltered life I lead.'

'There's something else,' Bailey said, wanting to comfort him. 'My sources are Ryan, via a lady in a domestic violence unit, strictly confidential, you understand? Your cleaning lady is dealing with her own problems. She's left her old man and holed up in the place where her brother lived. Her husband, according to her, does not know the existence of the place. It's on the same bus route,' he added irrelevantly, thinking of the convenience of the family Eliot. 'Does that make you feel better?'

'Yes, much. I still feel I should have a word with Mr Boyce.'

'Ah,' said Bailey. 'I thought I might set Ryan on him.'

Alistair looked surprised. 'Is that wise?'

Bailey sighed. 'I doubt it.'

'How's Helen?' Alistair asked, shaking himself, changing the subject with evident relief.

'Fine,' said Bailey, a shade over hearty. 'Very busy.'

Dear Cath, I'm sorry cleaning is a bit difficult today, because of the painter. He's only doing ceilings, I'm supposed to do the rest. If you could just clean what you can, and the kitchen windows. Suggest if nothing else, you sit in the garden and have a rest. If tendency to weed comes over you, don't resist. By the way, if you ever want to come here during the day, you know you are welcome.

That was early in the week. There had been a note in reply:

Dear Helen, I gave the painter a hand, hope that is OK. Will come back tomorrow afternoon and do some more if that is also OK. I like painting. Is £5 an hour all right? PS I know where there is a good carpet shop near me in Clapton. It is on the 59 route.

OK? It was brilliant. Helen West's domestic talents included an ability to slap paint on walls, applying extra to gum up cracks, but it took a while to get going. It was an act of economic conscience to limit the decorator to the difficult bits: it did not follow that she relished the rest. So to find, along with Cath's poorly written note, evidence of the first coat covering the bedroom walls in a colour called golden white, was a discovery tantamount to the finding of treasure. There is nothing, Helen realized, quite as exciting as the sight of pristine paint. Beat sex, beat everything, and if Bailey chose to persist in stand-off mode, that was fine, too. He was welcome to sulk until it was all done, and with the unexpected bonus of Cath, it would take a week rather than a month. If Emily Eliot's curtain lady worked with similar speed, as promised, this would be a seven-day revolution. Then Helen kicked the rolled-up carpet in the living room. She had thought it would do. Cath's broad hint in the note she had left could not have been clearer.

It was such bland carpet, piecemeal from where the blood-stained parts had been replaced, and she did not want to think about that.

Cheap carpet, Clapton. Number 59. Take Cath. Good for her, she clearly likes this stuff, might also get her to talk. An outing. Two days off booked already. She shivered in anticipation. A trip to buy carpet had all the flavour of gun running. Cath's obvious energy with the paint meant she was well. No need for immediate concern, just a niggling doubt.

Damien Flood had moved around during his life. He had been dedicated to impermanence and achieved it through a measure of deceit. Putting down roots was anathema. Which was why a one-room flat at the top of a high-rise council block, easily obtainable even on a long waiting-list, because no-one else – not a pensioner or a mum with baby, or anyone who resented burglary, or had no stamina for the stairs – wanted such an inaccessible space. Damien did not mind a place where it took forty-five minutes on a bad day to put out the rubbish. He had another gaff, grace and favour of Mickey Gat: he had drifted between a dozen more in his thirty years of riches and penury. Cath said Damien had a death wish: he liked the high places from where he could fling himself, and he denied himself the anchors which would ensure survival, such as bricks, mortar and the love of a good woman. On the last point, there was less conjecture. Why settle for one woman, when you could run a string of them?

Not that he seemed to do that either, not in public. Cath could no longer remember his public persona, only that she had never seen him with any serious attachment. Nor could she quite recall him in any other setting but this one, from which a serious girlfriend, however besotted, and however low her expectations, would surely recoil. A single room, with mattress and armchair, a kitchenette at one end with a selection of other unmatched chairs abandoned round a white melamine table. A poster on the wall, shelves made with breeze blocks. A bleak bathroom. The whole place was drab, unkempt without evidence of heavy dirt, lived in by a man who washed his clothes and his person with obsessive care and left the rest to itself until just before it began to rot. No wonder the council had showed no interest in getting it back. Cath doubted if Damien's erstwhile landlords even knew he was dead. Someone had given her the contents of his pockets some time after he died; it might have been one of his friends, it might have been a policeman, but the packet included his keys.

She had given the Mickey Gat keys back straightaway, via Joe, but she never admitted having this set. As far as she knew she was the only visitor here when Damien was alive, and the escape route it provided was heaven-sent now, a sign of divinely orchestrated protection, evidence that Damien's soul might have gone to the right place. There was nothing about home she missed, apart from the telephone. On a wall in the living room, there was a hole where a socket might have been. Cath realized with a start that she had no idea how to get one connected. Then she shook herself. She was not going to stay here for ever. It was like living in a greenhouse far above the world, while she craved the spaces below, away from the milky light, the windows with nothing but view, the slight swaying in the wind and the movement of the water in the brown lavatory pan.

Cath closed the door softly behind her, moving in the early morning heat which ascended the building, like smoke up a chimney, towards the lift. Today, it worked. She felt safer than houses at this hour in the morning. No-one else seemed to recognize the light of day before noon, and only then, she thought, nose wrinkling in disgust at the smell and the graffiti, to go and get some booze, collect the giro, or admit the social worker. On the tenth floor, the door opened to admit a white mother and black child. Both cried softly all the way to the ground.

Cath got on the 59. She felt both tranquil and resigned. She had the nagging doubt that this would be the morning Joe came to find her at the Eliots'. He had left her in peace for three days, but Emily Eliot would surely help, surely tell the man Cath was taking a week off, something like that; Joe would not leave the Spoon for long in the morning, because he was frightened of Mickey Gat: it would only be a short call, and in the afternoon Cath would be safely cocooned in Helen's basement. There was enough to do there for the rest of the week and she wasn't thinking further ahead than that.

Jane Eliot greeted her on the doorstep. She was wearing a gold cardboard crown (courtesy of McDonald's) and her mother's old silk dressing-gown tied in a lump round her middle and still trailing on the ground over her bare feet. She put a finger to her lips, ushered Cath inside with the imperious gestures which seemed to confuse royalty with courtier, then stamped her foot angrily when Cath exploded with laughter. The little darling: she looked so sweet and so guilty and the sound of Cath's laughter, strange to her own ears, startled and amazed them both. Jane forgot where she was.

'What's the matter with you, Cath? You never laugh.'

She had all of a child's resentment against inconsistent adult behaviour. Cath gave her a hug, another upsetting action. The child smelled like a perfume counter.

'Well, I am today. Where's your mother?'

'Out. Dad had a day off work, so they said, sod everything, they were going out. Without us!' The indignation was profound, although little Jane had already decided there were ample compensations for parental absence. It was something worthy of revenge. 'Mark is supposed to be looking after me,' she added. 'Mummy made him promise faithfully, but she didn't know about his hangover. He's gone back to bed. You'll look after me, won't you? We can play.'

'Where's your sister?' Cath asked, beginning to sense alarm as she looked upstairs and saw a trail of listing paper cascading down like a banner. Jane stamped her foot again impatiently.

'It's all in Mummy's note, silly. In the kitchen. She is staying with her stupid friend. They're going swimming.'

'And you', Cath stated firmly, 'will drown in big trouble when your Mummy comes home.'

How much big trouble became apparent some little time later as Cath whistled through the long skinny house. Her own feeling of joy at being given responsibility, this accolade of trust and this freedom, was beginning to wane even before she reached Mr Eliot's study. There was so much to do in three hours, plus keeping Jane happy. Since she knew the futility of trying to wake a boy with a hangover, Cath did not attempt to rouse the trusted guardian, Mark. She judged the carnage wreaked by a younger and jealous sibling to be fairly thorough. But, above all, Cath who never resented work and was given this small element of control, wanted to honour everyone, prove her own worth. Happiness gave her energy. She wanted to protect the baby from a scolding and also succour the errant older brother; she wanted to be all things to all of them, because they loved her and she wanted to love them back. Onward Christian Soldiers.

At the door to the study, the room supposed to be sacrosanct, resolution failed. The child had scattered the papers. She had untied the bundles Cath had seen in there, bound with either pink or white tape. Some of the tape was round her wrists, a little more round her ankles: she was a gypsy princess, decked in scraps. Cath did not understand paper. She could read and write better than most teenagers, but she was confused by the quantity; knew she could only restore some semblance of order and felt a brief surge of pity for poor Mr Eliot, who worked so hard and was always so courteous.

Jane was downstairs, exhausted by her labours and mesmerized by the usually forbidden daytime TV. Cath began to sort and tidy. The room smelt of perfume, all at odds with the masculine air of the desk, the solid chair, the old pen-and-ink set and the anonymity of Alistair's computer screen. Cath moved with precision and speed, pulling papers into rough piles, not looking, but judging by familiarity of typescripts and creases in the pages to get them into some sort of order. She was coy in doing this, averting her eyes from the written word, until from the depths of the mess, she caught sight of her own name. Not Cath. Mary Catherine Boyce. Joseph Boyce, listed next in alphabetical order in the index. The rest of this bundle was more or less intact. Cath felt her heart shudder against her ribs. She began to read. Continued to read as her back rested against the wall, her legs splayed and her lips, ready to laugh again, mouthed the words.

There was so much about the aftermath of her brother's death she had not known. Joe had shielded her and she had welcomed it, believed him when he said it was better not to know, to forget everything as soon as possible. He was dead; nothing else had any importance. Joe had taken her to identify the body, a formal identification, Damien's lovely face so perfect. She did not understand the words of the doctor with all the initials after his name, but she understood the photos of a golden-haired man with his entrails falling on the ground. Cath clutched herself, feeling the rising tide of nausea, bit her lip, and carried on. Joe's statement was precise about times, emphatic about how he had left early in order to come home to her. Her statement contained the times he had told her to say. She had taken his word as gospel. Joe Boyce, saying how he loved his brother-in-law, but the man did not have time for him. Lies, all lies. Damien always had time; Joe had always envied him, that was all. Joe was such a liar.

'What are you doing?' said Jane from the doorway.

'Nothing,' said Cath, shuffling the papers so the photographs remained hidden. For God Almighty's sake, why didn't Mr Eliot lock his study door? Children could not help it if they were untrustworthy. Nor, at this moment, could she.

'Only there's a man at the door, asking for you. I said I didn't think you were here today, but I'd go and look. Are you here?'

The child was cunning. Cath wondered where she had got it from. She pretended to yawn.

'Oh, he must want your mother, selling something she doesn't want, I bet. If I come and talk to a man at the door, I'll have no time to play with you. Go and tell him you've had a good look round, 'cos you know I'm usually here, but your mummy is really cross because she's got a note from me saying I've gone away for a week. Ask if he knows where I am. Can you do that?' Cath winked, roguishly.

'Course I bloody can. What do you think I am, stupid?'

The child flounced. Little actress. Cath gave it three minutes, standing on the landing, listening for the dull echo of the front door closing, then went down.

'He went,' said Jane, with all her mother's authority. 'I asked him if he'd like to come in for a cup of tea, just to make it seem real, but he didn't want to.'

'Good girl,' said Cath, making her voice echo an indifference she did not feel. It could only have been Joe; he would have to try once, and she could not have faced him.

'I've got to tidy my room,' Jane announced. Cath was surprised; the effect made her calmer. Even a child was strong enough to guard against Joe.

'Why's that, then? I thought you wanted to play.'

'That man at the door. He's the one who comes round when I'm messy, so he knows my room's messy now. We scare him off with perfume. Actually he only looked in the window once, but I tell everyone it was more than once, and he left something in the garden. Want to see?' She paused mid-flood. 'Daddy doesn't believe me. Do you believe me?'

'No,' said Cath, 'not a word of it. You've probably told fifty stories about that man, all of them different. What did he look like?' Oh, the shame of it. Joe coming round here and looking in windows like a thief, tainting this perfect house. How could he? But Cath thought more about Damien, haunted by the vision of him captured on celluloid in the study. I should take those photos away, Cath was telling herself. Take them away, if I dared, and hide them. No strangers should ever have seen Damien like that, all naked and ugly. It was shameful.

'This is what I found in the garden,' Jane was chanting, sick of subterfuge, television and anything short of exclusive attention. 'This thingy.'

She made a feint at Cath's toes with the sheathed, rusty bayonet. It looked as lethal as her toys. Cath regarded it with anger and horror. It was obscene for a child to brandish a knife in fun.

'I only think that man left it here, ages ago. Absolutely ages. Who else would leave it? Daddy says it's very sharp inside, though. Want to see?' Her eyes were full of teasing challenge.

Cath's hand was raised in sudden nervous rage, ready to slap. She brought it down instead, heavily on the girl's shoulder, shaking her roughly, ashamed of the action and the look of hurt she had caused. She turned the gesture into a clumsy hug, but Jane was not mollified. The hug turned into a pat: Cath struggled for self control, gained it.

'How lovely,' she said, still more sharply than she intended. 'Let's play with something else, shall we?'

Bailey stood with Ryan outside court number four, Snaresbrook. The outside of the building looked like a bishop's palace: the inside bore witness to extensive refurbishment. None of that old Victorian lavatory tat Bailey rather liked and Ryan detested. It was modern, spacious and dignified, but nothing altered. By noon they were in their third hour of waiting their turn as witnesses in a case which had taken a year to come to trial: they had no idea how long they might wait and the one thing which united them was stoicism. Since they could not discuss the facts of an ancient episode of grievous bodily harm on a shopkeeper, they read their newspapers, *The Times* for Bailey, four-minute bursts with the *Mirror* for Ryan, who was harbouring, as usual, a sense of grievance unalleviated by Bailey's silence.

'I know what I was going to ask you, guv,' Ryan said, bored to death with scandal. 'You know yesterday? Going to see that Mr Eliot? Can you tell me something? Do all those barristers have rooms like that? I mean, a mess. I can't see how he'd ever find anything in there, let alone read it, but he had read ours, hadn't he?' Ryan had been dying to discuss this phenomenon since Bailey had abruptly abandoned him in the Temple; Bailey had forestalled him all morning.

'They don't have much space,' Bailey said. 'Eliot takes papers home, most of the time. I must remind him to give them back. What does it matter if they work out of chaos? As long as they get it done.' Ryan sighed with a theatricality Bailey found irritating, like many features of the boy, which made him ponder from time to time the random nature of affection between human beings. It remained so senselessly selective, not based upon virtues or admiration; it came out of the blue and landed him with loyalties often undeserved. He would have run through fire to rescue Ryan from danger without having any real idea why, especially at this moment. He put down the newspaper.

'And speaking of conferences with barristers, Mike, your manners were bloody awful yesterday. You were either sighing like a tragedy queen or grinning like a monkey, and the expressions in between ranged from pout to boredom.'

'I only grinned when he said there was nothing wrong with the case, didn't I? When he said he thought we'd done what we could. What's wrong with that?'

'Everything.'

'No wronger than him saying he couldn't take a case because it might risk his wife's cleaning lady. I never heard such crap.'

The doors of the courtroom opened. Three barristers in wigs emerged, followed in drabs by others without fancy dress. The barristers seemed to sense the brooding presence of two police officers and moved away.

'What's going on?' Ryan asked, enlivened by the prospect of movement, however minimal. Bailey caught the expression of ardent satisfaction on the face of the defending barrister, nodding with his opposite number, both in earnest conversation.

'It probably means the judge has got the hump and our brief is copping a plea to actual bodily harm.'

'But that bloke had a broken skull,' Ryan protested.

Bailey shrugged. 'So?'

'So,' said Ryan, without lowering his voice, 'the whole fucking system stinks. Wigs or no wigs.'

'Sit down,' Bailey hissed. 'I was only kidding.'

Then one of the lawyers came towards him with an ingratiating smile, and he knew the yoke was on them. He stared up at the vaulted ceiling of the magnificent *palais de justice* and tried to imagine it was a cathedral.

Helen and Cath stood under the white ceilings of Helen's flat. Decorator gone, job half done, Helen was turning round and round, as if she was staring at the ceiling of the Sistine Chapel.

'I think you've done enough, Cath. You'll be knackered.'

'No I won't.'

'Isn't it wonderful?' Helen murmured out loud.

'It's white paint,' Cath murmured prosaically.

Cath remained unscathed by paint. She seemed weary, preoccupied, but she worked with quiet precision. Helen had emulsion in her hair: her hands were stiff with it and a blister raised itself on her right forefinger.

'I've left him, you know,' Cath remarked idly.

'Oh. Would you like some tea?' What else was there to say? 'I expect he wants you to go back, does he?' she added.

'I expect so,' Cath shrugged. 'That woman you sent round was very helpful. Mary. She gave me a lift.'

It was on the tip of Helen's tongue to say she had sent no-one. Then she thought of interventionist Bailey, the man who never let anyone know what he was doing, and held her tongue. Cath had her own version of events: let her keep it.

'What are you going to do?' she asked gently. They were back to back in the kitchen, Cath cleaning a brush. The repeated shrug was felt rather than seen.

'I dunno. It doesn't much matter. Did you take down that address I gave you? The carpet place?'

Helen was beginning to realize the existence of a code. Cath could no more come out with a straight series of statements than she could fly over the moon. As soon as she had said anything personal, she needed to change the subject. The listener could not prompt or initiate, only hope for the thread to be renewed.

'Do you really think I need new carpet, Cath?'

'Yeah, if you can afford it, why not?' Cath gave a surprising, if grim, chuckle. 'Make the place really nice. Catch a man, that way. They like to be comfortable.'

'You sound like Mrs Eliot. She says the same thing.'

'I bet she does.'

They spent a lot of time, in between silences, talking about Mrs Eliot. Cath was never warmer or more animated than when talking about Emily, Helen realized. Mrs Eliot this, Mrs Eliot that, as if the woman were somewhere between goddess and patron saint. And a better role model than me, Helen thought. She often forgot, in her own milieu, how a career woman was not everyone's idea of a heroine. In Cath's eyes she was a slightly deficient spinster.

'Do you think I need her advice, Cath?'

'No more than I need yours. Are you going to get that carpet? Only if you want me to show you where it is, you'll have to come on the bus.'

'I've got paint in my hair,' Helen protested.

'Suits you,' said Cath.

She wondered if it did, this casual scruffiness which made her at one with everyone else on the bus, churning through unfashionable London. Down St Paul's Road, into Balls Pond, Dalston Junction, where the crowds hanging round the stops, newly risen from bed in the mid-afternoon, waited less for transport than simply for the sake of waiting. Into the nettlebed of Hackney, Helen silent, Cath, animated for Cath, treating her companion to a muttered commentary, given from behind the back of her hand as if it was confidential.

'They don't go out to work around here, not much, anyway. Don't know how they live, really. No self-respect. Look over there. That's the leisure centre and all they do is vandalize it, terrible. That's where my brother was killed in a fight. Don't worry, not far to go now. That's where I'm living now,' gesturing to a high-rise block on the left. 'Right on the top. They don't go to work from there, either. I bet you'll get a good bargain in this warehouse. I did, but Joe was sick on it. If they scc anyone coming in with money, they'll fall over backwards.'

The code continued to invade this anecdotal account of Cath's life and times. First there would be a clue, a statement, a throwaway line, hidden in the midst of several sentences of banality, gems to be picked out of the dross. About how much she loved the Eliots, especially that Jane, how Joe did not know where she was in the afternoons and then, look at that dog, woman, shop, driver, tut tut. Some people got no respect, have they? This apropos of nothing, until finally, 'I hate this bus, you know, I do really. If Joe wants me back, he'll have to do something about this bus. And this is where you get off.'

There was nothing anyone could do about the bus. It moved of its own volition, snarling and wheezing, with a conductor suffering from a summer cold and seasonal indifference. It stopped and started, swallowed and disgorged. The engine throbbed; passengers shuddered in unison. A shambling drunk lurched on the bench seat downstairs, yelling at the window until the conductor yanked him up by the scruff of the neck without a word and he fell silent. Two overstuffed women, large enough to fill a seat each, sat in front of them, squeezed so tight that their laughter passed through acres of skin, loud and infectious. Amid a feeling of uncomfortable voyeurism, unused to travelling without a phalanx of commuters, Helen could see why Cath both hated and loved it. There was just too much life on an urban bus. Far too much. And that was all she understood.

CHAPTER NINE

B ailey looked at his watch; the unfamiliar action surprised him. Perhaps it was the fast-running clock which had confused him, wearing itself out for days with its frenetic telling of next year's time. He had cured the problem and the clock ticked in accordance with his watch, the hands crawling round the empty spaces of time at ordinary speed, and he now felt oddly disappointed. Real time, time without a purpose, hung heavy. It composed itself into units, each requiring a separate input of duty, pleasure, labour and necessity. He was clean, he was fed, he had done his work for the day, and unless he went to see Helen, the mending of another clock would be the last positive pleasure of the evening.

He sat on the enormous sofa, covered with tapestry cloth, the only spark of colour in the room, and surveyed his spacious domain with satisfaction. On balance, though, he preferred this room in winter, when artificial lights softened the harsher utilitarian edges and made everything glow. Looking forward to winter, and looking at his watch to dispel the restlessness induced by endless daylight, was surely a sign of depression. And he was not depressed, except by his own failures. He was simply at sea, armed with the engine of his own self sufficiency. Bailey, mid bottle of wine, decided it was too late to go to Helen now, he wouldn't be safe to drive.

He had himself and a book, a bottle and some music. No laughter, no discussion, none of life's non-essentials. He was sorry for people who could not cope on their own. He usually enjoyed it far too much.

Joe Boyce could not cope. He shivered and sneezed, could not catch his breath as he sat on the bus, felt as if his heart was jumping rather than beating. There were no fingernails left to chew. At other times he was hit by a peculiar lethargy and sat behind the bar with his mouth open, resembling, so Mickey Gat said in tones of ill-concealed disgust, some poor old geezer in the middle of a stroke. Mickey Gat, finding him thus on a Monday morning, was short on sympathy, the way she always was for anyone in her employment who could not work. Joe had no illusions about the profit motive and the rules of his employment, but Mickey's attitude hurt. It was one Joe had seen, heard, felt through his skin a thousand times before, condescension from the large person to the small, the officer to the non-commissioned, the boss to the wage slave, his father to himself. The hearty slap on the back, the smile, the jeering, all of it geared to stop him from doing what he wanted to do, which was weep.

'Women,' said Mickey Gat. 'Ungrateful, aren't we? S'pose she's a bit upset, is she? Did you give her that perfume or what?' Then roared with laughter. More boxes appeared in the back room of the Spoon and Fiddle. Another huge hand landed between Joe's shoulder blades, like a soft mallet being tapped against his spine, either as warning or solidarity, Joe did not know and could not have articulated a guess. Mickey did the dreadful business of tapping her nose. 'Mind you behave,' she said, roguishly, 'while your old woman's away.' Dear Mickey; so much one of the boys, she had become an honorary man.

When Mickey's grey Jaguar had slid away, like a sleek lion after a carnivorous lunch, Joe mustered his courage, and it was then, cutting the lemon clumsily so the juice ran round his bitten finger stumps, that he screamed. Anger had exhausted itself over the first few days. He had shouted and paced round the empty flat; he had examined the boxes in the attics, gloated over them, taken comfort from their bulk, made himself drunker than a skunk, yelled out of the top window, 'Good riddance!' while all the time the fear gripped his ribs. Joe Boyce cannot keep a wife. Joe Boyce cannot get it up. Joe Boyce retains nothing he holds dear, not a friend or even an enemy.

Now he sat with his head lolling, desperately sober after Mickey Gat's bonhomie, unable to go for the bus which would take him home. Trade was slack: summer holidays. Today it felt like a personal insult, as if the drinking public at large knew what a failure he was and shunned him like a leper. Joe did not quite know if he should feel grateful for this, since, all of a sudden, Cath's defection seemed to mean that he had something to prove. Hard men, friends of Damien Flood, do not sit around weeping for wives. He was half asleep on his feet, too immobile by far to manage a yawn, wired up, and ready to spring, a jerky mess who was dangerous to know, when in came the man he called Colonel Fogey. Half cut at five in the evening. The fact that the old colonel, if indeed he had ever borne such a rank, was never in any condition other than half cut or quarter sober, did not improve his chances because all Joe could remember was Cath ticking him off for poisoning the old boy with cocktails.

'Attenshun!' the colonel announced as he swayed through the door. Sunlight meant nothing to a man steeped in India. Or so he said. Joe looked at him with the sourness of entrenched dislike, as he sashayed towards the darkest corner, humming. 'Shun!' he repeated, sitting with a suddenness which clearly alarmed him. The colonel had a figure like a frog, a trembling jowl; his shirt-tails hung out slightly before and aft, his pathetic linen jacket, worn ragged over the decades, seemed to bear signs of rust, while his trousers, pleated into permanent creases, bore ominous stains around the crotch.

'Beer, boy,' said the colonel, tapping the table and looking round the empty room for an audience, raising his patrician voice. 'Beer, old chap. Now!'

It was some dim remembered vision of the pristine cleanliness of Cath, the way she wiped vomit off the walls and ironed his shirts, which made Joe see nothing but red. Filthy old scroat, banging the table and issuing orders. No money to spend and nothing to offer but drunken platitudes in an upper-class accent, no memories but good ones, no voice but the kind which issued orders. Joe went towards the old man, bearing a half of strong lager. Carlsberg, the alcoholics' answer to the problem of sitting still. He poured it over the colonel. Then he crashed the glass on the edge of the table, leaving a jagged stump protruding from his fist. There was so much flesh about the colonel's face worth the mashing. Joe's hand trembled; he longed to plunge the glass into the smoothest part of the high dome of skin stretched over the forehead, could feel in advance the satisfying crunch of shards against such a bare expanse of bone. The colonel's terror, enough to cause hesitation, made his flaccid belly shake. The trembling moved from his wobbly thighs to his chest and then to his hands; Joe paused, closed his eyes, unable to stop. Then a hand fell on his shoulder. Another relieved him of the glass.

'Haw haw haw,' said a voice behind his back. 'Very funny, very funny indeed. Nearly had us all convinced, eh, old man?'

Joe stood, helpless. A male figure emerged from nowhere, clouted the colonel round the shoulders, and bent down towards him.

'A joke, sir, innit? Good, innit? Why don't you sit out in the sun, sir? Drinks on the house.'

Colonel Fogey was helped from his chair, led outside, his leader grabbing a towel off the bar as they went, talking all the time, like a burbling drain, not glancing back. Joe stood in a trance, looking at his own shaking fist, still seeing the lethal stump of glass. He had just about recognized Ryan, the cheerful man who had taken his statement all those weeks ago, fucking copper, nice enough, not that nice. His brain, shocked by the wash of violence, began to reel when he realized what he might have done. He registered the sudden sunlight streaming through the door, the presence of the other man, the sound of the colonel outside, giggling like the child Joe had met this morning, and a voice with a clean mint smell, familiar, without being bossy.

'How do I get the man a drink, guv? And another towel, if you would.' There was a pause in which he found himself responding, thrusting five towels towards Ryan's clean breath, holding a glass beneath the optic which poured whisky in singles, doubles and trebles. Whisky was the colonel's favourite whenever his pension allowed. Joe gave him a treble.

'That's enough, ta. Great.'

Joe watched this small-statured Boy Scout, of equal height but probably lighter than himself, whisk the glass away to the great outdoors. There was a distant murmur of traffic, nothing which threatened half as much as the imagined whisper of Mickey Gat's Jag over the cobbles. The world was taking some time to come back into focus. He had the same desire to cry that he had felt in the early morning, when he expected to hear the discreet rustle of Cath leaving the bed. Outside, the colonel had found a companion. There was an earnest sort of chat going on, punctuated by the old man's dreadful guffaws. He seemed to have fully recovered. His presence outside, drying out in the sun, stinking like a brewery, would keep custom at bay for an hour.

Ryan slid onto the stool opposite the bar with long-practised ease. Bailey had said the bill was on the house, also the taxi home. Ryan did not know the purpose of this luxury, but he might as well enjoy it. Joe swivelled his head round and reluctantly looked him in the eyes. He met nothing but a cheeky grin, sympathetic.

'Pint of bitter, please,' said Ryan, putting a note on the counter. It was clear he was not even going to press his advantage by demanding free drinks. The desire to weep was almost overpowering Joe. Not sobbing as such, simply a surfeit of tears, stored overlong and oozing out of the corner of his eyes as he pulled the pint and sat down again.

'I'm sorry about that,' he mumbled. He did not know if Ryan would assume he was sorry about the tears or sorry about the fact that he had almost taken the old boy's eye out.

'I didn't see anything,' said Ryan gravely, neatly covering both possibilities. They sat in silence for a moment. Ryan looked around the neat little snug of a bar, nodding approvingly. Joe Boyce liked that too. He was proud of the Spoon and Fiddle, never liked the implication made, however obscure, that the place was a shade effete, not a proper pub with music and all the trimmings, but a sort of club like bar for the civilized of Kensington.

'Nice,' Ryan remarked sincerely. 'Very nice. Now, what's up with you? You look all in, mate, you really do.'

It was too much for Joe. Ryan's dimly remembered identity as a copper was all but forgotten. He poured himself a drink, blew his nose on a napkin, slumped.

'My wife's left me,' he said bleakly.

Ryan leant forward and touched him lightly on the arm.

'You and me, both,' he said. 'Don't tell me about it.'

So Joe told him.

At five in the afternoon, wearing a pristine white blouse, perfectly fitting skirt and a fair quantity of perfume, Mary Secura had sat in front of the desk of her divisional commander and been severely admonished for discreditable conduct. There was no particular sting in the tail, bar a reference to the fact that her next career move was under review and perhaps two years of domestic violence was long enough for anyone. He was kinder than she thought he would be, inclined to accept that the blame for Mr Rix remaining inside a fortnight longer than he might have done rested with the Crown Prosecution Service, who were easy to blame for everything. Mary was not sure what she had done to effect a relatively easy escape. She supposed it might have been her immaculate record, until the commander's over-warm hand-shake, almost culminating in an embrace at the end of the interview, indicated it might have been the perfume after all. She went back to the office and phoned Ryan for the celebratory drink he had promised, but he was out. So much for the return of favours. There was nothing for it but to go home. Back to the maisonette shared with Dave who would be on night shift. Great.

She went inside and shut the door behind her. Ryan would be home with the wife. She could have phoned her mother, but she only did that when she had good news. Everyone else had someone. Not her. It was not fair. She was the only person in the world at home with nothing to do. Then she remembered Mary Catherine Boyce at the top of her tower block, hiding, and, with a tinge of guilt, felt better and angry all over again.

Helen West's concrete floors were spattered with paint round the edges. She supposed designers got the desired effect of minimalist mess by accident. Magazines were full of illustrations of rooms resembling a wasteland, with a piece of lacey net twisted round a curtain pole, leaves on the floor and little else but an iron chair; scenes which suggested devastation. If she left the flat as it was, most of it thinly coated with the wash of golden white, she might win a prize. The current state would appeal to Bailey, not to her, apart from the carpet samples. They were in one-foot squares, leading from the front door into the living room, scattered further up the hall like stepping-stones over a stream, so that she found herself jumping from one to another. Footsteps were trailing home up the road: she could see varieties of feet passing the basement window, and felt the absurd desire to rush out and drag them in with the question, Look, tell me, which colour do you like best? Whatever she wanted they could deliver and fit by the end of the week. Cath was right. Cash buyers were greeted like lords. Stock without customers, the trader's nightmare. The stuff was so cheap, it could have fallen off the back of a lorry. Just you wait, Bailey, just you wait.

She had insisted on a taxi, to drop Cath home and to carry the samples. Cath had not resisted. Past the leisure centre (which looked more like a prison or a warehouse), turn left, right and right again. Cath went, clutching her talisman bag. She had looked, suddenly, incredibly vulnerable. The thought of her going into that enormous block, outside of which gangs of children ran screaming, filled Helen with pity and frustration. Closing her own door behind her, spreading out her stepping-stones, she was glad to be alone. It was better than many a version of the same evil.

Cath thought there were few evils as bad. The lift did not work; she trod up twenty floors, pausing for breath at each landing. There were no open spaces in the block, it felt like climbing up the inside of a tunnel, the air becoming rarer with each fifteen steps. She could hear murmurings behind doors, steps rushing along walkways. She looked out of the glassed-in stairwell at the first, third, fifth floor, and then did not look again as the ground receded, intensifying a sense of remoteness from all which was real. How had Damien managed here? Nicely, she thought to herself, angry with him.

The top two floors were empty. Down a long corridor on the penultimate floor, there were the sounds of someone working, the whine of a drill and the thump of a hammer. Some of the doors were reinforced, amateur self-protection which could incarcerate as well as deter. Her feet crunched over a small quantity of broken glass as she approached the last flight and a wave of homesickness assailed her. Then she heard the echo of more feet and shuffling on the landing above. A cough, the sound of someone listening. She paused.

For a glorious moment she thought it was Damien, waiting outside his own front door for her to arrive, and it was that illusion which made her fly up the last stone stairs, her feet clattering, before, on the last step, she realized what a row she made, what a dream it was and how she had denied herself the possibility of retreat. She was suddenly afraid, but also, despising her own silliness, careless and aggressive, not bothered about who it might be. She also had the slight sensation, an instinct founded on nothing, that whoever waited there with such patience and lack of subterfuge, could mean no harm.

Mickey Gat was looking out of the window on the landing, her huge presence blocking out the light.

'That you, Cath?' she enquired pleasantly, turning back to the view. 'It ain't half a long way down there. Must take you half an hour to get all the way up. Got a cup of tea, love?' The shocking pink of the shell suit hurt Cath's eyes.

She did not speak or smile, merely fiddled with the locks and opened the door. There was still the numbing sense of disappointment that it was not Damien after all, and it was still too soon to wonder what Mickey Gat might want, or even feel a suspicion of her presence at all. Of course Mickey would have known all Damien's hidey-holes; it was natural she should, but less natural she should climb all those stairs.

'Not very cheerful is it, love?' she remarked as she sat on one of the ill-matched chairs at the table. 'I suppose you could make it nice, though. I mean, if you was planning to stay.'

The kettle, a cheap piece of tin, boiled quickly on one of two electric rings. Enough for a single person. Cath's packing from home, to Mary Secura's surprise, had included little else but cleaning equipment: bleach, Jiff, cloths, window polish. Plus, as a sensible afterthought, a sliced loaf of the type which would last a week, margarine, tea and powdered milk.

She was at ease with Mickey Gat, always had been. Women were never a threat, however big. She had been used to a big brother, found a kind of gentleness which seemed to grow in proportion to human size. She had always known where she stood with Mickey Gat. Damien Flood's sister, was where. To be treated with respect on that account, but, like all other women, fundamentally unimportant and completely dispensable. Mickey Gat would never debate the point of whether a woman had a mind or clearly defined needs. She knew she had these features herself; for the rest, she was as chauvinistic as her fellow man and even more contemptuous.

'What can I do for you, Mickey? You didn't climb all the way up here for nothing.'

'And I didn't tell Joe where you might be, either,' Mickey said, cunningly.

'You were only guessing. I could have been anywhere. I got friends too, you know.' She thought of Helen West, the nice Secura girl, the Eliots; they gave her strength. A fragile energy, but still a help.

'I'm your friend,' said Mickey, as if injured by the prospect that she might ever need any other. 'I was Damien's friend. I loved that bloke, Cath. Just like you.'

Not quite like me, Cath thought. Fierce love it had been. The love for the only person who ever really mattered. No-one had loved Damien as she had done.

'So what do you want, Mickey?'

'I went to see your old man this morning, doll. He tells me you've up and left him. Well you must have done, mustn't you, or you wouldn't be here, would you?' Mickey laughed, shaking to a standstill as Cath's face gave no answering smile.

'Well, truth is, Cath, he's in a bit of a state. You'd be shocked, Cath, honest you would. I know he's not much of a man, but I mean, could you, do you think, reconsider?'

'What do you mean, he's not much of a man?' Cath retorted, stung into an immediate defence.

'I mean, he's only a man, Cath, not a saint. I wasn't criticizing him, honest. We all have our ups and downs, don't we? You've got a nice home, Cath, you can't give it up just like that. I don't like seeing him in this state, Cath, really I don't. There's no telling what he might do. And he's a good-looking fella, you know. There won't be a shortage of takers, Cath, and I'd hate to see you left on your own. Damien wouldn't have liked that.'

Damien had not liked the idea of Cath being on her own. I can't always be with you, he'd said. You gotta find someone nice, Cath. I'll always be there for you, but this isn't the way to live, Cath; you need more than me to love. A woman on her own, Cath? C'mon, it just isn't on, is it? She could feel a great sinking of the heart. Damien had always been right. A woman on her own was an eyesore.

'You mean you want me to go back to a man who knocks me around, because if I don't he won't do his job properly? That's more like it, isn't it?'

Mickey spread her hands and the gesture seemed to fill the room. Her wedding ring winked. Honesty was always her policy when she could not get away with a lie.

'Well, that's part of it, Cath, to tell the truth. Blokes like Joe are hard to find, you know. I can't run that pub without him. He's the only one understands them kind of customers. And if he's knocked you about, well, I'm sorry, but it's better than him running off with someone else.'

'I've got a job,' Cath said fiercely. 'Two jobs, and I'll get more, see if I don't. I got people who need me.'

'Career woman, now, are we? Joe needs you, Cath. And you need Joe.'

It was true, she knew it was true, but she was not going to admit it.

'Tell you what,' Mickey continued. 'Give it a few days. He needs a lesson, right? You've got to show him who's boss, right? Make him treat you special. Then he's going to meet you, take you somewhere really nice for a night out, and you can talk about it. That's all I'm asking, Cath. Do it for me and Damien, won't you? How about next Monday? Meet him at the Spoon. I'll tell him, give him the evening off.'

Cath knew she had no choice. If she did not promise, Mickey would tell Joe where she was and Joe would haul her all the way down all those stairs by the scruff of the neck and no-one in this block of flats would even notice. Besides, as a compromise, it was not so bad. She liked the thought of Joe being in a state. She nodded.

'There's a good girl then.' Mickey smiled. One large hand disappeared into the pocket of the shell suit, pulled out a wad of notes and a box. Perfume. She could see it clearly. Fake Estée Lauder. When Damien worked for Mickey he had given her perfume every month. Joe had taken it away, like all gifts from Damien.

'Buy yourself a nice frock, doll.'

The price of supremacy: one hundred pounds in cash. A man

needs a wife so he can do real work: other women are merely bought and sold. Mickey Gat lumbered to her feet and went to the door. As if in response to the authority of her presence and her demand for convenience, Cath could hear the distant whining of the lift, working again.

Emily Eliot suppressed the urge to slap her daughter. She could not bear the child whining. The need to slap a nine-year-old was not one she always withheld, although she had never administered a blow which could injure. A sharp hand was a good thing to have up your sleeve, catharsis for mother, humiliation for child, the ultimate in tame punishments, reserved for truly disgraceful behaviour. Which this was not, quite, and it did have some excuses. Children get you all ways, she had tried to explain to the few friends who were without progeny. They drive you to leave them for half a day, but cannot bear you having time to yourself; you have to make it up to them later and still they punish you.

Alistair had gone back into his chambers but he would be home again soon. No-one coming in this evening, so maybe dinner *à deux* and an early night? That was before she saw the study, but after she had understood that Mark's role in the supervision of his sibling had been to ignore her entirely. Raised voices, challenges, surly defences, accusations of ingratitude followed, also the banging of doors. On the sidelines, little Jane fumed. No-one had time for her. Not even Cath, who had become so preoccupied she put sugar in the lunchtime soup. The same Cath who had shaken her, almost slapped her and then refused to play. The insults had come thick and fast to Jane's pride and Cath's contribution was the worst. It was sunny, but Mark would not take her out. He said the light hurt his eyes.

All this emerged in a whine to which her mother paid scant attention. And when Jane was dragged to witness the carnage of the study, to which she had added, once Cath had finally woken Mark to resume control and left. She had done it, despite Cath's dire warnings, because she was fed up with Cath too, and the day's frustrations had reached the eye of their own particular storm. Not only was she being ignored, something she resented with all her mother's passion, but she was also going to be punished.

'Do you realize, you little horror,' Emily was saying, keeping her fists bunched against her sides and her voice ominously calm, 'just how long it will take your father to sort this lot out? Did you think of that, you selfish little . . . ? Do you know how hard Daddy works, and do we have to lock doors to keep you out? I feel like locking you in.'

The recitation stopped at that. Emily was gazing at the open drawers of the desk, making a mental inventory. Presents lurked in there, wrapping paper, surprises, Alistair's own cache of things to be dispensed. By an unwritten rule, she was not supposed to raid this desk either, but she was, of course, familiar with the contents. Her eyes were riveted: Jane could see her mother deciding, perhaps a little too late to put it into effect, that this might be an occasion for a clip round the ear, after all. She saw the direction of her mother's gaze and a self-righteous cunning froze her expression for an unseen instant.

'What's the matter, Mummy? What did I do? Why are you shouting at me?'

'Because you . . .' The disingenuity of Jane's limpid gaze made her pause. 'You've made a mess,' she finished lamely.

'Mummy, I didn't, not really. I came in to get some paper, that was all, Mummy, I promise it was. Oh and I took some pens,' she added with convincing sheepishness, nodding towards the top drawer where Alistair kept the lurid marker pens vital for annotating papers. Emily remembered him saying he did not know how his profession would live without such pens.

'Cath told me off,' she added in hushed tones, scuffing the carpet with her sandal, 'because I'd been in before and she'd tidied up once already, she said. She chased me out, but then she stayed in here a long time, reading, I think. She told me to go and fix my own room, and I did, Mummy, I did. She was horrid today, Mummy; she smells of bleach. Shall I bring back the pens?'

'Get out of here. Go down and watch TV. Don't move.'

Emily stood in the centre of the room, somehow overwhelmed with disgust. She had an intense feeling of losing control. It could have been Jane's mention of that lingering, cheap-soap, clean-but-not-entirely-pleasant smell which so typified Cath, and which Emily had told herself explained her own aversion to being within inches of the woman in any closed space. A snobbish aversion, as slight as her turning away from the sight of Cath eating bread and butter open mouthed, but one which created a *frisson* of revulsion if she thought of Cath poking around among her things. The same reaction applied, only in intensified form, to the idea of Cath touching things personal to her husband. Emily could share her privacy if she chose; in his absence, Alistair had no choice, no-one to defend his domain except his family. Cath had no business putting her stubby fingers and her ever-so-humble body in this small and exclusive room, however messy it had been.

And besides, everyone in Emily's house had to be subject to Emily's control. They could be perfectly good or perfectly bad, but they had to accept rules. And they had to be nice to her children, who were the very stars of her existence. Emily allowed herself to seethe, aware that she was being a bit of a control freak, fanning herself into indignation because she should never have been out of her domain long enough to let anyone take charge of it. Her command of them all, her single-minded mission to find them the best people in the world, brooked no renegades and took no captives. Poor Alistair. Poor Jane, treated with such unfairness, even though she was being honest enough to admit minor theft and trespass; that was brave, wasn't it? Emily the mother ignored the fleeting glimpse of guile she had seen in her shamefully neglected child, cut out the sound of her whingeing, instead she concentrated on the empty drawers of Alistair's desk, and in her search for a culprit, allowed a horrible suspicion to develop.

It grew as she made a comprehensive search of the corners of Jane's room. The child would not have the imagination to hide perfume anywhere else, since no-one in this most open of households would condone deceit. Jane's ground-floor bedroom contained no secrets. The marker pens were scattered on her bed in a litter of scrunched-up listing paper, and Emily's fury curdled into more guilt. How could it have occurred to her to blame her darling child for emptying the perfume drawer and interfering in the privacy of the study, how could she? The sad logic pointed to Cath, left with responsibility, taking the chance to pry and steal, and, even worse, leaving darling Jane to carry the can. That is what people did when they were poor, acted poor, smelled poor, but it did not excuse such conduct or mitigate the betrayal. The anger rose, swelling against the new target. No-one crossed the boundaries of Mrs Eliot's house rules without dire consequences.

It was enough to ruin the evening. Mark went out, deciding that the best cure for the remnant of his hangover was to try again and the best cure for parental disapproval was to earn even more. Jane was subdued, sweetly affectionate, her sister merely sleepy. They were a family with all hysteria spent and the relaxation of Emily's half day off seemed a thousand years old. Instead of an early night, she and Alistair drank far too much wine, which rendered them sleepy and philosophical. He was worried, she had noticed it at lunch, where her own gaiety had disguised his preoccupation. She had mentioned over supper, well after Jane's hurried goodnight to her papa, about the devastation of the study, cured for the most part before he came home, drawers firmly shut. She didn't want to linger on the missing perfume, because she was not supposed to know, and because what she was going to do about it was her decision alone. She did not mention Cath, either, any more than he did. There was a story in the paper he read out to her. A man leaving his family to work as a missionary for three years, what did she think of that?

Not much, she said shortly, not if his children were still dependent, no, she did not think much of that at all: it made her frightened. She did not add that she already felt under threat, for her judgement, for everything.

Are people with families allowed no other loyalty? he asked. Is there nothing beyond that? He was thinking of loyalties to his clients, giving up on a case because it was too close to home. You could not abandon care of anyone else, could you, simply because you had children to protect?

Yes, you could, said Emily shortly. Your family came first: sod anyone else. That was the whole idea. And if he wanted to be a missionary, would he take Jane with him?

They did not talk much after that.

Give a man a drink and he will talk until he drops. Ask a man who can mix a cocktail to give you a demo, and there could be serious damage, so Ryan concluded. Joe Boyce could not only mix them with dizzying speed, using up his resentment of Mickey Gat by being free with her ingredients, he was also keen to sip. It certainly improved his mood. First he assembled a concoction he described as a Scotch Kiss.

144

'One fluid ounce best Scotch, blended, any kind will do, but the better the ingredients, the better the drink, one fluid ounce Tia Maria, half ounces Malibu and pineapple juice, skip the fucking pineapple and strawberry on the side. You can't make the same cocktails with Irish or Canadian, you know. What do you think?' All the measuring had been done by sleight of hand, a buzz of liquid slopping into blender with precise ease.

'I'm sorry, I think it's disgusting,' Ryan said.

'Go and give it to the colonel, then.' The old man still sat outside, bawling at passers-by. He accepted the slightly foaming glass with indifference. Ryan wondered if he was suffering from shock.

'I can tell what a man like you needs,' Joe was announcing from behind the bar, hands everywhere, sipping a single malt himself. 'Something simpler. I like anything based on whisky, myself. You got a preference?'

'Oh no,' said Ryan jovially. 'Whisky every time.'

'People have gone off cocktails, you know. Gone off most things I'm good at. Here, try this.'

Ryan sipped. He liked it. Bit sweet, but he liked it and by hell, it packed a punch. 'Yeah,' he nodded. This one would not go to the colonel.

'Think I'll have the same,' Joe mused, 'while I'm thinking. Rusty Nail, they call it, silly name. One ounce each of best Scotch, I mean best, and an ounce of Drambuie. They got separate cocktails for Japanese, you know. Get a few Japanese in here. Lovely people. All smaller than me, thank God. Now, what next?'

Ryan had been under the impression that cocktails, certainly those he had ever bought for women, were to be sipped, savoured and made to last. Joe's Rusty Nail did not linger long enough for rust to form. He was fiddling with an ice bucket.

'Straight Irish, two ounces whiskey, must be Irish, though for this one, I'm not quite sure why. Has to be aged for five years, the Irish, so it's much better. Two ounces of that, what a waste when I come to think of it, plus half ounce each of Pernod and curaçao, couple of dashes of bitter and maraschino. Some people love it.'

Ryan merely liked it. They gave the second to the colonel, who had commenced singing hymns as the light began to fade. A few homegoing customers braved his barricade, lingered briefly while

Ryan and friend moved on to Whisky Sour, Boyce style. Whisky and lemon juice, without sweeteners, suited Ryan's taste best, but it could not beat the sweetness of the Glenfiddich which followed. Someone came in and expressed concern about the colonel. They got him a taxi, paid the fare in advance, and then, with a sigh, settled back where they were. Ryan kept offering to pay. To his secret relief, the barman just as consistently refused. The plant, situated to the left of Ryan's elbow, would never recover from his carefully spilled libations, but he had slid into the confidential stance, propping his head on his hand. Coming in here was like going on a building site, he had decided. If you did not have a hard head, you needed a hard hat. By anybody's standards, he had consumed a lot and the night, if not young, was youthful.

'Problem with my wife is, p'raps I should say was,' Ryan said, lying, but prognosticating on everything he knew about Mary Catherine Boyce, 'she got too independent. Got a job, see? I think when they use their heads, it goes to their heads. Everything they got in the fanny, well, that just dries up. She didn't like being touched, see, only she was wearing all these short skirts. To go to fucking work, I ask you. Should be ashamed, I told her. Scared to have kids, is what it was. Have kiddies and get dependent. Why fucking not? I asked her. It's me paid the fucking bills for five years, all for no fucking . . .'

Ryan had three children, the apples of his eye, fathered on a wife far more competitive than himself. He recognized the truth of that without a trace of guilt, and found a certain enjoyment in his new persona. After all, it did not really matter what he said. He was humble enough, and had done it often enough, to know that inebriated exchanges between men did not include the complicating factor of one really listening to the other. Women were different, and so was Bailey. He remembered Bailey with a rosy affection, forbore, wisely, to mention him. Joe was squinting at the ceiling. The tears had left his eyes, but his face was pink.

'Trouble with mine is all about her being fucked up by her brother.' Ryan wanted to sit up straight, remembered he should not.

'Wife's got a brother,' he volunteered. 'Fucking nerd. Comes round, tells me what to do.' Joe nodded.

'He told her what to do, all right. Or rather, he didn't. Didn't tell her what she should do. When she was about fourteen. Could be younger, she wouldn't say.' His head maintained a constant nod.

'You gotta be joking,' Ryan muttered. 'C'mon.'

'Nope. She got pregnant, right? Went wrong, it died. 'Course I didn't know till after I married the bitch, did I? Well, I knew she'd got this scar on her belly, an' I knew she wasn't no virgin bride, who wants one? Made me sorry for her, to tell the truth, I wanted to look after her. Only I didn't know he was the one should have looked after her when she was having it, poor cow didn't tell, there was no-one to tell 'cept him and what did he do? Nothing! Why didn't he look after her? Why didn't they get him home to stop some bloody doctor on duty for sixty hours making a fucking mess of it? She told me she wanted to die. And that fucking Damien, where was he? Learning to box in the fucking Army or something. Our hero. Everyone's hero. Wanker.'

'What could he have done?'

Joe's tears had somehow resumed, which meant a wet face, vivid with sincerity as he held a glass under a spiggot, one glass then another, banged both generous measures of best malt on the counter.

'Could have done?' Joe yelled. 'Could have done? Never mind what he could have done, what could *she* have done? She could have stopped fucking loving him for a start, couldn't she? And did she love him? Did she, all the time: Damien this, Damien that . . . Where the fuck was he when she was fucking needing him? Off the fucking planet, is where. Winning some tournament, is where. And she still thinks he's god, is fucking what. They were like that, those two.' He doubled the first two fingers on his left hand making a sign more of solidarity than obscenity. 'Like that,' he repeated.

'You mean, like that?' Ryan repeated the gesture with the fingers of his right hand. 'I mean really, like that?'

'He ruled our fucking lives, I mean really,' Joe said. 'Really. What he said went. My job, my gaff, my car. My woman.'

'Can't have been nice,' Ryan commented, still slumped.

'No,' said Joe, turning back to the optics. Amazing, Ryan thought, how his hands were so steady while the rest of his body jerked and twisted the way it did. Just amazing.

'It wasn't nice,' said Joe, with a turn of sobriety. 'It wasn't nice at all. I mean he introduced me to Cath, but I hated that fucker, you know? Hated him. Like fucking poison.'

'Give us another of that malt, will you?' was all Ryan said. He was already poisoned. May as well get worse. He needed something to cope with a horrible sensation of shock. Plus something he did not dare admit: pity for the man, and fear, plus a sensation of half truths not quite making a whole, a man talking in code.

He missed his wife and wished he was going home to bed.

CHAPTER TEN

I t was soft and safe but the light hurt his eyes. There was
Bailey, with an evil look, promising there were always means
to make a man talk.

'What did he tell you, Ryan?'

'Leave me alone, will you? He told me some things, not
everything. There was something more; something he wanted to
boast about, apart from the cocktails. Something he was proud
of, but guilty about. I don't know. He's done something heroic,
that man, and he wants to tell. Let me sleep.'

'I think he's wearing his guilt in the wrong pocket. Guilty about
the wrong things. Proud of the wrong things, too.'

'Were you always convinced he had something to do with
killing Damien Flood?'

'Was I? Did I say so? It had to be someone full of hate.'

'Well, he knows about hate.' Ryan's eyes were closing: the lids
felt like heavy coins.

'His sister might have hated. It was Damien's baby she had,
when she was only a kid herself. There's a birth and death
certificate with Flood's name on, I found them. Looked like
Damien posed as husband. Who would know?'

Ryan opened his eyes. 'Oh Jesus Christ Almighty. Why didn't I

149

think of that? Jesus. What a clever old man you are.' His eyes closed again. News of any kind, however exceptional, remained subject to other needs. He murmured to cover a kind of embarrassment. Bailey murmured back.

'Oh no, the sister loved him all right. But I don't think our Joe has any idea whose baby it was. I think he might have said.'

'Are you sure? . . . For God's sake, let me sleep.'

There was a roll of thunder: Joe twitched in his own bed, dreaming of glory. Technicolor dreams in rancid sheets. Damien Flood, the golden boy, covered in green blood. The same handsome Damien, adored by little Joseph Boyce, who had clung to his coat-tails, and then been presented with Damien's sister, like a gift from heaven, so comely, so sweet and so much in need of protection it would make a man of him and admit him to the inner sanctum of Damien's gang. Joe Boyce, showered with the stardom of that wedding, all his needs provided for: a job, a place; until, apart from the goods in the attics, his whole life revolved around Damien's hand-outs, Damien's contacts. And still his little wife did not really love him. Perhaps with that scar on her belly she could never let herself be loved, never believe it, but when it came to loving, she was just like the rest: Damien came first. Bastard.

So, in his dream, Joe took command. He came out of a cloud of memories, each more humiliating than the last, until the dream took over.

There they would be, a band of brothers, drinking away a good time. Only in the dream, Joe would not be the servant, the trooper for their colours, with alcohol the only bond between them, never equality, although he would still be the one who left to go home first. He would do that by choice, not because he feared to be left behind.

Damien would come out of the Gents, zipping up his trousers, then slap his arms round the shoulders of the other two men before walking out ahead of them, swaggering; the woman clearing up behind the bar following with her eyes the sight of his small buttocks and thick, blond hair gleaming gold against the white of his shirt before she turned back to emptying ashtrays. How can a man walk as he talked, slurred, but bouncy? The friends would be taller, lankier, neater and somehow less impressive; even from behind, Damien had a certain charisma. A little drunk, yes; as drunk as he ever was, never disorderly, ill humoured or loud, never a really dirty joke or piece of rudeness. He might have been going to seed a bit, but he did so with an element of youthful dignity and he had a laugh which echoed joy.

Joe could not shake away the dream. He had refined it, through a thousand half dreams, into a kind of visual reality, so that once he stepped out into the open, he could actually feel the chill of the air, damp with winter drizzle, or hear the distinctive sound of a diesel engine churning uphill as they crossed the road to the car park next to the leisure centre. It was dark in there. Joe, watching from the shadows of the trees, anxious, curious, wanting to go with them, knowing they should not have laughed at those lads, nor taken their money.

Then the three kids, snarling like cats, pouncing with such a lack of skill that Joe pitied them, empathized with their futile aggression; they were kittens, not tom-cats, so pathetic even with their broken pool cues, it was like setting flies to attack a wall, but there was nothing inevitable in this dream. So the first youth, the runt of someone's litter, a boy without facial features and bluish skin, sprinted forward, felled Goliath, and Joe was surprised. He almost leapt out from behind that tree and ran to Damien's aid, until the incubation of three years' hatred forced him to stay still. Eughh! He could see himself, covering his eyes and listening to the sounds: grunts, groans, fist on bone, short sharp screams, the same sounds of the power he could only ever exercise over Cath and only then with appalling shame. He felt hot, boiling inside his jacket, despite the cold of the rain around the bare trees of the park. When he removed his hands from his face, to the sounds of running footsteps, the stink of breath still reverberating, he could not believe that Damien, the immortal, was still there. They had both shifted places, him retreating, Damien staggering breathlessly into the dark of the park, lying down to rest against a tree, looking peaceful, presenting to any man who hated him enough, the perfect opportunity. Uncannily perfect, with someone in the wings, neatly poised to take the blame. In all his dreams, Joe was never without the satchel he carried, but in this dream, it contained the bayonet he had sharpened, brought along for no other purpose except to show it to Damien. Damien had said he was interested in all that stuff, but he wasn't and Joe never got a word in edgeways. Running feet, shouting in the distance; the flatulent sound of far-away bus brakes and the murmuring of the trees, a thunderous silence, Damien, groaning, but still oddly graceful.

Joe turned in his bed. At this point the dream was more day-dream than a vision of the night, the focus was clearer; he could hear words, although from a distance, voices without intonation or individuality. What would he say? Would he say, See this, Damien? See this? I brought it for you. See this? Watch Damien's eyes widen, his face, even with the graze on his forehead, taking on that look of familiar welcome. 'It's you,' he would murmur. 'Yes, it's me,' Joe could hear himself say as he stabbed him the first time, in the chest. He was so muscular there, it was as if he did not feel it. Then there would be Damien again, murmuring something like, 'No, no, don't,' as his great hands came out like a pair of pliers, and gripped Joe by the shoulders. 'Don't do this, Joe, please. What did I do wrong, Joe, please?' Too late to stop, the wrong kind of knife, sharp on one side, not a dagger, but a heavy blade, took all his strength to get it out, relieved at the lack of blood, standing back and wanting to retreat. And then a moment of terrible reality, when Joe could not think of a single thing which Damien had done to deserve this. The blood came out like a fountain and that toneless voice again, loud, almost a scream. 'Cath . . . Oh, my lovely Cath, save me.'

That was the point of perfect clarity, when the dream became completely sensuous. Joe, plunging the bayonet as hard as he could into the softest bit of belly, the part of Damien which showed how he had gone downhill, sloping into a suggestion of fat. Joe looking on with wonder as he saw himself using both hands to drag the blade from left to right and back, feeling the connection of bone, tissue soft and hard, and whenever Damien said, Cath, digging in further until he felt the spine and still the bugger would not die. The mess was extraordinary, the emerg-ence of the contents of that tight abdomen something akin to a newborn child and the staccato, wailing sounds, more than similar. Cath, Cath: Damien still repeating her name, refusing to stop and refusing to die, until Joe could not bear the sound, yanked away his clumsy weapon from the groaning lump with the ever-open mouth, toppled with the effort, saw himself rolling over in the wet grass, away from the blood. Not looking back as he wiped the blade, stumbling away from that voice, still calling in the rain, hands clawing at the red raw spillage of life.

Joe landed on the carpet by his bed with his fists bunched against his chest, his body rigid. Then he opened his eyes to the smell of whisky vomit. A captive fly buzzed against the window. He made the experiment of trying to stand, pushing himself onto his knees, then straightening his torso, then levering himself to his feet with the support of the bed. Once upright he felt stable for a moment, then crashed sideways onto the mattress, and lay there staring at the ceiling. There was no thunder, except the reverberations inside his skull. The fly buzzed; the light through Cath's home-made curtains showed the features of early dawn.

It was a dream; a nightmare of glory. Only a dream. It could have happened like that. If they beat him, he would have to confess it had happened exactly like that; he would be terrified to confess, but proud of it, too. Then the evening before the dream came back to his mind in a series of slow images. Talking to the man in the Spoon. He had not boasted, he had only wept. The man had felt sorry, got him home safe and not on the bus either. So everyone was safe, now and for ever, but if the dream was true, why on earth was it that he could not remember what he had done with the bayonet? Dreams were untidy, short on practical details; that part remained blank, shocked into oblivion. Joe was as bitter as the whisky taste was sweet. No-one would ever come looking for him now. No-one would ever look at him and see the hero.

The mists had cleared. Ryan knew that coffee in the morning was not the best way to treat a surfeit of whisky the night before, but it was all he wanted and Bailey made the best. Ryan rose from his bed of pain on the couch with exaggerated groans, in fact feeling fine, all things considered, better than he supposed he deserved. The conversation of the early hours caused more confusion in his brain than the alcohol; in the meantime, he had been dreaming of women in violent, pornographic poses and it blurred his memory. Bailey was talking: Bailey could talk through a storm, flood or fire, without raising his voice. Ryan blinked hard, shook his head and looked round. The colours of the sofa on which he had lain attacked his eyes; everything else was light and bright. It was so clean in here, any smell must be his own, not dirt or dust. Thinking what a good little housewife Bailey was, and what an efficient host, did not cut him down to size. Or stop him talking.

'You agree with me, then?'

'Of course. About what?'

'About Joe Boyce being violent, out of control. Devious, dangerous.'

Ryan shook his head again. 'I didn't before. Thought he was a harmless little bloke who took out his frustrations on his wife once in a while, that's all. Until I saw him with the broken glass, ready to do some poor old sod in the eye for nothing more than speaking out of turn in the wrong accent. Yes, he's violent. More than average. Violent enough to do that kind of damage to Damien Flood.'

'And if his wife goes back to him, she would be in danger too?'

'Doesn't follow. He loves her.'

'He must have loved her brother once, too. And if it was Joe who did it, she'll remember something, won't she? When she's finally recovered from the death, she'll think of some niggly little detail. She'll remember how hubby didn't come home at quite the time she says in her statement. How he went straight to have a bath and left early the next morning with his clothes in a bag, something like that.'

'It rained,' Ryan remembered. 'It was raining when I got to the body.' His case, he thought bitterly; my case with minimal supervision from you. Bailey letting him spread his wings only to gum them later. Blood running away into the ground; the dead man's yellow hair plastered against his head.

Bailey made more coffee. 'Enough danger to the wife for you to get your PC Secura officially involved.'

'Are you going to arrest him?'

'Who?'

'Joe Boyce.'

'On what grounds? There's no more evidence than there ever was. Even if Mary Catherine Boyce told us interesting things, we'd be nowhere near.'

'So what's all this for?' Ryan yelled. 'Why have I got this bloody headache?'

'I needed to know, that's why. Do you need a clean shirt?'

*

Cath had not been allowed the luxury of open grief, but she had still been grieving, wandering in a daze, a constant fog, like someone high on tranquillizers, floating along at the same level as other people's knees, never quite able to raise her eyes or concentrate for more than a minute. Even in the Eliots' house, wandering from room to room to fetch something and forgetting when she got there what it was. Sometimes, sitting on the bus, she would find herself surprised at the sight of a landmark which she could have sworn they had already passed. Today, she could see it all clearly. Joe had not let her cry; when she had cried he had hit her and then cried himself as if to say, what about me, what about me?

Cath sat on the 59 in a state which approached contentment. Not happiness, Cath had long since forgotten what that concept was, but a state of anxious resolution which she felt called for some self-congratulation, although she could not say why.

Handling Mickey Gat, keeping a hundred pounds of her money, learning that Joe missed her? Better still, being left independently in charge of Mrs Eliot's household: that had been a source of pride, too. Proving indispensable to Helen West added some weight, although that was less important. Cath dismissed to the ante-rooms of her mind her own sojourn in Mr Eliot's study, although she was half-heartedly aware that it was the most important thing of all and would have to be disinterred, later. The immediate impact was clearer, because it brought a measure of relief. All those papers in the study could only mean that nice Mr Eliot (and, it followed, his wife) knew more about Cath than she could ever have guessed; knew about Damien, for instance, had some measure of what she had suffered and how brave she had been these last months, so that when she took the momentous step she would take this morning, of asking Emily for help, she would not have to begin at the beginning, because in the information stakes, she was halfway there. How kind and sensitive of them both to mind their own business. In the midst of all this concluding, planning, swaying with the bus, anxious, but confident, it never occurred to Cath that the first-name-only terms which prevailed in the relationship between cleaning lady and cash-paying employer made it unlikely that anyone would automatically connect her full name on a page with the Cath they knew, or that if they had, they might fail to tell their nearest and dearest. Cleaning ladies were treasures with telephone numbers; their full names, their identities, apart from idiosyncrasies, remained in a kind of limbo. The more reliable they were, the more anonymous.

The sun touched Cath's face through a smudged window; she thought briefly of what it would be like up in the eyrie in winter. Yes, explain, calmly and briefly, what her situation was and ask for help. How easy, and yet how difficult a concept that was, but it was not as if she was asking for much and certainly not for anything they could not give. She would like more work, enough to fill three afternoons a week, babysitting, anything they could arrange for her, with all their friends. Emily had fixed her up with Helen West, hadn't she? and there was surely more. Plenty enough to allow her to squat in Damien's flat until she could find something better. Mustn't overburden Mrs Eliot, though, she was a busy woman; ask Helen West later about things like dole money and all that stuff, or take up the offer of that friend of hers, Mary somebody. What a calculating customer she was becoming: she'd be making lists next. The Eliots loved her: she was family, they had often said so. Today, she would accept the accolade, break the habits of a lifetime. Ask for something.

With the bus moving into the smoother reaches of Knightsbridge, it all seemed simple.

She let herself in with the key, smelling the household warmth which was so different from the warmth of the sun, carrying scents of burned toast, soap, feet, and the promise of cheerful voices. She put down her PVC carrier bag, which she always carried regardless of need, and made for the hall cupboard and the Hoover. She always did that first thing, so as not to be seen to have to wait for some special instruction and in any event, there was never a day when this hall did not need cleaning. The house was silent: it seemed almost a shame to waken it into life with the bad-mannered noise of a machine.

Despite her activity Cath was anxious to reach coffee time. Emily Eliot was not. She waved over the noise of the Hoover, disappeared rapidly to the upper regions, put on her make-up and made a list. Ask Hormsbies to supper: frightful people, but their daughter gets on well with Jane and we've been there twice. Write to your mother and thank her for Mark's present. Buy new clothes for Mark, although he does not deserve it, must be his fault he's growing out at the knees, or has he actually cut those jeans? Emily threw her pen across the room. This was procrastination. Get on with it, woman, get on with it. There had never been a motto better suited to a wife: she should get the words emblazoned on a T-shirt.

'I want to talk to you,' she yelled, over the noise of the Hoover. Where was Jane, subversive, eavesdropping little brute with a passion for dirt? Ah yes, waiting for the friend who was coming for the day, and arranging her room in accordance with what said friend would find most admirable. Cath beamed at her, followed her meekly, while Emily felt irritated. Worse still, when Cath sat at the pine table in the ktichen, she fingered with evident, if critical, affection the surface she had scrubbed so often. Honey spilt at breakfast, a shower of crumbs left by Alistair, cocoa pops spilt by someone. Same old stains on the ceiling, food hiding in every crack.

'Mr Eliot's room,' Emily began, putting bread and butter on the table, fumbling with a jar of instant coffee.

'Yes,' said Cath. She grabbed a piece of bread, talked hurriedly with a full mouth. 'I was going to tell you about that.' She looked round, a trifle shifty, looking out for Jane, waiting to say how the child had only been looking for paper and was very sorry, and hadn't she herself put it all back more or less right? Emily looked at the open mouth, nauseated. On cue, Jane came sidling in. No hellos, just a sideways shuffle, clinging to the cupboards.

'Look what I found, Mummy.'

'Where?'

'In Cath's bag.' She held aloft a boxed bottle Estée Lauder, White Linen. Mickey Gat's bribe, which Cath had dropped in there, intending to give it to little Jane, who liked that kind of thing. Emily got up and switched off the kettle. She put back in the bread bin the remains of the granary loaf which Cath ate with such relish, amusing the children who could not understand anyone who did not prefer biscuits.

'I think you'd better go, Cath. I'm sorry about this, but it's best all round.'

Cath stared dumbfounded. She had begun to laugh, her face contorted in a smile which would preface an explanation about how anyone was welcome to Mickey Gat's perfume, since none of it was real, despite the labels, and it wouldn't last five minutes on a camel, although it was still lovely if it was free; and there was Emily Eliot, fumbling in her handbag and handing her five twenty-pound notes, crisp from a cash machine.

'A week in hand,' Emily said, her voice as crisp as the notes. 'Don't worry about the Hoover, I'll put it away.'

Joe was right then, wasn't he? Joe was right about a lot of things, including people in big houses. Cath stood on the doorstep, clutching her bag. Her head seemed to be shaking with a life of its own, turning left and right, right and left like some weary old dog suffering from blindness. She had money in her fist, her bag on her arm; she had never left a house with such speed and she had no idea why. She wanted to sit on the steps which led down to the street, but the thought of lingering where the chill of their cruelty could contaminate her further moved her on. Wandering, she remembered to put the cash in her purse, the second one-hundred-pound bribe she had received in twenty-four hours: at this rate, she would be rich. Cath sat on a doorstep five doors down.

They knew, was why. The bad things as well as the good. With their clever wit and all their knowledge they had decoded it all. About she and Damien shoved out to care, shuffling around in the same bedsit when they ran away; the brother with convictions for theft, and the baby that never was. They knew everything there was to know about the potted life-history contained in the statement of Mary Catherine Boyce. And from the pinnacle of their omnipotence they had decided she was not worth the butter on their bread. Four hours a day, sometimes more, five days a week for a year, uncomplaining Cath would do anything, and she still wasn't worth a hearing. She found herself looking down the road which led into the mews where the Spoon and Fiddle sat; but resisted the temptation to walk down there, find Joe and say you were right after all. She had sat on cold stones for more than an hour: she was strong enough to move out of range, but all the morning's resolution was gone, leaving nothing but a residue of duty. The afternoon was promised; another hundred yards brought her to the number 59, and the golden yellow walls of Helen West who could not paint her own bathroom and did not have a man.

She had had enough of the PVC bag, too: Mrs Eliot had given it to her last Christmas. Cath prepared to shove it in the bin by the bus-stop, felt the weight at the bottom, looked inside instead. Resting on her umbrella was the wee bayonet Jane had shown her yesterday. Get rid of rubbish on the cleaning lady. Cath felt a moment of complete panic, but then it fell into perspective. There was no malice in the child, no knowledge, no accusation; only the contemptuous action of getting rid of something which disturbed her. Just like her mother, getting rid of clothes infected with moth. It was a gift of fate, nothing sinister in it, only contempt.

Bailey could not settle. He found himself in that vacuum created by useless knowledge which he could not share for lack of proof. It would lie on his brain like indigestible food. No-one inside the police force wanted knowledge which led to nothing. He could tell the collator at the local nick to mention Joe Boyce on the files, brief each relief to watch out for him, but what good would that do? Bailey was angry with himself for setting a hare he could not catch; he had disturbed Ryan to the marrow of his bones, for nothing. There was no-one to save and almost no-one to tell. He sat at his desk, drumming his fingers, and looked out of the window into the back yard which steamed with heat and exhaust fumes. He heard laughter coming from next door and thought of his uncluttered home. Then he thought of Helen's.

Well, he seemed to have cut himself off from solace there. She would have given him a good objective analysis, would she not? Yes, in normal circumstances, but perhaps not when it was so close to home. Bailey knew he was refusing to give her the benefit of the doubt, knew that in some way he was on the brink of disaster with her, and that part of it was his own fault for saying he would not see her until the weekend, let her sort out her own household mess, leave him out of it. Selfish, yes, but she had agreed with it. She knew damn well his offers of help were half-hearted. Bailey did not like change. He disliked it, perversely, as much as he disliked staying still.

The leisure centre park where Damien Flood had died was no great distance from the police station where he had landed, peripatetic animal that he was, that morning. There was a monumental pile of papers on his desk: there were other more recent murders, but he could not let this last case lie. Somewhere soon, he would be moved on to new professional hunting-grounds, despite his own resistance, in the same way that life was going to shift Helen and himself into another gear. He wanted something settled before the revolution he could sense on the horizon, like the promise of a storm. And he did not want that boy convicted of murder when all he had done was a feeble attempt at revenge.

Walking round the perimeter of the park, Bailey found it difficult to imagine it in the depths of winter. There would be fewer places to hide. Trying to translate the appearance of a place into another season was like trying to look through binoculars the wrong way round. Now, in the afternoon, it was a vision of innocence. There was a small playground beyond the tennis-courts; mothers sat with babies in prams, and if the peace was disturbed by shrieked commands, 'Val! Get down off there!' 'Danny, stop that, now!', often punctuated by imprecations not suitable for the ears of children, there was nothing sinister about it. It was a multi-coloured scene of racial harmony, paralleled in the crowds on the tennis court, kids mainly, playing games without discipline, using this space like any other space. Animals herding, Bailey thought, making lowing sounds to one another, enjoying the sun.

He found the place depicted in the photographs he had memorized. The tree which had supported the body, the scrubbed grass around it leading to the cinder path. Cut through here and you got to the pub, go the other way and you came out almost next door to Joe Boyce. He had not realized the distances were quite so small; it surprised him, but there was nothing else to discover. He was not quite sure what he had expected. A bunch of flowers to commemorate the scene, perhaps, as if Damien Flood had been a fallen hero.

Whatever else he was, Flood did not warrant much status. No-one was going to erect a statue to commemorate every mugging in this place, but it seemed a good idea. A commemoration of victims, Bailey thought, amused by the idea. He went back to his desk and phoned Helen at hers. Out, he was told, in tones of disapproval. Day off, for painting her flat. Unavailable for comment.

*

160

They sat in the kitchen eating a scratchy and early supper, baked potatoes with cheese, salad, which Cath ignored in favour of bread and butter; no wonder she was starving, as well as plump. Helen was thinking how Bailey was perhaps wise to stay away, because a kitchen full of chaos was not conducive to trust, appetite, confidence or condolence, not as far as Catherine Boyce was concerned. The talkative Cath of yesterday was transformed into the red-eyed misery of today, energetic, yes; communicative, certainly not. Arriving earlier than expected, she gave her brief news and then said she would get on with the painting.

I'll speak to Emily, Helen had said, sick with fury; how could she do that to you? She did and you won't speak to her, Cath said fiercely. Please. After that, all Cath would discuss was carpets. She moved from one of the stepping-stones to another, nodding approval, making her own choice and then changing her mind, as if her battered ego was taking refuge in playing games, finally agreeing that Helen had chosen right. And if Helen West thought she might loosen up and discuss the intimate details of her life over a plate of bread and butter, Cath was not going to oblige. She had wanted to do that this morning, and look what happened then.

The silences were uncomfortable. Cath could feel Helen's disappointment and her helpless desire to make amends: it washed over her like a balm both prickly to the skin and comforting, until, within the strict confines of her ability, she relented. She spat out, in her own code, the conclusions reached on the number 59 from Knightsbridge to here. Conclusions formed while sitting on doorsteps which remained cold despite the sun, contemplating the death of still-unformed hopes.

'You see? It ain't no good at all, trying to do without a man, is it?' she burst out. 'No good at all. At least, as long as I had Joe, other people couldn't push me round. Still, I suppose I'll get used to it. I gotta get used to it, haven't I?'

Helen thought of Redwood, the tyrannies of work from which Emily Eliot was so immune, and frowned.

'Having a man never stopped anyone pushing me around,' she remarked.

Cath was not listening. 'I need something new to wear,' she announced. That sounded positive.

'Yes, you do,' Helen agreed, no longer surprised by the illogical sequence of Cath's announcements.

'Make me feel better. You always feel better if you try. Isn't that right?'

'Sure you do.'

'We're going out next Monday,' Cath stated flatly. 'Joe and me. For a chat.'

'Is this the first time you've left him?' Helen asked, sadly. Cath managed to shake her head and nod at the same time.

'Once before. That wasn't any good either. This time I gotta manage. Get myself looking nice, at least.'

Helen thought of leaving Bailey and all the times it had been on the cards, never more so than now, because their needs seemed to have become so incompatible. That was all any of them were, men and women both, nothing but a series of needs to be met by a series of ever-more-disgraceful compromises and, in the light of that, she realized how powerless she was to help Cath in any but the most small and practical of ways. People do what they will: you cannot make them trust or do what is best for themselves.

'Monday?' she queried. 'I suppose that's as good a day as any. Somewhere nice? Come on, Cath,' she was trying to be cheerful, finding it a strain, trying to break an unbreakable code. 'Tell me, what's your idea of a nice time? A treat?'

Cath looked down at her bread and butter, replaced the last morsel on the plate, held it captive there in case it should escape. She felt nothing but despair. She could not think of the last time she had been happy, apart from when she had lost herself in work, or, dawdling at the Eliots' kitchen table, had watched Jane in the garden; and that thought, more than anything, made her want to cry.

'I think,' she said, swallowing quickly, trying to emulate Helen's smile, 'I think my idea of a real treat is never again going on the number 59.'

'That doesn't seem much to ask,' Helen said.

She thought, in desperation, Is there anything I can offer to do which will help? Anything?

'Does your new place have hot water, Cath?'

'Not so's you'd notice. I manage.'

Helen imagined the vacuum of the weekend ahead. Wondered what a woman did at the top of a block on a sweltering Sunday.

'If you could help me part of Saturday, Sunday too if you like, Monday if you can make it, Cath, that would be great. We'd finish everything, gloss paint the lot. Hang the curtains, put everything back. I can't do it on my own. Then I'm sure I can get you loads more work, and anyway, there'll still be plenty to do here. The garden for a start. OK?'

It was the right kind of offer. Practical. Cath nodded with vigour. Helen wished she could like her. Find more in her own heart than a guilty kind of admiration. It was true what Bailey and Mary Secura both said in their separate ways. She did not understand.

CHAPTER ELEVEN

'**D**o you know what they print at the bottom of Crown Prosecution Service letters? They've got this printed line. It says, "Working for Justice". They must be out of their minds, printing that. What a nerve.' Mary Secura stared at her own hands holding the drink, noticed her bitten fingernails and hid them under the table.

'Helen West told me how she got a letter back from a bloke. Said he couldn't see how that line at the bottom of the letter had anything to do with the rest of it. Why don't we have something like that at the end of a letter from the police? You know, a little something to tuck inside the summons, like they give you with the big electricity bill, telling you it's all for your own good, really.'

Ryan smiled at Mary Secura's mockery. 'We used to have a recruiting slogan,' he said, 'years ago. "Dull it isn't." They put it on the bottom of posters in the Tube. Wasn't true, either. Another?'

Amazing how quickly his hangovers seemed to flee these days. Maybe that meant he was a real alcoholic instead of pretending, or it could have been that the two days spent in the bosom of his family since the last binge had effected a cure. More likely, it was the simpler pleasure of Mary's company, what with both of them grousing and putting the world to rights. Ryan would have preferred Mary with hair ruffled and no clothes on at all, but a man cannot be picky. Since that sight was not on the menu so far, he was perfectly prepared to make do with the company of a woman who felt as hard done by as he did himself. There were many routes to bliss: this was only one of them. No-one ever told you what a positive pleasure it was to sit down and moan.

'Think you'll do all right with Bailey,' he hinted. He was going to go on and add how he had put in a good word, but then avoided the chance to tell a downright lie that Mary was likely to detect. The two of them were having a pleasant evening and Ryan did not want to spoil it. PC Mary Secura was reeling from the discovery that her career was in the lap of the gods, who rated the weight of brain power and dedication rather less than perfume and a short skirt. She was remembering her admonishment, uneasily tempered by the overlong handshake, followed by the reaction of her policeman partner at home, who had acted as if she had laid a dozen men by lunchtime on a Monday: boiling with angry shock, wondering about the impact of her disgrace on his own career, all that shit. In the tide of these resentments, the face of Shirley Rix swam up like a picture of a drowned woman with her hair floating away, and with that image there swelled all the furious love Mary still felt for her chosen career and her chosen victims. Apart from the Rix incident, she had always played it by the book; now there seemed less point and she looked at Ryan with a greater appreciation of alternative methods for getting any damn thing done.

'It isn't just a job, Mike, is it? Not just nine to five, do what you can, surely not? Yes, it is, I can see it written in your face. Working for justice, hey? What a laugh. Last time I saw Justice was a punch-up at a party where the right person got a fat lip.'

Ryan sipped his drink. Not a bad pub, not as nice as the Spoon and Fiddle, source of his last hangover. He thought he might take Mary there another time provided it changed hands as well as management, since a pub owned by huge Mickey Gat and managed by a bloke he might have fingered for murder was not a place he would take a respectable girl who was spoken for. He tried to recall what Bailey had said to him the other night, about the enormous pleasure of having a conversation free of double meaning, innuendo and at least three motives. A luxury too complicated for Ryan. Speaking for himself, he never had conversations like that, especially with women.

'How are you getting on with Mary Catherine Boyce?'

He waited for her to say she thought this was a social conversation, but she didn't. Mary mixed business with pleasure, without noticing the difference. She took work home and also out for the evening like other people would a baby. She would be hell to sleep with, Ryan thought; she would talk about work in her dreams.

'Went to see her today, as a matter of fact. We had her husband in the Unit yesterday, claiming we'd kidnapped her. He'd been tearing the flat apart, he said, not a bad flat either, if you don't mind leaks, and he'd found one of our leaflets. So we calmed him down, sent him to Everyman – clinic for violent men. But, of course, he'll never go. Cath's been out most of the week, working, she says, and I know where, good for her, not many of our ladies work or even know how, even less their mothers, wish they did. So, we talked about getting her tenancy legal and we talked about getting benefits and I might as well have been talking to a brick wall, and then we talk about getting a solicitor so she can get a formal separation, and then, stone me, calm as a cucumber, she says she's going out with her old man on Monday, and what should she wear? I swear to God, I could've killed her. What do you do? I mean, what do you do?'

'Give up,' Ryan volunteered.

'Sounds about right. Not easy, but sure as hell, right.'

Ryan had never had an abstract passion for justice. It was some moving standard way out there on the horizon while he enjoyed his job for the freedom, the powers and the occasional moment of influence. He could feel such a moment coming on, right now. He could also feel the guidance of Bailey's philosophy, which had a rough translation along the lines of, if you obey most of the rules, most of the time and then have the patience to wait, you get them in the end. Ryan could see the advice in purely picturesque terms; an old family motto, carved in wood around some old grizzled buzzard, which leant the whole idea a kind of respectability, although he himself had never quite got round to believing it. There was always a quicker way to work for justice.

'Listen to what I found out about that poor cow's husband,' he began. Ryan forgot, in the telling, that truth was a virtue, while conjecture was not; he revelled instead in this wide-eyed, female audience far younger and sexier than many who had made him cast discretion to the wind. All right, so Bailey and he, the other morning, had dreamt up a scenario which was more acceptable as an explanation for Damien Flood's murder than the one on record so far. The tale Ryan now told Mary included details of how he had checked with the Boyce neighbours, only to discover that Joe Boyce had indeed come home on the night of the murder much later than the times underlined in his statement and that of his weeping wifc. Despite the row they made themselves, the downstairs neighbours knew that the Boyce partnership never took a bath at night, except this once, when one of them did and the bath leaked through the neighbours' ceiling. It was the first time that had ever happened, not a leak, the sort of flood you get with an overflow: someone had left the thing running, but would they come to court and say so? Never. They had only remembered because it was the day before Giro cheques and because of Joe's uncharacteristic humility the next morning when they mentioned it. Since then, he had reverted to type.

Ryan did not add that he had only got thus far by threatening a full-scale drugs raid, not in his power to activate, nor did he stress that these late and unreliable enquiries were ones he might have thought to make in the first place, soon after the death. Bailey would have done so, but Bailey, at the time, had three or four major enquiries. You could get to hate Bailey's example if you worked for him long enough, which in Ryan's case was not yet.

Mary Secura lit her fourth cigarette, smoking as if she only did it to make herself feel worse, a woman with a guilt problem, scratching it raw through amazement and outrage. In her company, Ryan came to share her frustration, it passed between them like a buzz. His story rendered her shell-shocked.

'He kills her brother and she's worried about what to wear on their grand reunion,' Mary murmured. 'If that don't beat all.'

There was a vision dancing before her eyes of going to the Boyce household, ringing the bell, standing back, waiting for the blood to come over the doorstep. Or going, as she had done once, to a house full of hungry blue bottles, swarming round a corpse. Cath would be one of those; the type of battered wife who goes on claiming love, ignoring the cut-off point, leaves, returns, leaves and returns until she is finally carried away in a coffin. And then the man pleads he was provoked.

167

'Don't suppose she has any idea of what Joe might have done,' Ryan suggested.

'Don't suppose you have much hard fact either,' Mary replied, but he could tell she was hooked. She could see Joe Boyce as a murderer all right. She could see all husbands as potential murderers; the job had got to her brain.

'You going back to see her again? Like, over the next twenty-four hours?' he asked.

'Could do, I suppose,' she said, stretching and yawning like a glorious, aerobic-exercised cat. Think of that in a leotard, Ryan told himself; better than no clothes at all, leotards.

'Fancy a curry?'

She seemed to recover herself, shuffle slightly like someone who had heard these unseductive lines before.

'What's your wife doing this evening, Mike?'

'Spanish class.'

'I thought', she said as she swept up her good handbag from the table, planted a kiss on his forehead and stroked his cheek in a way which made him feel dizzy, 'she might have been home, ironing your shirts. You're a star, Mike. Thanks for the drink.'

Alistair Eliot went to the pub on his way home. He knew that he did not stop at the Spoon as a panacea, or even because two days without a professional cleaner had turned his house into a minefield of things on which the average man could break his neck. He stopped because he no longer wanted to get home, on acount of a row with Emily which had passed all boundaries known before, and because if home was no longer a source of comfort, his conscience was worse. How could she have sacked that poor woman for stealing perfume? Perfume was simply not important enough to warrant such action against someone so loyal. In a proper job Cath would have been given warning. His anger had been one of bewilderment, a disappointment in his wife, even before he remembered that Emily had not known exactly how unfortunate Cath was. It did not matter, he had said, who possessed the perfume hidden in his desk drawer; sacking Cath still stank. Poor Cath, he had kept on repeating to Emily's evident displeasure; poor Cath. She is not poor Cath. She smells, she's irritating, she has bad table-manners and she's a thief!, Emily had yelled, aggressive and defensive. A thief!

And you are scarcely better, he said gravely, to treat her in such a fashion without a second chance or any attempt to find out the truth, listen, evaluate or learn why someone who so clearly loves and reveres you should behave in such a way, for so little.

I gave her a hundred pounds and she took it, Emily flashed back. Isn't that what you lawyers call an admission? Only an admission of need, he replied: supposing you were innocent as charged, wouldn't you have taken the money? What finished it was when he told her of Cath's situation, bereaved of a close brother, beaten by an otherwise loving husband. To Alistair's amazement, Emily had said that made no difference at all. She was not duty bound to take on other people's problems; she did not want them in her house any more than she wanted carpet beetles. Which all explained why Alistair went to the Spoon, with some vague and woolly idea of doing good by explanation. Or parting with another hundred pounds, something along the lines of atonement by word or deed, in full recognition that whatever he did would be clumsy. It was a cloudy, muggy evening; the flowers in the window-boxes drooped, reminders of how everything comes to an end, even summer, slipping slowly past the sell-by date. Alistair sat by their suffocating smell.

Joe Boyce had watched his hesitant steps down the street as he stood by the mullioned windows polishing glasses. In contrast to the days before, his mood had become benign. He thought of Mickey Gat, in here yesterday, purringly kind, saying now, now, Joe, I got news for you. Joe had somehow forgotten to take offence at the fact that Mickey Gat knew the whereabouts of his wife while he himself did not: it seemed perfectly acceptable in the order of things, this female solidarity, a reminder that Mickey was one of them, after all. Condescending, yes, but also acceptable as long as Mickey Gat did not lord it, only said, humbly, that she was acting as go-between and wouldn't it be a good idea if the two of them started all over again? Joe and Cath, starting with a clean slate and a special night out, Monday? She misses you something dreadful, Mickey Gat said; she does, really, Joe, she keeps saying so, but you gotta behave these days if you want to keep a wife, and you gotta start as you mean to go on, so next Monday, evening off, show her the town. Joe nodded, sweating with relief, trying not to laugh when the paw produced perfume again. If only Mickey would not do that, forgetting the last time and the time before.

Over twenty-four hours, though, the facts got blurred and Joe's old arrogance began to surface. The prospect of next Monday evening had undergone a subtle change. It was no longer a gentle, tentative experiment in which he would treat his little wife like gold dust and let her know how much he cherished her; it was becoming instead a *fait accompli* in which Cath returned to him and said she was sorry, ready to come home and resume normal married life there and then. Joe decided he might accept her apologies, but then again, he might not. It was not himself who required forgiveness: it was her.

So Mr Eliot came at a good time. Joe Boyce was getting back into the driving-seat, feeling magnanimous and perfectly prepared to overlook the fact that a favourite customer had not been in for a while.

'Hello there, Mr Eliot! How are you? No, stay where you are, sir, I'll bring the usual.' Alistair was nonplussed by the bonhomie. Joe sat with him, the same old scenario, only this time with one of them deeply uncomfortable.

'I gather my wife wasn't working for your wife last week, Mr Eliot. She was staying with relatives, you see, I hope it wasn't inconvenient. Only one day, can't remember which, I forgot and called with a message for her, something I wanted her to get on the way home. I talked to your daughter, silly me. Cath will be back in harness, any time now.'

'Oh.' The expression made Alistair wince.

We are all at cross purposes, he thought, every one of us a little mad, each of us with a piece of puzzle in our hands, while the truth floats up there like that big, black raincloud. Alistair knew part of the story, Bailey knew something, Helen West another thing and this man on the opposite side of the table was in possession of his own version entirely. Alistair drank his token half pint and made small talk, thinking how you could not apologize to someone who was entirely unaware of anything deserving it, even less to a man who hit his wife. He rose to leave, giddy with confusion.

'Wait a minute, sir,' said Joe, tapping his finger to his nose, Mickey Gat style. 'Take home a little something for Mrs E, will you?' To Alistair's ill-disguised horror, Joe Boyce presented him with a box of perfume. Ma Griffe.

'Plenty of that in our house,' Joe whispered conspiratorially with a frightful wink. 'Not quite the real thing, if you see what I mean, but it does the trick with the wife.'

Alistair could only stammer thanks. He was even more bewildered. Why should Cath steal perfume when she had so much already?

There was a mirror in Damien's place: Damien would never have left the house without looking in a mirror, not even if he had been in a state of Saturday-night fever. Now Cath stood in front of the mirror, crying in the way she could only ever have done in private. Helen West had meant well: she had found Cath the promise of three jobs and kept her fully employed painting gloss paint on windows, making a new home, taking up those lovely curtains, keeping up a stream of chat, and then, with the usual carelessness kept for such gestures, doing what Emily Eliot did, turning out her wardrobe in Cath's direction. What made Cath weep now was not the pile of clothes she had brought home on the bus, but the thought that, unlike Emily Eliot, Helen West, whom she had rather despised, did not give away what was strictly surplus. She gave away her best things, only pretending they were no longer needed, when what she had done was select garments which would fit and look good on Cath's lumpy figure. Cath was finally moved by the subterfuge, and by that under-ground flat which did not sway with the wind, heat like an oven or reek with loneliness. She had the fleeting notion of asking Helen West to give her the cat, watch the silly woman hesitate for a moment and then say, Yes, of course, Cath, if you treat it nicely and you think it would help. She would, too, the stupid woman.

Crying made her deaf, until the knock on her door made her freeze. She heard shuffling steps outside, a firm rapping repeated. It was too late to put out the light and simply pretend she was not there. Cath shut her eyes in panic: it couldn't be Mickey Gat this time. What was it Damien had told her about what happened here when youths, high on glue or worse, broke in and found nothing to steal? They smashed bones, that's what; old people living here barricaded themselves in, burned to death when they could not get out. The knock was repeated, someone was calling her name, a female voice, soft, but demanding. Cath opened her door to Mary Secura.

'Just passing,' Mary remarked. Even Cath could tell it was a lie. No-one was ever just passing a place where you had to climb twenty flights of stairs.

'You look nice,' Mary remarked with unflattering surprise. So I do, in a way, Cath thought, turning back to the old wardrobe door which served as mirror. Nicer than usual in a cream-coloured blouse and a full skirt which twirled round her calves in a rich, dark floral print. She could only think of one thing at a time. She stripped off the blouse and dropped the skirt to her ankles, totally unselfconscious of her semi-nakedness. Mary Secura gasped, then coughed to hide it: she had seen worse by way of violent injury, but her eyes were transfixed by the scar on Cath's belly. Ugly, puckering, disfiguring in the minute it remained revealed, before Cath pulled a loose dress over her head, buttoned the neck and turned a circle.

'Not as good,' she muttered.

'You could get that scar fixed, you know, Cath, if you wanted. Wouldn't cost you,' Mary volunteered, casually.

'I don't want to, thanks,' said Cath, looking at her for the first time. 'It's mine. Think I'll keep it. Joe doesn't mind it.'

Mary was not listening. She was in another planet, hovering above the hemisphere, disorientated by the height, remembering how far away she had left the car which might not be there when she went back. She sat on one of the uncomfortable chairs, letting the handbag drop.

'Cath, how is it you can leave that man and even think of going back? I want to leave mine without ever going back.'

'Well, more fool you,' Cath said.

'I came to tell you something. About your man, Joe.'

'I know all about him.'

'No, Cath. You think you do, but you don't. What time does he normally come home? What time did he come home when he went out drinking with your brother?'

Cath was fussing with the dress.

'He always came home just before pub closing. Fridays, he went out. He usually gets time off on Fridays.' She was mumbling, looking slightly alarmed, staring at the mirror and seeing not herself, but the photo she had seen of Damien in Mr

172

Eliot's study. The irritating voice of Mary Secura came from a distance: Cath wished she would simply go.

'Did he ever carry a weapon, Cath? Like when he was carrying money from the pub? Might have needed one sometimes. He was jealous of your brother, Cath, wasn't he?'

Cath undid the top buttons, turned in front of the mirror.

'We're going to have a nice time, Monday,' she chanted. 'Me and Joe. Talk things over. Mickey Gat said. Going out, we are, somewhere special. He promised.'

'Did Joe ever keep a weapon at home?' Mary continued inexorably. 'Up in those attics of yours? Something which could just about cut a man in half?'

'Who asked you here?' Cath shouted. 'Get out! Get out before I kill you!'

She gestured towards the window with a stubby finger, but the window would not open. She stood by the glass as Mary's voice continued. It was a long way down: Cath could feel herself wanting to jump, to float before she hit the ground, and still Mary went on talking.

'Out on the piss,' Bailey said, looking across the road. It was what Helen called his loud look, full of challenge, the kind of look which would make anyone behave worse. She had long since decided she was a coward. If she met a mugger she would smile and say, of course, have my purse, in the same way she would pretend to laugh if she were teased. She would have skirted round the herd of half-drunk youths who jostled them on the pavement, and although Bailey also preferred stand-off to confrontation, the lines on his face did not indicate the same degree of acceptance. It was a Saturday night out: the place he had chosen to eat was rarely so crowded and the wait for a table irritated him. They should have been dining *chez* Eliot, but words had been spoken between Emily and Helen which had put the invitation into abeyance. Bailey could not understand why Helen did not simply shout down the phone, Emily you got this all wrong, in the same way he would have yelled at Ryan and then forgotten about it, but women were women, and their diplomacies a mystery. In pursuit of food, he had invited Helen well into his own territory, a terrain uneasy on the eye, ugly, craggy, uneven, good in parts, foul for the remainder, the restaurants not for the rich and famous, especially the latter, since no-one would know who they were.

The inside of Arrivederci made Helen sigh with pleasure: Bailey could watch her relax, before her long, paint-stained fingers fluttered in indecision over bread and aromatic olives and then fished for a cigarette in guilty postponement of more fattening pleasures. When in this Italian ambience, one ate like a Roman; the plants were dusty and the proprietor a tyrant who could not stand small appetites. Persons who tucked his napkins under their chins, cleaned the dish of olives and ate the bread were served with alacrity.

I love you looking jubilant and greedy, Bailey wanted to say, and I am sorry for my evasions, equally sorry for yours this week. He thought they were up to date on Cath the cleaning lady, he had told her most of what he knew, including Cath in her high-rise flat receiving advice from PC Secura. He knew rather less of what Cath had been doing in Helen's house for most of the week. Since he had, as she put it, flounced away from the mess, access had been either unsought or denied, but all distractions forgotten, she was as sunny as the weather this Saturday night. Bailey placed his hand over hers, wanting to say something momentous, not as yet articulated; something which contained apology and declaration. She used the other hand deftly, to stroke the corner of his mouth.

'Black olive,' she said. 'You messy eater. Have you mended that clock yet?'

'Which clock?' He had thirty-seven clocks at the last count, not including sufficient pieces of clock to make five more, and he had still fallen into this strange habit of consulting his watch.

'The one which races us into the next decade.'

'I forgot to show you. Yes, I mended it, but it's given me a neurosis.'

He was hungry, not only for the food, but for the humour and the intimacy of trust she always offered, along with that heady formula of mutual respect. I have abused that mutual respect, he thought; she knows it and so do I. I have also abused the time-honoured tradition that if you do not keep on asking a woman to become your wife, she will find another man, or at least, another way of living.

The proprietor appeared, looked warmly at the dearth of

bread. Helen opened her mouth to speak but Bailey looked at her warningly, in the knowledge that in this place you ate what the boss told you to eat. The moment for making an effort to say something personal was past. He felt it slip like the taste of garlic on his tongue, hid the biting sensation in a question.

'Listen, what exactly are you doing to your flat, Helen? Tunnelling for freedom? Knocking down walls?'

'I'm turning it into a brothel,' she said seriously. 'Grand opening night next Tuesday, I think. Don't rely on a discount.'

He laughed, but his heart sank. Lamb, the proprietor had ordered. You havva the lamb and eat it all. His spirits lifted at the prospect. Bailey looked at the contentment of her face and wondered if it still had anything to do with his presence.

'How much did Emily Eliot help with all this interior design?'

'Think I can't do this kind of thing on my own, do you? She helped quite a bit, to tell the truth. You know Emily can't stand indecision. Go shopping with Emily and there's no hanging about, no luxuriating in choice. And she always knows someone who knows someone who gets things done cheap. It's an art. She's clever.'

'She wasn't very clever with Cath.'

Helen was silent. 'Do you know, I'm glad to be single?' was all she said. 'I'd hate to be a megalomaniac wife and mother. Mothers run a closed book. They shut the world out, close off anything inconvenient, as if being mum in charge of a family is so self-justifying, so sanctifying, they never need have a conscience about anything else. Some of them make me sick.'

Prejudiced, judgemental, politically incorrect, leaping onto a band wagon and waving a flag: the Helen he loved.

'You see them in shops and cars,' Helen continued angrily. 'Expecting everyone else to give way. Look at Emily. She'd put Cath in prison without a backward glance if it meant motherly peace of mind and, what's more, she wouldn't even regret it. She owes Cath nothing. Cath isn't family. Beware the family who says you're one of us. They never mean it.'

Bailey was enjoying this. 'We're talking about the survival of the human race,' he objected.

'No we aren't. It survives all by itself. Probably because people without families have to devote themselves to looking after those who have. And then get splattered all over the pavement and reviled for not being normal. I'm going on, aren't I? This lamb is good.'

'I wasn't wanting you to stop.'

'What irritates me so much is that people like Emily feel superior and make me feel inferior. She has the right to pig-headed intolerance: I don't. Do you know what she said to me on the phone? She said . . .' Helen swallowed. 'She said she pitied me. If I had kids, I would understand.'

'Now that,' said Bailey, 'was unwise.'

Saturday was passing into Sunday. Upstairs in the flat where Joe Boyce lived, the air was stuffy underneath the eaves, lit by the streetlight and a moon the colour of milk. There were shuffling sounds from the attics: nervous laughter, whispers in the half light and sounds like the dragging of a body, something bumping downstairs from the top floor, slowly, pauses in between as one box after another hit each step in turn. Gradually, they grew bolder, less concerned about the noise. Pause, thump, pause, thump: unrhythmic but certain, repeated time and time again.

The neighbours downstairs turned off the music to listen, then decided to turn it on again lower, so they could hear at the same time as pretending they did not. They kept the door closed. Has he killed her then? one asked in a stage whisper; has the bastard finally done it? Mesmerized by the prospect, until they heard more muffled laughter and a sharp command from above their heads, herald of more shuffling, thumping on the lower stairs which passed their entrance and on out into the street. They turned the music up a notch and wished their front-room curtains did not hang in shreds with gaps in between they had never noticed before. The sound of removals did not mesh with the music, but the bass had more resonance than the footsteps going out into the road, laden, heavy. Had he killed her? Had he, the bastard who yelled at them for the noise but never turned it down himself when he belted his wife all round the kitchen? Had he really? Of all the half-stoned theories which passed across five sets of lips, not one included the suggestion that they should do anything other than listen. One of them had been drunk since noon; three others were slightly high and the fifth not a day over fourteen, with no wish to go home to mother. She shook, choked on a cigarette, drank the cider and looked for the darkest corner. When she could no longer stand the suspense, she crouched by the gap in the curtains and watched while the others watched her watching.

She turned back, scorning them for their huddled circle and exaggerated dread of a second visit from the police in one week. They had done nothing wrong, had they? She danced across the room in the same eerie light which lit the attics, put her thumb to her nose. Naa, she said, nobody's dead. It's only all them boxes he keeps getting delivered. He's only moving them out, doing a flit. Or more likely, he's getting done over. They collapsed into giggles. Nothing to worry about, but still she gazed back to the street where the burglars, one of whom had heard Joe Boyce boasting in a pub somewhere, loaded the van; and when it pulled away, she waved, as if to say, take me with you.

Saturday had slipped away and with it, the word 'weekend', which meant very little to Joe Boyce, the last passenger on almost the last bus wheeling across London, with his head resting against the cool of an upstairs window as the number 59 raced past empty shops at one fifteen, rattling his anaesthetized bones, only just keeping him awake. Fuck you, up yours, he kept on repeating to himself, singing little snatches of songs for as long as he could recall the words. 'Onward Christian Soldiers, marching on to war' . . . 'Hit the road, Jack, ain't you coming back no more, no more?' And somehow, 'God rest you, merry gentlemen', in memory of the colonel who had been in this evening and treated him as if he was lord and master. Oh yes, young Joe was on the up and up, and then the bus turned the corner like a frantic sniffer-dog on a scent and almost tipped him out of his seat. He was not drunk, merely tipsy. *In vino*, as Joe had told the colonel, tapping his own nose in the manner of Mickey Gat, does not always mean *in veritas*, hey, old boy? Memory's not so good with drink aboard, is it, old son, but didn't we have a good time the other night? Rather, said the colonel, suddenly a trifle uncertain about why his drinks were still generous, and, incidentally, free.

Not drunk, merely Brahms and Liszt, still capable of making sweet music. Maybe Cath would be home, unable to wait until Monday because she really could not stay away. At home, sleeping like a baby. He could not think in anything but clichés and he was singing, 'Hello, Dolly' as he walked, not stumbled up the stairs and saw the light on.

No double lock either, but the emptiness inside was like a punch in the stomach, repeated as he went from room to room, wailing, 'Cath, where are you?', his voice echoing from floor to ceiling. A joke, that was what it was, a joke, the house looking like this, rooms emptied not only of physical presence but of almost everything else too. There were table and chairs, carpet on floors, kitchen stuff, sofa, bed, all Cath's second-hand things. Nothing in the attics but drip-stained floors and the rubbish of packing.

There were old wardrobes in the attics, Cath again, but the doors which were formerly jammed shut by the weight of things piled outside them were now hanging open. In one of these, on top of listing floorboards, he found the last box of all. Damp to the touch, full of army insignia, his beret, three olive-colour sweaters eaten by moth and three old bayonets, the last of the collection.

The white moon winked scorn through the window as Joe Boyce stood and wept for the loss of his only possessions and for the dreams which had gone into the acquisition of a thousand useless things. He wanted to plead with the thieves, then replaced his misery with bitterness. None of this would have happened if Cath had been at home, doing her duty. Then Joe became maudlin again, then bitter.

Wife, come home. He was nothing without her; felt he had loved her since the day he was born, counted on the fingers of both hands all the things she owed him.

And at last, sinking into sleep, he could remember where he would have put the other bayonet, the one in his dream. Upstairs in that cupboard. So the only good thing the burglars had done was to take it too.

CHAPTER TWELVE

H elen saw them through her office window, spotlit in the
cruel gaze of early Monday morning. Something was going
on.

On the other side of the road, secretary for supervisor number
two (without spectacles), entered her own little box of a room,
stage left. The secretary to number one (office Lothario, with
specs), sidled into her own room at the other end of the floor. On
each of their desks was a red rose faded by the weekend, the
blooms variously disposed in a glass vase and a blue mug.
Simultaneously, each woman adjusted the flower in its recep-
tacle. Then for reasons unknown, both ladies moved from their
cubicles and marched straight across Helen's line of vision to the
opposite end of the floor. The meeting in the middle resembled a
square dance and was obviously something of a mutual shock.
They handled it well, smiling distant smiles and looking hell bent
on important errands. Number two's secretary carried a sheaf of
paper towards the copier standing next door to number one's
office, while number one's secretary seemed destined for the fax
machine. Once ten steps beyond the other, and hidden by open-
plan screens, each raced into the other's room and began
rummaging around in the desk. They made swift, unskilful

searches, leaving a trail of fingerprints of which Helen did not approve. Then, each of them decapitated the red rose belonging to the other. Helen sighed. She could have told them that they both kept the cards given by number one, he with the specs and the scholastic air, in the top right hand drawer. Also, they both sat on his knee. Also, he took one of them out for drinks and promises on Wednesdays, the other, Tuesdays and Thursdays. She could have saved them coming in early on Monday. All they had to do was wave and she would have answered in Morse code.

The two ladies passed again in the middle, heads high, no greeting this time. Other staff had arrived, filling up the space. One of the women was crying.

Helen turned her back to the glass, regretfully. The sun rose a little higher. The day was all but accounted for: two hours form-filling, the relentlessly stupid, bureaucratic curse of working for cut-price, ill-managed justice, then a funeral, then the last of home improvements. Not bad for a day off which Redwood would resent because it was summer and she did not have children.

It had taken some time to get Shirley Rix arranged for her passage from corpse to ashes. The husband had made a fuss, said he wanted horses with plumes, until he realized fuss meant money and he only got a small grant for a fiery consignment to mother earth. Mr Rix might have been as sad as Mary Secura, but his primary symptom was resentment. He sat on one side of the Chapel of Rest, still bearing signs of prison pallor among persons looking slightly tanned, his son sandwiched between himself and his own mother with a smattering of hunched family behind, while on the other side was Shirley's crowd, planning kidnap of the child and so full of hate they could scarcely say their prayers. The arrangement into combat zones was more appropriate to a wedding. Mary Secura, braced, but not motivated to keep the peace, bristled when Helen West slid into the seat beside her.

There was the disembodied sound of pre-recorded organ music and the sensation of being crushed by the queue waiting for the next one outside.

'What are you doing here?' Mary sniffed. 'What did you have to come here for?'

'Same as you. Showing respect.'

The place stank of flowers, the lingering perfume of exotic blooms, tributes in wreaths and hothouse bouquets. More sweetly from home-grown bunches of roses, sweet peas from allotments, backyard scented stocks predominating over sterile lilies.

'How did you know this was going on?' Mary hissed, her voice drowning in a languid hymn. Helen was wishing religious culture could catch up with the times: in a building with supermarket windows, it seemed odd to be playing music which belonged in a dark church.

'You told me. You phoned me and told me, last week. You barked, remember?'

'I still don't understand why you came.'

'I didn't want you to think I'd forgotten, that's all.'

They stood, filed out. There was a short, sharp squabble at the exit door, swiftly shushed into ominous silence. Shirley Rix's son ran to his maternal grandad, he was yanked back none too gently and began to cry. He was a beautiful boy, Helen noticed, eyes like brown saucers and hair like a smooth thatch. They all breathed better, dispersed more quickly out in the heat, while the next queue moved in. Helen and Mary Secura sat on a bench, smoking; they watched the rest climb into cars while an older man rearranged the flowers, as if looking for his own.

'That one over there,' Mary said, 'is under the impression he is Shirley's dad. He could be right. Shirley didn't think so. He wouldn't listen when she wanted help. You've seen the photos: what do you think?'

'Don't know, doesn't matter,' Helen said. 'But it did occur to me to wonder whether Shirley's gorgeous little boy is really the same blood as the man who reckons he fathered him. I mean, look at them. Not remotely alike. Shirley had quite a past, didn't she? I'm not examining her virtue, you understand, but if it ever came to needing to remove that boy from his dad's care, well it might help to question Papa's territorial rights. Can't hurt Shirl, can it? Suggest it to the family. DNA testing would prove it. Filthy thought.'

'Christ,' said Mary. 'I never considered that.' She shivered, not quite knowing why it was so uncomfortable to either like or admire Helen West, setting herself against it.

'You know DC Ryan, don't you? He told me you were beaten

up once. By a bloke. Is that true? That how you got a scar on your forehead?'

'I bumped into something.'

Smoke wreathed upward through perfumed air.

'You came to this funeral for me, didn't you? You're watching me.'

'What's so important about you? I came for Shirley. In case no-one else did.'

'Oh fuck off. You're just like every other lawyer I ever met. A bloody liar, only you do it nicely. Got to be an angle, I mean, you've got to want something, haven't you? All right. I admit it. I've been to see your cleaning lady.'

'I never asked you to do that.'

It was in her throat to say that she did not actually know how to utilize police power to her own personal purpose, that the ambit of her authority was smaller than any of them dreamed and that she had spent two hours filling in forms to stress her role as cog in wheel; but sitting on a warm wooden bench, with a view of a garden full of mourners drifting round like blossom, she could also sense the futility of trying to turn prejudice into realism.

'Course you didn't ask me to see her,' Mary mimicked her voice. 'Not in so many words. Can't accuse you of anything so straightforward, can I now? Only it just happens to be Ryan, Bailey's sexy little errand boy, who comes down to me and asks the questions, doesn't it? Now is that coincidence or is it not? Don't answer, I don't want to know. How's the decorating, by the way? Does he like it?'

'Not in any way you would notice. He's scarcely seen it.'

'I gather from her, Cath Boyce I mean, that the place looks great and she's been helping a lot.'

'Yes, she has. Still does. I thought the best thing I could do was keep her busy and give her money. I don't think anyone goes to heaven on my counselling skills.'

Mary stubbed out her cigarette, grinding it onto stone with a neat heel.

'Cheap labour, isn't it? Still, I suppose it's better than no job at all. In answer to the question you meant to ask, your Cath seems fine. She got the long straw, after all. Such as, a man who hasn't yet got round to hitting her in the face, somewhere to go when she left and no kids for blackmail fodder. More than most of my ladies get in a month of Sundays. Not frightened either, our Cath.'

'Yes, she is. How can anyone not be frightened in her situation? She's left him anyway. I wish I knew when people should stay or when they should go, but I hope she stays away.'

Helen said this with regret. It seemed such an indulgence to let Bailey traipse across her memory: Bailey's distance, Bailey's removal from anything, his taciturnity, followed by openness, making her feel like an occasional convenience in his life, not an influence.

'I didn't say anything about Cath,' she began. 'I didn't come here to talk about her. Cath has her own willpower. I don't want to talk about Cath; I don't need to talk about Cath, I'm not even good on double motives—'

'Nor am I, but we all have to pretend we aren't, don't we?' Mary interrupted with a laugh so loud it fluttered the lilies. 'Anyway, I'll tell you what you want to know, in case you didn't already. Your cleaning lady is getting reunited with her old man this evening. Whatever he's done, she still loves him. So she's going out tonight, meeting him from work, all dressed up in her glad rags. From what I can see, you've even provided her with the frock; she showed me. Good gear you gave her, you gotta be made of money. Or guilty as sin to be giving away stuff like that. She says you haven't paid her.' Another drag of fresh cigarette. 'Haven't paid her for all the work she's done. Painting, all that.'

Helen was calm, growing calmer. Seeing Cath take home all those clothes.

'You're making this up as you go along, Mary. She's certainly cheaper than a decorator, but that wasn't why . . . What do you mean? Sure, I gave her clothes, that's my business, and I always pay her far more than she asks.'

Mary took no notice.

'Well anyway, she's going out with the little fucker tonight. The man might have killed her brother and she's going out with him like a virgin girlfriend, full of hope, outfit provided by the Crown Prosecution Service to save money all round, I ask you. Don't offer me a hanky while I cry, I've got my own.'

She was back into that big bag, diving deep down in there among the radio, paper handkerchiefs, the scarf, the notebook and all the detritus of a woman who carries her life around. The

183

thing looked like a punch-bag, Mary could have flung it round her head and thrown it like a hammer, she was strong enough and sufficiently angry. Helen ventured one more question.

'Where is she meeting him? Cath, meeting her old man?'

'I thought you would know,' Mary spat. 'You probably made them a dinner reservation.'

Helen stood up, shook out her skirt: there were petals in the folds of the cloth. She thought of Cath, morose and uncommunicative the whole weekend, giving nothing away.

'Enough, Mary. Enough. If you can tell me how I can help Cath, I'll listen, but otherwise, not.'

Mary had fallen into silence, wanting to spit or apologize, the way she always wanted things too late, and then went on, making them worse.

'Advice? About Cath? Strikes me you already gave it. There's nothing you can do. She'll help herself to freedom, or she won't. Besides, you wouldn't want to stop her painting your windows, would you? Just don't interfere. You won't make it better. No-one can.'

Do not interfere. Bailey remarked this very English precept, which was honoured the length of the number 59 bus route, more so in the environs of Knightsbridge than in the neighbourhood of Mickey Gat's pub, but still honoured. The failure to interfere, or even to offer information so that other people could interfere, was indigenous to the brickwork wherever he looked. In Mickey Gat's place, it was more a question of the punters not being good at framing facts or concerns into words. Greetings and jeers were often confused. Monday lunchtime was less than crowded; boredom made Mickey herself more than usually articulate.

'Where's your little friend, Mr Bailey? The one who has to go home to his wife, so she can wash his ears?'

'Day off,' Bailey smiled. 'Probably taking his kids to a park, so they can learn how to mug the others.'

'That's not nice talk, Mr Bailey. Sit down, will you? Nothing happening here.'

They sat, huge woman and slender man. With no-one watching, Mickey did not insist on the male ritual of making her guests drink. Both of them nursed orange juice.

'We haven't got this right, you know. We haven't got this

right at all.' There was no need for Bailey to specify what he meant.

'Well, that makes a change, doesn't it? You don't often get things right, you lot. What's different now?' Bailey was quiet. Mickey's sigh was the last breath of a hurricane. She smelled wonderful. No fake perfume for Mickey.

'I loved that man Damien like a brother, Mr Bailey. Weren't a lot I could do for him though, except help him look after his own. So I got the flat for his sister and a job for the brother-in-law and I still take an interest, Mr Bailey. You can't stop taking an interest just because people get killed, can you? I dunno what you want to know. You just seem to ferret around. You even look like a ferret. My dad used to run them.'

'Just talk to me about Damien. Anything which comes to mind.'

As he spoke, Bailey was wondering idly how Helen would manage in a place like this. He was faintly surprised to conclude that she would manage very well. She would shake Mickey Gat by the manicured paw, cope with the extraordinary apparition without unfortunate comment, probably accept the perfume with a beatific smile and then offer to draft her will.

'I think they were all right, you know, Joe Boyce and Catherine. Damien worried about them, though. I mean Joe didn't want his wife to get a job, would you believe, but she went on about it until Damien told him, let her do what she wants, for God's sake, she ain't going to run away. So Joe agreed, but it had to be him found the job, somewhere near where he worked, so he could keep an eye on her, come home on the bus with her, that kind of thing, although I don't think it quite worked out that way. You know what I mean? He's so jealous, that Joe Boyce, he even went and looked in the windows of the place she works, one night, just to check. Silly bugger. He told Damien that, when he was pissed; Damien thought it was funny, so he told me. Last year that was, soon after she started. I suppose we all get jealous, don't we, Mr Bailey?'

Mickey leaned forward for her drink, tapped her nose. 'So I upped his hours at the Spoon and made it six days a week, of course. Gave him less time for mischief. He's all right, Joe, really.'

'Are you going to keep him on there?' Bailey made his curiosity sound mild and inconsequential, showing no real signs of impatience, as if this information was incidental to what he might have wanted.

'Course I am, why not? He's reliable. Anyway, I thought of what Damien would have wanted. Best thing for his sister is for Joe to stay in work and her to stay where she is, with her old man. It's not good, a woman being on her own.'

'Oh, has she left him then?' He knew that perfectly well, but it was always wise to feign ignorance with Mickey.

Mickey nodded sadly. 'Yeah. She went to stay in Damien's gaff, but I've had a word with her. And him. So they're going out on the town tonight; I even gave her a bit of spending and him a night off. Women, you know, they sometimes make me ashamed. You know . . .'

'Yes, I know.' Bailey guessed what was coming next. 'Like cats, if you don't feed them.' Both of them stared at their unwanted orange juice, weighed down by their own wisdom. Bailey rose and stretched.

'So you don't know a single person who might have had it in for Damien?'

Michaela Gat shook her head, looked up at Bailey's height.

'Unless it was someone envied him. Damien was good at a lot of things, he was even ace at selling perfume down the market. He could do five hundred quid a day, could Damien. Dunno why Joe Boyce never wanted part of the action. He's a sensitive.'

'That must be why he hits his wife.'

Mickey shrugged herself to her feet.

'That's up to him, Mr Bailey. Shows he loves her.'

They were standing shoulder to shoulder. Mickey looked Bailey up and down as if examining a horse before a race.

'No, you're still in good shape, Mr Bailey, I'll say that for you. When you getting out of the police? You're wasted in there. We come from the same place, you and me, and look what I've done with my life.' She gestured the room, expansively. 'And then look what you've done with yours. I got a nice house in Wanstead, with a family and a swimming-pool, and you got fuck all. Shame, really. Let us know when you need a proper job. I could do with a useful ferret and I pay proper.'

With that accolade, they parted, Bailey smarting, despite laughing. It was a strange sensation to be pitied. Humiliating to be seen as the servant of another, and thus, a failure.

By mid-afternoon, the heat at the top of Bevan House was stifling. Mary Catherine Boyce had washed herself in cold water, although she had already taken a bath, courtesy of Helen West, before leaving that home for this. She had been tempted to stay there, change her clothes and go out for the evening, but it seemed a liberty which could only lead to well-intentioned questions, so she came home. Helen had given her too much cash, as it happened, but if she did not deserve it for pacifying the carpet men, getting up at dawn, hoovering after they had gone and flogging back here on the bus in an afternoon of stifling heat, well, Helen would not grudge it.

Cath had dusted the mirror in order to feel better about her view of herself as she confronted it. She was so pale. Make-up, then: she had a little of that and Helen's bathroom cabinet had revealed a few supplies so clearly abandoned it was high time they were recycled. Cath did not have much skill with the art of *maquillage*, but a fingerful of eyeshadow and some carefully applied mascara made such a significant difference, she blushed at the sight of herself, emboldened to tackle the clothes. In the days when she loved clothes, she had preferred heavy coats, good woollens and colourful legs, not flimsy cotton. Summer was a time for girls; winter favoured women. Not bad all the same: black blouse, the cascading dark floral skirt, shoes with slight heel, all of her streamlined, taking the view of herself up from the tiny ankles, skimming full hips. Pity she had to take that little PVC bag with her in the absence of anything else convenient, but just as well. Joe might not be able to recognize her without it, and besides, it was fate which had given her something to carry in the bag.

She wished it was perfume, found herself searching Damien's one-time home in case he had some of it still hidden away, then shook her head in front of the mirror, chiding herself for the regret. What a terrible gift was perfume, always given by a man to make you wear it and please him, while you stank of blackmail; but in memory of long-past gifts, memory of Damien, she wished she could add a spray to her wrists as a kind of charm.

The bus would smell less sweet. She and Joe were going out on the town and she was going to act like a lady so she could be treated in the same way. In the heat of the afternoon, she walked slowly down the stairs, so as not to perspire, practising an elegant step as she turned left out of the central portico and made for the leisure centre in the near distance. There were always taxis cruising there.

When Helen opened the door to her own flat, her toes felt the tickle of new carpet. The front door moved across it stiffly, dragging on the pristine surface of deep gold. The door to the living room had been removed and left with a notice attached. All the rooms seemed slightly smaller, the ceilings closer, while her feet sprang as though on a trampoline, from room to room, before she kicked off her shoes in case they were dirty. Gold and blue, reflecting colours onto the white ceiling, even the kitchen painted, the window-panes mended and shining clean, the chipped surfaces polished within an inch of life and everything suddenly respectable. It felt like being given a prize, a parcel containing a ton of self-esteem, and for all that, it did not feel quite like home. There was the odd piece of furniture which looked as if it had strayed from the film set of some historical kitchen-sink drama into one of modern romance and, for a minute or two, she felt the same way herself. Outdated. The whole vision gave her the desire to comb her hair and tidy herself up a bit, just so she would match. Even the cat was infected. It came indoors via the flap in the kitchen wall and sat marooned on the floor, washing itself assiduously, then leaping onto the table, crouching with the close observation of a judge. The tail moved, sleek and ominous, while the cat cleaned her paws.

All right, Joe Boyce admitted to the colonel, I am, as a matter of fact, a bit nervous about the evening in hand. I mean, wouldn't you be? My wife walks out on me, leaves me to get burgled, decides to make it up in her own time while all I can think of is how we've lost everything. Everything, mate, I'm telling you, everything we ever wanted, including a whole lot of stuff I never even knew I had, see? Shameful, isn't it? Only she isn't ashamed, not her. They never are, are they, wimmin?

They were seated outside the Spoon. The flowers had the scent of decay about them; Joe had bombarded them with mineral water during the afternoon recess and the lobelia, in particular, seemed to resent it. Mickey had a man come and do the flowers, but the man's visits made no allowance for this kind of heat and Joe reckoned flowers had a thirst too, just like the colonel and himself.

You could talk all day to the colonel, Joe decided, provided he said nothing back, only made agreeable nods and grunts. He had done nothing much else since coming in here at three in the afternoon, cunning old bird to realize Joe was there, too, and just the company Joe needed. Somewhere along the line of the week's traumas, Joe was inclined to fuss the colonel like a dog so old and loyal the owner becomes impervious to the smell. The colonel had not moved in an hour: Joe had been in and out, recounting episodes of his own life with increasing indignation. Dear boy, the colonel murmured in receipt of each drink and each anecdote. Dear boy, how absolutely frightful for you.

His pose had become statuesque, if an egg-shaped body could ever be thus described, until, when Joe emerged with yet another for both of them, he found to his surprise that the colonel had leapt to his feet. Leaping was not his style; the effort made him pant, his voice was both slurred and distinct and all the same his heart was in it.

'Madam,' he said, 'charmed, I'm sure.' There was an attempt to sweep a bow which almost turned into a curtsy. Cath helped him back to his seat. She was bold as brass, sitting outside there as if she owned the place, looking up at him, raising her sun-glasses; Cath, in sun-glasses over painted eyes, smiling with a red mouth, sitting with her legs crossed and her bag under the iron chair, fanning herself against the heat. She looked a different woman: Joe did not like to think that time spent away from him could have done that.

'Hello, Joe. If you aren't going to say hello, do you think I can have some water? I'm parched.'

Echoes came back to him . . . Joe, could you make me tea, I hurt all over, Joe, please . . . He looked at her, goggle-eyed, unable to move as she made conversation with the colonel. Nice weather, isn't it? Yes, a bit hot, ma'am, but better than being cold, hey? Oh yes, surely, I hate the cold, don't you, but what do you wear when it's like this? The plants still drooping in misery behind them, as if Joe had given them gin rather than water; Cath smiling like a stranger, straight into the eyes of another old man. All that was bad enough before Alistair Eliot walked by. Joe shot inside, thinking it was all too much to bear: it was as if his allies had all gathered together to shoot him; his wife looking positively sexy, his friend come by to reprove him, everyone looking at everyone except himself, redundant amongst them all. Still the hanger-on, not only at his own party but every other he had ever attended.

Alistair Eliot smiled at the duo outside the Spoon. They looked like a nice old man and his daughter, he could see himself in that role when Jane was grown up. He did not recognize Mary Catherine Boyce in her smart outfit, although she stirred some dim memory in his more than usually distracted state; she had nothing to do with the Cath he had met so often in an overall. Different women, different territory, however close. If he had had a hat, he might have raised it. Joe watched him go with relief, Cath, with bitter hurt.

'You can go fuck off if you like,' Joe said to the young man behind the bar. 'Cos I don't think I'm going anywhere. My loving wife, see her, outside? She's come in to help. About time she helped.'

The young man shook his head, tempted but remembering the size of Mickey Gat.

'Can't do that, Mr Boyce. I got orders. You've got to go out.'

Sitting outside with the colonel, Cath watched her own expectations fade. A posse of drinkers arrived out of their offices, chattering like starlings, ready to unload the day. The relief barman brought her water with lemon and ice, but Joe ignored her, until, after two hours in which her own immobility made her cold, despite the humid warmth, he came and sat down, sullen and silent. She placed a tentative hand on his arm, and then, jeeringly, he spoke.

'You look very nice. Planning on going somewhere special, were you?'

She felt for a minute as if her heart would break, smiled steadily, stroking his arm as if in supplication, and it was the suggestion of pleading in this action which finally mollified him, although he was already drunk. Drunk in the way Joe Boyce was at work, never quite showing it, simply possessed of a slight wildness.

'Come on,' he ordered. 'Off we go.' He marched down the

street before her, letting her run behind. 'We'll find a nice pub,' he shouted over his shoulder, watching with approval her attempts to keep up. There had been the suggestion of tears in her eyes as she sat with the colonel: the unfamiliar mascara was blurred. The hard-earned dignity of her entrance was diminishing fast. Already her blouse felt creased, the armpits sticky and still she held on to her PVC bag. They got as far as two streets away, into an establishment as far removed from the gentrification of the Spoon as was possible in the area. This one was full of tourists, young, impossibly handsome, brash and blond, girls in shorts grimacing at warm beer before they ordered more.

They stayed there for an hour, Cath on bitter lemon, Joe putting a couple more stiff ones down his neck, ogling the girls. Cath paid for the rounds without protest. Then they moved on, to another place, slightly worse and even more crowded. He led; Cath followed. Joe told her about the burglary, without otherwise volunteering much. He did not ask a single question about her welfare, what she had done, how she had been. She asked him if he had been eating properly and he said no. Her face grew stiff from smiling as Joe chatted to strangers in a long, almost ritualistic humiliation. In the last of four pubs, long after midnight, where drinking was still in full swing for a birthday party, Cath went to the Ladies and left him, via the back door.

The sky outside grew softly dark, then the rain stopped play for those bold enough to risk sitting out of doors in a London summer. Around Sloane Square, the cruising cars found other destinations and the streets shone with damp. In Emily Eliot's household, silence persisted. Jane was in her room drawing furiously on listing paper many hours after she was supposed to be asleep. Emily had long since gone to bed alone. Alistair was in his study, not exactly working, but staring at the wall, wondering about other trials rather than the one commencing tomorrow, worried about society, the universe, his household bills and any other subject but himself. He would have liked the oblivion of being drunk, to avoid having to conclude that there were times when he did not really like Mrs Eliot very much, even though he loved her.

Somewhere in the middle of a great deal of diffused guilt about what he might be doing wrong, Alistair saw himself walking past the Spoon earlier that evening, resisting the temptation to stop for a drink, noticing the old man sitting alongside that familiar face which had nagged him all the way home. Cath: he had it now, only it made the guilt so much worse. Of course it had been Cath, with that hunched way of sitting and that secretive smile, and he had ignored her. Alistair recognized the need to speak to some wise soul outside his family circle, to straighten out his own emotions. He could only think of Helen West or Geoffrey Bailey as those with the necessary degree of detachment to hear him out when he did not know what he wanted to say. He walked to his son's bedroom at the back of the house, noted that the window was wide open in the boy's absence. A lingering smell of cigarette smoke pervaded the room, explaining this sudden passion for fresh air; why didn't the boy just do it openly, instead of treating it as a clandestine pleasure? There were so many worse crimes, such as unkindness, brutality, dishonesty and wilful blindness.

The onset of rain made him feel better; he leaned out of the window. Down below, light shone into the garden from Jane's room, illuminating the churned earth outside her window. The perfume Alistair had accepted from Joe Boyce and failed, as yet, to show to his wife, burned a hole in the bottom drawer of his desk. He knew in his heart of hearts that his wife had acted on instinct, but he also knew that Cath, their victim, was not a real thief.

Cath could not move. Instead, she let two, three buses go by and stayed in the shelter, waiting for him. Joe Boyce had reached the point Cath had recognized on many an evening at home, all passion, all aggression spent, leading him into a state when he was as soft and floppy as a cuddly toy. Staggering to the bus stop, he was outrageously pleased to see her, affectionate, scarcely able to stand, the last remnants of recent memory gone. They stood beneath the awning with their bodies forming a triangle, he leaning into her, pressing against her for balance, while she braced herself against the shelter and let him slobber into her ear. 'Oh Cath, I'm sorry, Cath, I do love you, Cath . . . why do you do this to me, Cath, why did you . . . I love you, Cath.' A litany going on, interrupted once in a while with a curse about the non-appearance of the bus. The ignominy of her evening no longer troubled her: she had money for a taxi, but did not search for it, she simply stood there waiting for the number 59, late night bus, to take them home as if she had known it would happen this way, all the time.

The bus stormed into sight, bottom half empty, top deck one third full. There were a few stares of disapproval as Cath pushed and shoved to get Joe upstairs and all the way to the front, out of harm's way, with him giggling throughout as if she was tickling him. She sat with his heavy arm around her shoulder, almost pushing her off the narrow seat, still murmuring, I love you, Cath, you know I do, she shushing him as she would a child while the imperious conductor looked at their passes and ambled away, tongue clicking under his breath, shaking his head at the futility of the human race. And then, with a sigh, Joe slid towards the window and let his face rest against the pane. She had always marvelled at his capacity not only for instant forgetfulness, but also for unplanned, profound sleep. It was something she envied, rarely achieved and craved all the time.

Sleep softened the lines of his face, made his mouth seem generous rather than petulant. Cath stared ahead as the bus churned through the drizzle, past the deserted theatres of Shaftsbury Avenue where the lights gave promise of life still existing inside gambling parlours and slot machine arcades, the last resort of pimps, touts and those few still desperate for entertainment. In front of her eyes, night-time London took shape and showed shame: people bedding down in doorways, drunken revellers climbing on board for a few stops, restaurant waiters, the last to come out into the dark. By the time the bus reached Islington, it was almost empty again, ploughing a path east, rattling sleepy windows down narrow roads. Joe slid further down the seat, snoring. His hands remained crossed on his chest, his legs splayed, still allowing her no room for comfort. Cath turned. Behind her, near the top of the stairs, three other passengers also slept, one of them noisily. Joe's shirt had ridden up, exposing his belly. His trousers had slipped down as he stumbled up the stairs. Like his brother-in-law, he had grown soft in the stomach.

Cath leaned forward and kissed him on the cheek. I gave you the chances, she whispered. I gave you the chance to look after me, and you could not take it. I can't do anything else, my love. Then she felt inside the PVC bag and withdrew the bayonet.

Rusted, certainly, but sharpened again long after being ground to sharpness by some backstreet lathe, honed against stone, so that the blade was half the size it had been, whittled and ground to a shine. Damien had taught her how to do that, a long time since, when they had both learned how to make every single thing useful, even a bayonet. Joe or Damien, she forgot which: only men thought they knew how to sharpen a blade, something they learned in the company of other men.

She had her left arm firmly round his shoulder for balance as she plunged the blade into his belly. There was an inconsequential thought of how much more easily this could be done with a kitchen knife if such items were not, somehow, sacrosanct. As she plunged, with the same energy she applied to housework, she leaned closer, putting her hand over his mouth, the way she had done before when the conductor was looking, and dragged the blade towards herself, twisted, pulled it away, despite the resistance, then began again, left to right, systematically, the way she hoovered stairs. The large sheet of thin polythene, pinched from Emily's dry-cleaned clothes and now used as a kind of apron, rustled as she twisted the blade for the second time. Cath had a passion for cleanliness and did not want to get dirty: the skirt was important. Joe's eyes opened wide; his mouth bubbled with spittle; he struggled in weak spasms. She held him tighter; she had muscles like an ox. From behind they looked like a couple adjusting themselves for amorous comfort. The little barks he made could have been those of a man fondled intimately.

Before the blood cascaded, Cath covered him with the jacket which had been half off his shoulders when he wailed his way to the bus stop. She wiped her hands on it first. She looked around again before tugging out the bayonet, amazed at the effort it took, mumbling under her breath about the inefficiency of the thing and at the same time, examining the dark floral skirt and the black blouse for damage. There was little sign. The bus sailed past St Paul's Road and into Hackney. Cath waited for a moment, withdrawing from him fastidiously and carefully. She was a mile or so from home.

Fate had given her the weapon. She was governed by fate. A child had given her the knife. It was preordained.

*

When she alighted, five stops from the main terminal, surrounded and hidden by three teenagers in search of a club they had heard about up here which stayed open all hours, she looked like an ordinary little waitress coming home from a job rather than someone returning from a night out. She remembered not to open her mouth, set off for Bevan House. With the bayonet in the PVC bag, Cath walked smartly along the main streets, her little heels whacking the pavement in challenging sound. No-one stirred. No short cuts, no shrinking in the shadows. Walk proud: someone had told her that was the way for a woman to stay safe.

Halfway up the rising heat of the flats, wiping away the last of the mascara, blurred by tears into black channels round her mouth, she reminded herself how dangerous it was out there. Wept anew, because she had loved him.

CHAPTER THIRTEEN

H elen West was day-dreaming, playing several scenes over in her mind. Scene One: the door would open. Bailey would cross the threshold, gasp with admiration and fall at her feet. Scene Two: the pair of them hosting a party, without argument. Scene Three: herself, in this room, preaching hypocritically to Emily Eliot and Redwood about the joys of single life. Scene Four was the door opening again, but this time to admit a total stranger, a dependable-looking male with a chunky physique diametrically opposed to Bailey's own, carrying a bouquet of flowers as he murmured, What a lovely home you have, Helen; what exquisite taste; marry me tomorrow and never work again. Scene Five: even bigger bouquets. The next, possibly most realistic scenario, was the door opening yet again, Bailey waiting behind it, refusing to come in, while she ran across to welcome him and tripped on the new carpet. The last sequence was Bailey and herself sitting in the golden living room by the fire, like Darby and Joan. Then the film snapped.

Unable to make much sense of her own quixotic day-dreams, Helen was severely ashamed of them. Halfway through Tuesday evening, she had completed the final touches, added two new plants and some flowers in the kitchen. She was so impressed with the splendour of the flat, she had been tempted to phone Bailey and warn him that if he did not faint at the sight there would be dire recriminations, but that would spoil the surprise.

Day-dreams made her angry, they were yet another weakness. It was useless pretending she was not influenced by what she saw and read; she was not immune to the contagion of the romantic or the desire for security purveyed by mothers and magazines, even though experience had taught her to expect so little. Wedding bells were the music of the young. Helen did not want a solid Emily Eliot style ménage, but she did not quite know how not to not want it either, or how to close her ears to the blandishments of marriage propaganda. So here she was, a grown-up woman, more emancipated than most, mistress of all she surveyed in an elegant apartment with real food in the kitchen, waiting for her man with all the subtlety of a street-corner prostitute.

Dear Bailey, save me from an evening of contemplating nothing but my bank balance. Even if the effort was not entirely mine, will you please, for once, compliment me? Even if you don't love me, admire what I've achieved.

He had a key. She had taken off the dirty track-suit suitable for dusting books and hanging pictures, wore a casual shirt in loud stripes, clean jeans cut off at the knee and bare feet, the better to enjoy the carpet. Even in her present mood she could not manage frills, and added only enough perfume to mask the smell of cigarettes and paint.

Bailey administered a peck on the cheek and walked straight into the kitchen, the one place in her whole abode which had altered the least radically. He opened the fridge, ignored the ample contents, pulled out a lager and leant against the wall with a sigh.

'What do you think?' she demanded.

'About what?' He was staring into the garden. 'Listen, has your cleaning lady been here today?'

It was not a request for information, more an aggressive demand, and he was refusing to turn round and face her. Or look beyond, into the marvels of the hall. The hectoring tone prompted rising anger, chill anxiety and a spontaneous lie.

'No. Why?'

Cath had been here, to Helen's surprise, when she herself came home. They had coincided for half an hour; not long, so not therefore, quite such a large lie. The encounter had not been pleasant; she wanted to forget it until later.

'Husband was killed. On the bus, late last night. They forgot to check everyone was off, parked it. Found him this morning. No wallet. I didn't get called in to identify him until this afternoon. We couldn't find her anywhere.'

He made it sound like an accusation. Helen leant against the kitchen table, appalled.

'How was he killed?'

'Stabbed. Thoroughly. He might have survived, all the same, if he hadn't lain there and bled to death. By the smell of his clothes and the vomit, he was as drunk as a skunk.' He slumped against the sink. 'I don't know why I thought she might be here. People tend to come to you, that's all. I should have gone to her place and waited. Someone's got to tell her. I don't particularly want it to be Ryan.'

'You know I thought for a minute you were going to say she had something to do with it. Killing him, I mean.'

He looked at her vacantly, his way of telling a lie. 'Why would you think that?'

'I didn't . . .'

'Good. I've got to go.'

'I'll just get my shoes. Wait a minute.'

Bailey swallowed the last of the beer and turned on her. 'You don't need shoes. What do you need shoes for? What do you think you're doing?'

'Going with you. Look, I don't love her, but for all I know, I'm the best she's got. Better than some great big copper standing over her saying, Madam, did you know your husband's dead? Wait for me.' She was hurrying out of the room, like one of the scenes from the day-dreams, tripped on the new height of the carpet, before he was holding her by the arm, roughly.

'No! I'm not taking you anywhere. I'm not. I don't want you with me, understand? This is work. I don't want you going to places I have to go to, right?'

'But I want to go. For Christ's sake, it isn't me who'll come to harm. What are you doing which can't take a witness? If you don't take me, I'll go by myself.'

'You don't know where she lives.'

'Block of flats on the 59 route. Top floor, I've seen the place.'

'Which block, which number flat? Don't be silly.'

She put her arm across the door, stopping him, suddenly calm. 'Listen to me for a minute. You're going to tell some poor persecuted woman that her husband's dead. He might have been a bastard and she might not be what I'd call a friend but she's valued by me and she knows me, so why can't I come with you, even if I only sit in your car? The only reason is you can't ever really let me share the important bits of your life. You seem to want a dizzy little bimbo you can park on a bar stool without the meter running. If you can't give a better excuse, you and I don't go anywhere, ever again. Have you got that? I'll get my shoes.'

He shuddered, as if afflicted by cold. Helen felt the breeze and heard the slam of the front door before she was halfway back from the bedroom. She sat in the golden living room, ashamed of her own state of ultimately guilty rage. Judgement day. She was nothing but a little woman who ignored the world to paint her house.

Damien Flood's place had been turned over good and proper. There was a hole in the door to indicate where the lock had been chiselled out in clumsy fashion, noisily and slowly. No attempt had been made to resecure it: the damage was fresh. Inside, there had been precious little to steal: no video-recorders, cameras, computers, nothing to make the time spent worthwhile. There was a token amount of wanton destruction, even that limited, as if the childish burglars had grown tired: sugar and powdered milk dumped on the floor, slices of bread scattered, a set of makeshift bookshelves, put together out of planks and painted breeze-blocks, dismantled, two mugs smashed. No faeces or graffiti; no statement of envy pertinent in a flat as bare as this; instead, Bailey supposed children had used it as a temporary playground.

He noticed a print on the wall showing a bowl of daisies, a theme echoed in two tea towels hanging over a chair, as if someone had once tried to give a touch of personality to the anonymity of the place. Bailey felt his angry frustration die, felt only sympathy for the occupant. Wherever she was, life was pushing Mary Catherine Boyce to the limit.

*

The pity had grown to outrageous proportions by the time he encountered the inside of the real home of Cath and Joe Boyce. A young neighbour from downstairs tried to close the door on him, as if he was a Jehovah's Witness come to save her soul. Yes, she had been out all day; she'd said so before, hadn't she? And the place had been burgled on Saturday night: is that what he had come about? They had all heard the man who lived there walking round and screaming when he came home. He had paced round, crying and shouting most of Sunday, none of their business.

Bailey went upstairs, put his shoulder to the door. It showed signs of fortification, recently destroyed by experts, gave to the slightest pressure. There was nothing inside to indicate burglary, merely a sense of emptiness which was all the more pathetic because the living room, kitchen and bathroom on this floor bore such signs of strenuous, penny-pinching effort. Daisy print on the wall here too; shelves constructed in the same way as Damien's. There was the detritus he might have expected from a primitive married man left on his own for a week, a few unwashed dishes, grime accumulating on the draining board, all at odds with a significant smell of bleach. Bailey picked up a tea towel, patterned with daisies, he noticed, and used it to cover his hands as he looked through an old kitchen unit, battered, lovingly painted with gloss at some point in a venerable life. Lying among the knives in the cutlery drawer was an old bayonet. Bailey lifted it out with the tea towel, and moved into the living area to find better light. The pattern on the towel, those clumsy shelves, the print on the wall, somehow shocked him more than the weapon in the drawer. Damien Flood's hideaway, Joe Boyce's home: both somehow dominated by the same, feminine touch.

Bailey tried to imagine the time it would take to sharpen such an obdurate piece of metal blade designed for the forceful thrust rather than the delicacies of surgery. Someone at some time had ground this blade on a lathe to obtain such a cutting edge, refined by resharpening again for effective use. There were marks on the side of the breeze-block shelving; Bailey remembered his mother outside the back door, sharpening a carving knife against the wall.

No-one had ever searched this house: Joe Boyce had never been a suspect. Bailey could not see why this savage bayonet had been left, even by Joe Boyce. Joe could have kept it sheathed among the military memorabilia above the bar of the Spoon, or taken to carrying it again after he had been attacked on the way home; murderers were always fools, and yet nothing quite explained either why it should be the cleanest and most incriminating thing in an otherwise greasy drawer, or the pervasive scent of bleach which hung around the sink.

Then there was a footfall from above him, a plaintive voice, calling down querulously.

'Is that you, Joe? I'm sick, Joe, make us some tea. I hurt, Joe, I hurt all over . . .'

The voice echoed, and the air was suddenly cold. The voice spluttering, repeated the refrain. I hurt, Joe, make us some tea. It was a refrain like a chant; finally, it unnerved him.

'Come on down,' he shouted.

Poor bitch; perhaps she was so attuned to obedience, she would have obeyed the summons of a thief, provided he was male. The step on the stairs was weary; the figure emerging into the stuffy room, slow and shambling.

'Hello,' Mary Catherine Boyce murmured without rancour or surprise. 'If you've come to take any more stuff, don't bother. Someone else has had it all. Joe's going to be ever so cross. I should have been here, you see, only I wasn't. I was somewhere else. It's so hot today. Someone took all the boxes.'

It was the plaintive voice of a little girl, driven to the thumb-sucking habits of adult dementia. Cath swayed slightly, sighed and went on speaking, with difficulty.

'Only I'm a little bit drunk, see? I got it on the way. I thought if it worked for him it might work for me, even if I hate the taste. And then if he hits me, p'raps I won't feel it.'

She was grinning inanely, puzzled, entirely naked, with her hands crossed across her chest, her hair lank, her lumpy stomach folding over a puckered scar. She was shaking her head.

'It doesn't work, you know. I don't know why he ever thinks it does, does nothing for me.'

'I'm a police officer, Mrs Boyce. And Joe's dead.'

She began to wail, like an animal in pain.

He had no personal radio with him. The burglars had taken the fancy phone. There were enough reasons for him to ignore the formulae he should have followed, such as calling for help, getting in a female officer, all that. Instead, he turned his back on her, put the kettle beneath the tap and bellowed over the sound of running water and her desperate wailing.

'I'm making tea, love. Get some clothes on, there's a good girl.'

The pity had grown to a lump of gristle in his throat, choking. He was thinking of the lump of humanity, abused by his own kind, a pretty woman making herself revolting by being so pitiable. He was also thinking of Joe Boyce, rolling round on the top deck of an empty bus. Lying there and dying in his own vomit, perishing through asphyxia and blood loss, not from his clumsy wounds. Thinking too, how this woman had been a constant presence not in one home, but two. Would Helen's kitchen, or Emily's, ever sport tea cloths with daisies? As his mind raced, like his delinquent clock, he wondered how he would phrase his report to the Crown Prosecution Service, to lawyers like Helen, so removed but working in the interests of justice as far as they knew it, which was not as well as he. Thinking of the bottom line, insufficient evidence, or a plea bargain, plus all that destructive nonsense in between.

Helen had found the shoes and the car keys. This kind of car would be safe wherever she took it and since she felt as attractive as a leper, she was safe too. East. Away from gentrified houses and towards the urban edges of the metropolis. The number 59 droned past the end of the road; she followed it.

There was no sensation of following a star, like the three kings trailing through another kind of desert in pursuit of divine message, hope instead of despair; it was simply an alternative to doing nothing.

Light was fading at nine o'clock, diminishing with the slow reluctance which heralded the inexorable sunset of summer. Long shadows, heat stored in the brickwork, ragged flowers and brown grass between buildings, the trees of north London still green, the hedges of gardens still gallant. Helen did not feel self-conscious about following a bus. Late evening traffic was brisk and purposeful; no-one noticed. The bus itself skipped stops, skittish, like an antisocial cat. On paper, Helen knew these streets, some of them boasting real or faded glory, others history, others an ethnic dominance which was busy and brave in the dying light. Looking for landmarks, pausing, with the bus, parallel to playing-fields, watching a game of football on brown turf, moving forward again. She thought she would have been safer on the bus, without the shell afforded by a car, until she remembered Joe Boyce.

Major junction, red lights, where the youths came forward in a gang, threw water at the windscreen and began to wipe it off. Helen had no money, sat there revving the engine and on the change of lights jolted forward without payment. One shook his fist and yelled; the others melted back: wrong car. Hackney emerged through glass streaked with dirt and soap: the exhaust of the bus spouted blue smoke; and into the equation, as she saw where she was, came motorway signs, local signs, a distinctive pub and railway-station sign, and then the block Cath had pointed out emerged on the left. There was no-one behind to protest at her abrupt and ill-mannered manoeuvre towards it.

Top floor, Bevan House: that was where she was, strange Cath, and this was where a stranger parked a car. In between two other cars, one wrecked, the other in the first stages of renovation, Helen's car simply looked like a vehicle awaiting therapeutic attention. And this was where she walked on a sultry evening. Sauntered downhill, into a building, found a lift, pressed a button, waited in vain until someone ran past and rewarded her optimism with a two-fingered salute and a grin. She looked at the darkening flight of stairs to which he pointed. She knew these places on paper: she had a map of the city in which she lived, on paper. She could climb stairs, too.

She felt the scar on her forehead, she could never quite suppress the memories of fear and pain. She felt Bailey's contempt, and remembered at last what it was Cath had said. Going out as she was coming in, Helen somehow disturbed to find her back – yesterday had been the final day: Helen needed no more help than regular cleaning, Cath no more help than regular jobs. She had felt a sense of being taken over, something which had made her brusque, until Cath had said, humbly, she just had to see what it was like with everything finished. The sight of Cath, with a great big bin-liner, taking away left-over paint, without asking first, made Helen feel mean as well as angry. You didn't need it, Cath had said, all wounded and defensive; I thought you wouldn't mind. I'm going to do up our place, now I've seen what can be done with yours. No-one's going to interfere, this time. There had been no invitation and even less inclination to ask about Cath's grand night out with the old man. Emily Eliot did not know about that; Helen did not think anyone else did either, apart from Mary Secura, Bailey least of all. Big night out, special treat, the man drunk. Him coming home on the bus. Cath hated the bus. Cath knew when she took the paint that wherever he had gone, Joe Boyce was not coming home.

No-one had managed to find her, Bailey said. Because she had been hiding in Helen's flat until Helen came home, planning, getting the time wrong. And if Cath said no-one was going to interfere in her domestic plans this time, she could only have been referring to him. Him, the until-death-us-do-part man.

It was somewhere on the way back that Helen came to the conclusion that she would say nothing unless anyone asked. Even if Cath were guilty of collusion in a death, so be it. Even if it went completely against her principles and her belief in justice by the rules. Shades of Mary's bitterness. Mind your own business. Watch out for policy. The fact that in all her cases there had been one, potentially murderous, husband convicted out of the last dozen, with her watching Cath work up to new life without really offering help, standing in the sidelines, working in the interests of justice. About which they said, if it ain't broke don't fix it. Helen drove back to home, sweet home.

'I suppose she sent you, as well,' Cath said. 'She keeps on sending people.' The whine was still in the voice, the childish note gone with the tea.

'Who's she, Cath?' he asked gently.

'Helen. Lady I worked for. Decorating. Shan't go back there. She won't want me anyway. Very mean, that lady. Real slaver. Makes me work hard. Forgets to pay, have to fight for it.'

Bailey could not begin to equate this description of Helen with the truth, although he could see that Mary Catherine Boyce was in the kind of state where accuracy was unlikely and truth, if it emerged at all, would be accidental. It was the kind of accident he prayed for; truth, coming out of a side road before the driver noticed a wrong turning. He had underestimated her. Cath was accustomed to underestimation. It was a feature of her life, amounting to contempt.

'I don't like this tea much,' she grumbled. 'Did you put sugar in it?'

'Plenty. Cath, what was that bayonet doing in the kitchen drawer?'

'I couldn't throw it away, could I? I never throw anything away.' She looked at him as if the suggestion was vulgar.

'Oh I don't know. It's a good idea, sometimes, isn't it, throwing away things which aren't any use? Keeps the place tidy.'

She nodded earnestly, as if he had endorsed a long-held philosophy.

'But it's Joe's, you see. I was never allowed to throw away anything which was Joe's. I knew he had it, of course, even though he put it upstairs with all his other stuff. Burglars might have found it, left it out. He brought it with him last night. Showed it to me when we were in a pub. Told me I would get some of it if I didn't behave. We were supposed to go somewhere nice, but we didn't. He just got drunk.' She began to cry, a snuffling sound which produced moist eyes rather than tears. Bailey remained completely still.

'I ran away from him,' Cath said. 'I ran out of the last place the back way and went for the bus, only a bus didn't come. They never come when you want them. But he found me. He was cross. He got that thing out on the bus. I thought he was going to do for me. I was fighting him for it. I didn't scream, what would be the point and anyway, I didn't want anyone to see him, drunk like that. It slipped, went into his tummy. He was laughing. I didn't think he was so much hurt. I just thought I've got to get away and never come back, this time. Can I have some more of that tea, please?'

'You must have known you'd have given him a nice little scar, Cath. Like he gave Damien.'

'Yes,' she agreed, nodding vigorously, then clamped her hand over her mouth.

'And like Damien gave you, all that time ago?'

She was suddenly more composed. 'Oh, I don't know. That policewoman, Mary, she told me I could get that fixed, but I didn't believe her, not really.'

Bailey was silent, his mind running on again to the report. They would move him soon, he knew they would, to a life well above street level, full of endless reports. Reports which could not even

205

begin to place reliance on what a suspect said under the unfamiliar influence of alcohol, without being given the formal words of caution. You do not have to say anything, but what you do say can be used against you. The woman talked in code.

'I think I sort of knew about Joe and Damien,' Cath continued chattily. 'You know, things Joe would let slip when he hit me. You and your brother, bad as one another, that kind of thing. He had to go, he would say: he can't do that to you, and not go. Thought he meant Damien not being around when I was pregnant. He never knew it was Damien's baby. I didn't know for certain how he'd killed Damien until I saw him with that knife last night. I kept thinking, why didn't he use a proper knife? But I don't suppose he could. I would have noticed if he took things from the kitchen. I knew when I saw that old dagger thing. He would never have used anything new. He couldn't. It would have spoiled it.'

Bailey poured more strong tea into her cup. Both were orange in colour. He ladled into it three teaspoons of sugar.

'Damien got you a fine scar on your belly, didn't he? Then Damien is cut apart, the same way you were. No anaesthetic though. Joe did that. Did you kill Joe for revenge, Cath? For Damien, or for all the beatings he gave you?'

'Kill him?' Cath was wide-eyed, shaking. 'Kill him? I would never have wanted to kill Joe. Didn't cross my mind. I loved him. I loved him. You don't seem to understand anything. Someone else killed him. I loved him.'

'We'll have to go, Cath. May take a while. Do you want to bring anything with you?'

She looked around in a state of total confusion.

'I can't, can I? It's all gone, and I . . . anyway, I haven't got a bag.'

Bailey led her out of the house with the deference of a ballroom dancing partner, his mind still running ahead, going into overdrive. Get this place watched and turned over in the morning. Nothing doing, been burgled by an expert. Formal interview under caution, get a woman to do it. Even halfway sober, Cath could clam up in response to sympathy, couldn't blame her, really. Yeah, she'd done for her old man just like he did for her brother, but what if she said nothing, said she'd gone home alone? What he knew already showed she'd left some pub or other long before Joe. It would be, at best, a formal prosecution, with a bit of public attention because it had all happened on a bus. They wouldn't even get near a conviction for manslaughter, not with a battered wife, not with this kind of history. Formal result. A fable of the times, discussed in newspaper editorials for a day. At least that little boy on a murder charge might not go down for long enough to really learn how. He supposed that was something of an achievement, the best he was going to get.

'One more thing,' he said once they were inside his car, while she patted and stroked the seat, like a pet. 'Did you keep on going with your brother Damien, making love to him, I mean, after you married Joe?' It was a casual question, ending with a click of seat belt. Nothing said in cars would do as evidence these days; there would be nothing he could do with the knowledge. Cath's eyes beneath the street light shone like pools of rain on a white pavement.

'Oh yes, whenever he wanted. He was my brother. He would have told Joe about how I used to sleep with him before if I didn't. Joe loved Damien, you see, and anyway, I loved Damien, too. Most of my life, see, he was all I ever had.'

She settled back, a child on an outing. 'So I never wanted it to stop, not really,' she continued. 'Not even when he came to meet me in the park. Sometimes he frightened me, doing that. He liked to play games. Hide-and-seek in the park, in the dark.' She giggled, softly. 'He liked that.'

Close on midnight, Alistair Eliot phoned Helen West. He was as far out of Emily's earshot as Helen was herself; still both of them spoke in low voices, as if afraid of being overheard.

'Sorry to bother you.' Alistair so often prefaced statements or requests with an apology.

'Alistair, don't do that. I'm having an argument with Emily, not with you.'

He sighed. 'Yes, I know. Me and you, both. About Cath. That's what I wanted to ask about. Look, I think one of us should go and see her. Emily says she never knew where she lives. Do you?'

Shame came back and hit her like a punch.

'No, I don't.'

'Well, I do,' he said triumphantly. 'I've found it on a set of papers. Do you think I should go and see her? I feel so guilty about what we did to her. And then I saw her last night, outside that pub her husband runs. I walked straight past. She was looking smart, but so sad, Helen, and I didn't even wave. I went back today. There was an old man outside. Told me Cath's husband had ignored and abused her, dragged her away, later. Drunk. I could have saved her from that, Helen. I could have saved her, and I just walked on by.'

Helen had a strong mental picture of Cath, truculent and defensive earlier on. Got a better picture than she had ever imagined of that grand evening out. She took a firm grip of the phone.

'No, Alistair, I wouldn't go and see her. Not yet. There've been a few developments.'

'Oh?'

'Theft, wasn't it? Perfume? Well, I doubt if Cath would ever steal anything new, but she would take something second hand. And she can lie. Probably only when she's driven to lie, but all the same . . .' Gabbling. Wanting this kind man to understand something without giving him any information which might enable him to understand. Trying to talk in code, like Cath. Like Bailey did to her so much of the time. Alistair was suddenly cold. He sounded both puzzled and sad.

'You're like Emily,' he said. 'You've been talking to Emily. You sound like our judgemental judges. No imagination. They don't always listen, either.'

There was a full glass of red wine next to the phone in the hall. Helen watched it topple, did not move as it seeped away into the gold carpet.

CHAPTER FOURTEEN

On the tenth day of September, the charge against an eighteen-year-old boy was reduced from murder to one of affray and assault. The youth had grown fatter on remand: he was never going to play pool again. There was no member of the murder-victim's family in court to complain how this was a travesty of justice, and the family of the boy was too relieved to care. No public explanation was made, save a brief statement that the Crown accepted that there had been an intervening human cause in between the fight and the death; a man unconnected with this defendant in any way. Constructing a balance sheet which included almost six months in custody and a few minor convictions from the recent past, the judge gravely sent this miscreant down for a further nine months. An adequate gestation period, Bailey thought. In his pocket he had the letter picked up from his desk that morning, ordering his own transfer to penal servitude. From now on, he was handling complaints against police, and he would never be able to stop looking at his watch.

First thing in the morning, Cath lay in her own bed, curled like a snake in a warm burrow. A little snap in the air today: no incentive to get up. Better to lie where she was and open her eyes slowly, stroking her belly, moving her legs and arms to get the energy going, look around. This room was as far as she had got. She had painted the walls yellow, moved in the daisy print from the kitchen, bought, without a hint of guilt, a brand-new bed-cover the pristine white of snow. It was not the old alarm clock which had woken her, but this voice inside her head, Is that you? Is that you? Is this really you, lying idle?

Yes, this was the way she liked it. Bare and clean, like the living room. Mickey Gat said she was doing up the Spoon shortly, throwing out a set of table and chairs, as well as all the carpet. She did it each year, she said. Cath had told her, don't chuck the furniture: I'll have it. There was bound to be paint left over as well. Cath liked working in the Spoon: she was good at it, a quick learner. Mickey said, Yes, she would do. Better than Joe, as it happened. Mickey Gat knew all about women being better than men, especially if they had the guts to take over a man's job. Poor old Joe, always did have bad luck or judgement, but they had given him a good funeral. What a way to go. Some thug doing you in on the bus. Must be a loony, thrown out of one of those homes they kept closing down. Somehow, by an obscure and logical route, it came back to another version of 'them' and 'us'.

'We don't have to be friends,' Helen said carefully to Mary Secura. 'It isn't a necessary part of the arrangement and probably doesn't even help. But we have to be able to communicate. My boss says so.'

She grinned with a shrug as she spoke. Mary rewarded her with the ghost of a smile. There was more than a hint of the apology she could not bring herself to make. All that money Cath had. Of course Helen West had paid her. Mary was subdued, respectful even, she seemed to have lost some of the fire, like someone recovering from an illness. Despite the volatility of Mary in health, Helen was hoping that this convalescent state was temporary. The woman firing off in all directions was distinctly preferable. All Mary was thinking, in a state which bordered on guilt, still-remembered shock now overlaid with defensiveness, was how Helen West's ability to turn the other cheek was infuriating. Mid-thirties burn-out: that was Helen West. She did not want to be like that.

'This Rix case. I can hardly believe it. Shirley scarcely cold, and

210

he's got another woman and the other woman has made a complaint. Incredible. He must be out of his mind.'

'It isn't the new woman complaining, it's her sister. And he had her before he got charged with hitting Shirl. Sort of a sideline, really. I've got a feeling Shirl found out. That was the first cut-off point, I reckon, with the kid the final straw. Not the beatings.'

'Well, we're going to need some corroboration. We can't run this on a medical report and a complaint from the sister. Hearsay, all of it.'

Mary shook her head. 'We'll have to wait for the repeat performance then, won't we?'

'Unless the victim gives us a statement, yes.'

'OK. Next?'

It was not much of a mystery why Redwood was instigating meetings between police and Crown Prosecution Service (in their offices, of course, God forbid his staff should go to police premises), at an earlier stage in the case. After that mêlée next door, the police were suddenly allies. He had waxed lyrical in a meeting. You will all have seen the fight in the offices over the road, he had announced to the assembly. At least, judging from the crowds at the windows, most of you did. Two women scrapping, pulling hair, biting, actually drawing blood. Men joining in, if you don't mind; you could hear the shouting from here. Some fool on our staff, a young blood whose name I shall not mention, went over the way, to help, he said, because a poor man in spectacles seemed to be getting the worst of it. He received a black eye for his pains, so you see, we must have a policy. Which is, if you do happen to see nasty things occur either at court or in your daily lives anywhere, don't intervene; call the police immediately. The police are made for this kind of thing; they smoothed the situation in no time. They are there to control breaches of the peace, not us. We work in the interests of justice, which is a very different thing altogether.

Redwood had not seen the crowd in his room stuffing handkerchiefs in their mouths to restrain ribaldry, Helen, doodling in a corner. She wondered if she would feel violent if, after the recent absence, she heard rumours of Bailey with another woman. Among a phalanx of men in grey clothing, Helen missed Bailey. Would jealousy, however futile, make her want to scratch the face of another woman? She had closed her own eyes and felt savage. Yes, it would.

Mary was gathering files and photos, stuffing the notebook back into the bulging handbag, looking for escape. She was uncomfortable with the proximity of so many lawyers padding about, bloodsuckers in uniform.

'Sit down a minute.' She sat.

'Cath killed her old man on the bus, didn't she? You were in on the interview as the only female officer she knew. Tell me.'

'Nothing to tell. I gave her her rights, told her she didn't have to say anything, and she didn't. No-one remembers her being on that damn bus. The conductor refuses to remember what day of the week it was. Witnesses in the last pub they went to said she left before him, a good half hour before, distressed because he was drunk, spilt whisky on her skirt. There isn't anything to say they even travelled together. She went back to her brother's place, went out next day as usual. Place got burgled. So she goes back to the old man. Again. Only he was dead already and the first she knew was when Bailey told her. That was when she showed him the knife.'

'Bayonet?'

'That's it. Been chatting to Mr Bailey?' A note of anxiety entered her voice.

'No. Not much. More guesswork, really. And your friend Ryan.'

'Who?'

'Never mind. Are you going to tell me what you really think?'

Mary remained seated, wanting to leave. Perhaps she did actually owe this woman something, for her own misjudgement. For the fact they had once got on so well and needed to do so again. And because she was Bailey's bird, and Mary still wanted to work for Bailey; but chiefly because she already seemed to know so much.

'It doesn't matter what I think,' she said. 'But yes, I think you could be right. She could well have killed him. Poor bitch. I also think it doesn't matter. He deserved it.'

'That bayonet . . .' Helen began, then stopped. She knew enough about that bayonet. Ryan, when bumped into accidentally in a court corridor, was always pleased to see her, assumed she knew everything Bailey would know, and chatted with an amazing lack of discretion. All about this crazy bayonet which Joe Boyce had hidden from his wife and Bailey had found in a cutlery drawer. What an odd place to put it.

'Any large knife could have done the damage to Joe Boyce,' Mary said flatly. 'Nothing suggests that the bayonet ever left the house, or that it was ever used at all, except by Joe Boyce. Cath said she would have no idea how to get such a thing sharpened. It would need to be done by a powerful grinder in the first instance, I suppose. Joe played with things like that. It simply moved into the cutlery drawer after Cath had left. Cath said it repelled her, all Joe's military stuff repelled her. Let's face it, every cutlery drawer has a murder weapon in it.'

She stood again, looked out of Helen's window to the workers opposite. 'Close, aren't they? At least offices are safer than houses.'

'If you say so,' Helen murmured.

'Did you complete all that decorating you were doing?' Mary asked by way of ending on a casual note. 'Yellow, wasn't it?'

'All over. How's life at home?'

Mary was halfway out of the door. 'Fine,' she said airily. 'Just fine. I thought about getting rid of dear old Dave, but it isn't worth the hassle. A woman on her own. You know.'

Mickey Gat levered herself out of the Jag, bounced across the cobbles of the mews and into the Spoon. The place shone like a new pin, whatever one of those was, Mickey was not into needle-work. Cath could get a fair old shine on that bar: you could see your face in it, and Cath's face wasn't the kind of mug to keep custom at bay. Mickey hadn't been so sure at first, but now she was. Cath turned exactly the right kind of blind eye to all the boxes of counterfeit perfume in the back room, too: she didn't even dust them. It was about the right time of year to start stockpiling for Christmas. Mickey was on her way to Harrods after this, to get a few ideas. She wafted indoors in a cloud of Poison, the real thing, not her own brand, and almost collided with an old gent coming out. He wore a cap, raised it. Mickey reckoned only people drinking half pints did that.

'You want to be careful with these old lags,' she told Cath. 'Sit around all day, take up space and don't spend nothing. We want them yuppy types, that's what we want.'

Cath shook her head. 'I know,' she agreed. 'But yuppy types like seeing the old ones hanging around, see? Gives the place a homey feel. Besides, some people won't go into a pub if it's empty. You need a couple of ornaments to fill up the corners.'

For a moment, Mickey did not know if Cath referred to the custom or the décor.

'Oh, yeah. Suppose you could be right. I'll have an orange juice.'

'I thought we could get a coffee-machine,' said Cath. 'People think it sobers them up, so they have a coffee, then they have another drink.'

'Steady on, girl,' said Mickey admiringly. 'Steady on. Think I'm made of money?'

She was looking at the takings. Not bad, not bad at all, for the tail end of summer.

It was time to mend fences. Alistair had said so. You can't just lose friends, he said: they are too rare and too valuable. Please, make it up and ask them for supper.

'Whoops!' Emily sighed, voice a little high, body a little drunk, deciding that this was all so difficult she deserved another drink. Her mind was full of fearful imaginings, something to do with this direction about friend Helen West who was, after all, very easy to look at, admired by Alistair in his distant way and mentioned twice, obliquely, in the last week or three. Better get in there first. It did not do for a dedicated wife to have her man distracted the way hers had been. Such men were like a viral culture looking for a new plant: there was no telling what they would let grow on them. Besides she did have a conscience, even if it was not troubling her.

Dear Helen,
    OK, I've been shitty and over the top and I was devastated to hear what happened to Cath's husband, but I do miss you. Can we have lunch or something?

There was a pause, writer staring into distance. No, that would not do. She'd have to make it longer, chat a bit, to bring Helen round. Let her know that life was going on at the usual hectic pace, try and get Helen involved.

. . . Jane sends her love, to Bailey, little flirt . . .

Another pause, then Emily smiled and wrote with animation, the way she always could when describing children.

. . . She is a flirt, you know. You have no idea how children play with the truth. We're thinking of setting up a courtroom in the kitchen, where we test one another for truth or fib! One person's evidence against another's, it's the only way! Otherwise, it's amazing what you believe when you want to believe it. I don't know how I could have believed so badly of Cath, except for the funny bad manners and the smell, like school lavatories after a wash, would you believe. School or prison, but you know more about those . . .

Helen supposed it had cost Emily some to write what looked like a long letter in the middle of her oh-so-busy life, but since Helen was not mother, housekeeper or any of that herself, simply an observer, she could read her personal mail whenever she pleased, and it did not please her to do so immediately. She had all the time in the world. Even when the letter was accompanied by a peace-offering to make up for Emily's rash judgement, which may well have helped Cath on her way to desperate violence. Helen felt that Emily Eliot did not quite deserve forgiveness and conciliation by return of post. Nor did she want to plough through a missive of family news, designed to charm her. The rest of the letter could wait. So could the gift accompanying it, a small box, soap, perfume perhaps.

In the evenings the room seemed to have slipped back into familiarity with sinister ease. There was extra fluff and a fine coat of gold dust on everything, which Helen could not quite bring herself to clean. No-one else was going to do it, she was quite certain of that. Somewhere, floating around London, there were two sets of keys, Bailey's and Cath's, but she had needed a new lock anyway.

The place was still remarkably different, impressive even. After a few weeks, surfaces no longer quite so pristine, a few spillages and a bit of neglect, she no longer felt the need to wipe her feet when she entered or comb her hair when she passed a mirror. Golden light came in at the kitchen window, twinkled on the slightly smeared wineglass. Dishwasher next. The fridge still panted like a thing in labour and worked with only moderate efficiency, no real problem at the moment, since there was so little in it.

Which would have been why Bailey came to call, homing instinct working overtime, plastic bag in hand as if he thought he could use food and drink as a password after all this time. She saw his feet from the street, wondered what he would do if she let him discover how his key no longer worked and knowing she would not make him wait, waved from the window and let him in.

Scene fifty-five, take five. Bailey came in through the front door, tripped on the new carpet, righted himself and made an undignified entrance into the dulcet yellow wash of the living room, dropping the bag. The gasp was not quite one of astonishment, the words used merely the gentler obscenities uttered by someone who has just avoided failing.

'Christ Almighty. What have you done here? It's all clean. Yellow, is it?'

'I'm glad you like it.' Helen said. 'Nice of you to notice. You've seen it before, but I don't suppose you remember. Where've you been?' She spoke as if the absence had been hours, rather than far too many days.

He looked slightly hangdog, turned on his heel and made for the kitchen. She remained as she was. There was the sound of a cork popping, and more muffled swearing as he searched through reorganized cupboards. Her mood had been desperate, depressed, any kind of self-esteem notable by its absence; now she could feel herself lifting, like a balloon, the beginnings of laughter starting in her throat as she listened. So much for pride. Back he came with a tray of glasses, fizzy stuff.

'What are we celebrating?'

'We aren't. Yet. And if we do, it'll be because of being alive and halfway sane. There's fuck all outside to celebrate.'

Silence fell. One of the things she had always loved about Bailey was his comfort with silence. It never bothered him any more than it did her, and he needed silence in order to find the right words.

'She killed him and you fudged it on paper. Is that what you were aiming to tell me?'

He looked up at her in surprise, took a large swig of the wine, and coughed.

'Yes and no. Well, no, that wasn't what I was going to say first. I was going to say, I think we ought to get married. We'll just lose one another if we don't get married. Only I've got this clock at home, started going at the rate of a day every hour again, and I can't stop it turning round until you do.'

'You're a liar.'

'No more than you. You lied to me about Cath being here the day after Boyce was killed. She told me, in the car. For all I know, you've got the life history of a bayonet at your fingertips and you wouldn't volunteer that, either. You would if you thought it was going to lead me in the direction of the right result. Which is not, as I see it, a wretched little cleaning lady with a wretched life to date, being put in prison for doing to her husband what he did to her brother. Even if it could be proved, which it can't.'

She nodded. The affirmation was reluctant, but definite. Two years ago, she thought, I would never have agreed. I have always believed in letting a jury decide. Why did I change? Guilt warps judgement, or is it arrogance? Perhaps we simply grow more alike, more cynical.

'I was going to tell you . . .' she began.

'Shh,' he warned. 'Don't. Clean slate from now on, all right?' He was off, like a butler, for the bottle. She had large wine glasses; a bottle of bubbly lasted no time at all. Helen fingered the curtains next to her chair. All that effort and expense.

'I don't think you could live in the same place as me,' she called.

'I don't think so either. What's that got to do with anything? You can be married and not live in the same place. Bloody royals do it all the time. Provided we both know where the other one is and we get the hell out of it from time to time.'

'Sounds like a good idea, then. I should have asked you, a long time ago.'

He shot back into the room. 'Well, if that's yes, thank God. I couldn't go through that again. You must be mad, saying yes.'

'You must be mad to volunteer.'

It was stupid and peculiarly embarrassing to be suddenly close to tears. He brushed the hair off her forehead, kissed the scar, withdrew and grinned his huge grin. She noticed he was trembling.

'You know, I've been sitting in my poxy flat, driving nails into my head, wondering if I ever get anything right.'

'Oh yes, you do. It's me who doesn't. I don't do anything right.'

He laughed, a reassuring crow of joy. 'Who says? Well, you just sit there and be a deep, dark goldmine, then. What do you want for supper? Not yet. Later.'

'Food would do nicely.'

'I could fix you a nice sandwich,' Cath said winsomely to the colonel. 'We was thinking of doing sandwiches, quality ones, you know. You can get this lovely bread round the corner.'

He shook his head, politely. 'So sorry about your husband,' he said, for the fourteenth time. He had been saying it in various tones of disbelief for the last ten days, once the penny dropped. The colonel had a particular penchant for widows, even when the newness of their regime in his watering-hole meant the drinks were no longer free. She was kind to him though, liked the company in the afternoons, she said, made him feel protective and let him nod to sleep in the sun while there was still a chance. Nights beginning to draw in round about now, he told her, as if she had never had cause to discover such a phenomenon for herself. Had he been terribly insensitive to tell her that the grieving time would be over and that one day, she would be able to think of marrying again? He could hear himself saying it, minutes ago, before she offered the sandwich, so he had not caused offence, after all. Busy Lizzies, busy dying. Something new in the window-boxes, heavy-scented stocks. Made him dopey.

Cath eyed him, nodding off. He probably had a bob or two in bricks and mortar, she decided, but, for all that, he was still a shade too old. She could not quite see herself taking off her clothes and showing her scars for this one, sweet though he was, poor old thing. Pretty deaf with it, still a good listener, even while he slept. She needed a good listener who could not hear, patted his freckled hand as his eyes closed.

'You don't understand, Mr Colonel, sir. You don't really, which is all to the good, 'cos it wouldn't be a tonic for your health if you did. Course I'm grieving. I loved him. Or at least, I sort of loved him. Only there's grief and grief, if you see what I mean. I loved Damien, you see. I loved him to pieces. I couldn't have loved anyone else like that. He gets me pregnant, leaves me in the club, lets me get on with it, I lose the baby and get this sodding great scar. I can cope with that, at the time, anyway, see? Though you can never look at yourself the same way again. You aren't worth shit with a belly like mine. Least, that's what it feels like at fifteen.'

She sipped a Bloody Mary. Two a day of those was more than enough, plenty of Worcester sauce to give it bite, good for a girl. Better than lunch. This glass was cracked, she must remember not to use her muscles in the washing up.

'My one and only love,' she continued, dreamily. 'Sends money, comes home, looks after me, gets me the hotel job, and then, he gets me Joe, and Joe loves me. Does he ever? Till he finds out. Well, he thinks he finds out about me still going round to Damien, only he daren't say, just hits me. I mean, I didn't mind marrying Joe, because a woman should be married, Damien was right, you've got to put up with it.' So comforting, talking to the colonel. Old men, with old-fashioned values, they understood so much. About respectability, status, all that. Not like these yuppies in the bar.

'I thought he was doing it for my own good, see? Damien, I mean. But what I couldn't stand was when I came to realize he was just shoving me off. He used to keep Joe in order if I complained; I mean Joe couldn't help it if he couldn't keep his end up and had to fight his way out, could he? He was like that, and he loved me. Would have done anything for me, me for him, too. But when he got worse, and I went round to Damien with bruises, well, Damien didn't like me with bruises. Sodding great scar, yes, but bruises turned him off. And him a champion boxer!'

She let out a snort of laughter. The colonel stirred. Cath picked up the cigar left in the ashtray between them, and stubbed it out fiercely.

'Dumping me. Used to take me out at least, but the boys were better fun. Dumping me, so I'd stand outside the pub and watch for him and Joe, mostly him. After all he'd done. And all I'd done for him. Wanted to offload me, get rid of me. I was the only one who really loved him, and he wanted . . . What time is it?'

219

The colonel moved in his sleep. 'I'm *so* sorry about your husband,' he droned. Cath seized his wrist, looked at an ancient watch, put the arm back carefully.

'That's all right, early yet. I used to watch the time when I waited. Had a watch: Joe smashed it. Joe comes out the pub, always earlier than the others in case they leave him behind, see? Comes home that night in two minutes round that track, fit bloke, Joe, but angry, see? Tells me there's going to be a fight, crashes out indoors. Falls fast asleep, he could always do that. I dunno what I thought. Save Damien, I thought, silly fool he was in a scrap. But then when I ran across the park, I saw the tail end of the fight. I saw Damien waltzing away from it scarcely hurt, a bit out of breath, causing all that fuss for nothing, sitting down by a tree, and then I thought, you bugger, and I knew what I wanted to do. Give him back that scar he gave me, is what. So I did. I loved him. He loved me. Simple. He was doing wrong, dumping me. I couldn't live, knowing that. He'd walk away from me like he did from that fight, leaving everyone else with the scars.'

She patted her own stomach, drew in her breath to flatten it.

'Course I knew Joe had that bayonet thing in his satchel; he always did, he was so proud of it, I knew where to look.'

She looked at the cigar butt with regret. Smoke would be nice, but thinking of smoking was the equivalent to dirty thoughts and she did not have any of those. Dirty thoughts were almost as wicked as anyone thinking she would steal.

'Wouldn't stop screaming,' she clicked her tongue in disapproval. 'Never had any self-discipline. Took for ever and made me sweat, I can tell you. Ever such a noise. Didn't matter; no-one listens round there, I don't even know why Joe woke up to come out and look, but he did. He was quite nice to me, after, ran me a bath; but being nice – being ever so protective, wanting to pretend he did it – didn't last. He really wanted to pretend he did it. I wouldn't let him hide that bayonet, though. I put it in the only place I could think of, a garden. Where else could I put it? Where else was I allowed to go? And I gave Joe his chances, I did, I really did; I wanted him to be like Damien, wanted him to try to be as nice as Damien had been once, when he loved me the way I loved him, but he couldn't. And I couldn't stop loving Damien, even though he was dead. Never lasts, does it?'

'What?' said the colonel.

'People being nice to you,' Cath shouted. 'Do you want that sandwich, or not?'

He was too old. What a shame. Otherwise, he would have been ideal.

During the course of the night, the wind blew. Helen had forgotten to undo the grille which covered the bedroom window. The sound of the wind was reminiscent of a wild animal rattling the bars. About that time, they got up and ate scrambled eggs. Supper had been bypassed; once there had been fading daylight to hide the sudden, self-conscious nerves. Now it was dark. Autumn had begun to blow against the panes.

'I could live without those,' Bailey said, pointing towards the grilles with his fork before it speared a piece of burned toast.

'You don't have to live with them.'

'Nope, not every day, but there are better versions. Double glazing, better-looking stuff than that. I can fit it. Nice curtains you've got. Are they new?'

'Don't you notice anything?'

'You. You, always looking like you, whatever you put on. That's what I notice. You could call it X-ray eyes, but I also like what you put on. I also like you. You could chuck me out tomorrow, I'd still think so. I'd like you anyway. Oh yes, even if you get frightened and even if you lie. You've always got a good reason. Something to do with being a good woman. More than I could say about being a good man. Get this egg off this duvet.'

She was spilling the stuff in the effort to cut the toast.

'Mary Secura thinks I'm a burnt-out case.' He choked on the coffee, the thought trickling across his mind about whether he should tell her about an appointment in Police Complaints. Settling on an answer.

'She doesn't listen to what you say. Doesn't sleep with you, either. Thank God. So how would she know? Doesn't egg travel?'

Boiled eggs go off like bombs, Helen remembered. Scrambled, they only need to go as far as carpet level to bring in a cat with an addiction to butter. She scooped up the rest on her plate.

'Were we right about Cath?'

He got out of bed and ushered the cat out of the room. Kicked the fresh-painted door with his foot.

221

'I think so. Why? Don't you?'

'We didn't have a jury in on this one, that's why. There should be a jury. Evidence, all the safeguards which should come before judgement day. It feels arrogant.'

He nodded gravely. 'I know. I think I know. There are exceptions. Come here. I don't like doubt. I can't stand it. Did you hear me earlier? I once thought that if you didn't marry me, I might die, still think it once a day. You want a jury? You want a deed poll?'

Sweet morning, swelling against the garden windows, insistent to be seen. The first hint of a chill and a big, black beetle marching a path to suicide on the way to the kitchen. Far too much light in here. Helen West, soon to be a married woman, swanned in there, gossamer clad, walking on air, tired as all hell, fit for anything. Including yesterday's post, something to read while the kettle boiled. She was proof against anything. Even circulars, and the remnants of Emily's letter:

. . . Well, while you've been battling in your version of the real world, I've been labouring away in mine, and there's quite a lot I have to eat humble pie about. Such as discovering that my youngest child is a pathological liar, but maybe we should just call her creative. You see, I never believed she was CAPABLE of stealing the perfume, but it was her, she buries it. Alistair found it when he noticed signs of digging and went out there to see if the silly child had hidden this funny old bayonet thing which had somehow gone missing. When you tackle Jane about lying, she's perfectly frightful! She just makes up something else! Yes, she'd taken the bayonet (admittedly she'd found it in the first place, so I suppose it WAS hers really), but Jane being Jane, she HAS to say that she was only giving it back to Cath, because she'd seen Cath put it there in the first place. I ask you! Now that was the worst lie of all, because she'd always said some ghosty chap had put it there, oh, she's impossible. Mind, I'm glad to be rid of the thing, it was awfully sharp, and she would play with it.

Sorry to ramble on, but life is not a bed of roses. I do miss Cath. The bayonet incident reminds me of one of many reasons why. I mean, she would get things done for me, on her way home; she always knew places to get things done. Got all the knives sharpened for me one day, something I suppose you can do in the East End easier than round here! All blunt again now, of course, and the kettle doesn't work. Now please don't mind if I ask a favour, but I know you, loyal old thing that you are, you might see Cath in her troubles. Could you give her back this perfume? I know now she never stole it. It's the best I can do as an apology. She must have brought it in with her on the day Jane found it in her bag. We know it can't be ours, of course, because it isn't the real thing . . . ! That's what started us off, wondering about Jane.

Helen read with her hip propped against the work surface, found she had turned to face the wall with the corner of a unit pressing into her stomach, painfully. It was a rounded edge, but it hurt. So did the contents of the letter. She needed the concentration of that slight pain in order to think. Of Cath, and her unreal perfume, and her odour of sanctity. Secreting in a garden a knife she would know how to sharpen, the knowledge of which she denied. Why hide it if she did not know Joe had used it?

Because she had used it?

'No,' Helen said out loud. 'No, no, NO!'

She went back to the bedroom. They had promised each other they would break their habit of keeping secrets.

Bailey was still asleep. Sleeping the slumber of the just. To which she was no longer entitled.